P9-DNF-065

EVERY ANXIOUS WAVE

MO DAVIAU

EVERY ANXIOUS WAVE

ST. MARTIN'S PRESS NEW YORK

This is a work of fiction. All of the characters, organizations, and events portrayed in this novel are either products of the author's imagination or are used fictitiously.

 For information, address St. Martin's Press, 175 Fifth Avenue, New York, N.Y. 10010.

www.stmartins.com

The Library of Congress Cataloging-in-Publication Data is available upon request.

ISBN 978-1-250-06749-4 (hardcover)
ISBN 978-1-4668-7586-9 (e-book)

Our books may be purchased in bulk for promotional, educational, or business use. Please contact your local bookseller or the Macmillan Corporate and Premium Sales Department at (800) 221-7945, extension 5442, or by e-mail at MacmillanSpecialMarkets@macmillan.com.

10 9 8 7 6 5 4 3 2 1

First Edition: February 2016

FOR MY FATHER,
GEORGE DAVIAU
(1910–1992),
WHO, BY THE STRETCH IN OUR YEARS,
MADE ME A TIME TRAVELER

I'm so glad I waited for this.
Every nervous moment worth it.
Every anxious wave rode through
To find me lying safe with you.

—Sebadoh, "Kath"

EVERY ANXIOUS WAVE

1

ABOUT A YEAR before the time traveling began, before I lost Wayne and found Lena, Wayne DeMint stumbled into my bar for the first time. He figured out I was the guitarist from the Axis and affixed his khaki-clad keister to my barstool. Night after night, beer after beer, he shared with me and whoever else showed up the content of his dreams: crying kittens, *bukkake,* broken-toothed pirates with bloody bayonets, his dead mother chopped into bits. When closing time came he always wanted to stay, like a kid who didn't want to turn off the TV and go to bed. "I'll mop!" he'd offer, so most nights I sat up with Wayne as he sloshed mop water across my wooden floor. We'd crank up the jukebox and talk about bands, true love, failure, and the past. Mostly the past.

A bar is not a mental health facility, but I never had a dog growing up, and so I listened to Wayne. Wholesome, Midwestern

Wayne, computer scientist, he of the kindest smile and most generous bar tips.

Wayne and I shared that common affliction plaguing single men with limited prospects and self-destructive tendencies: we regarded our pasts with such love and loss that every day forward was a butter knife to the gut. Our twenties had been full of rock music and courage. The future made us older, but our wisdom was dubious. Wayne and I avoided the pain of tomorrow with alcohol and old rock bands. Pavement on the jukebox, the heavenly reddish glow of neon signs, and sentences that started with "Remember when . . ."

THE TIME TRAVEL business had started by accident.

One stupid afternoon a month ago, I couldn't find one of the prized army boots that I had bought from an army–navy surplus store in Boston for sixteen dollars in 1991, when I was twenty-one. The red laces that I'd put in them, due to vague anarchist leanings, were still intact, and even though time had worn away all the tread, those boots were both comfortable and comforting. They represented the very best parts of my life, and having one go missing was more than I could bear on a Sunday afternoon fifteen minutes before I needed to open my bar. Crawling around on the floor of my closet, pushing aside piles of dirty clothes and old magazines, I found myself falling feetfirst through a hole in the floor. Falling and cold. I thought it was from mixing bourbon with cold medicine, but then I landed with a thud on a familiar wooden floor. I had landed at the Empty Bottle, a rock club near my bar. The stack of *Chicago Reader*s by the door bore a cover from months earlier. A look out the window revealed barren trees and cars dusted in snow.

When the band took the stage, I realized that I'd been at this show three months ago, in February. A pack of talentless teenagers who played covers of Liz Phair songs like they meant nothing began to tune their guitars, looking for all the world like the smug bastards my friends and I were in the early 1990s.

The real kicker of this experience, the one that makes me clench my ass cheeks together and cry for my mother, happened when I saw myself leaning against the bar, tipping a can of PBR toward my mouth, glaring at the band with eyes of white-hot contempt. The blood rushed to my face. For the first time in my life, I could really see myself. All of myself. I saw what a bitter, pathetic sad-sack Karl Bender had become. Even at the ripe old age of forty, I still hadn't mastered the art of shaving; I had whisker skid marks on my face like a teenager. Had Meredith, the woman I was attached to for most of my twenties, known what I would turn into when she dumped me like a bag of trash back in '96? I took the hardest look I could: the stained teeth, the gut, the whole ugly package. I'm prone to self-loathing, but I had never hated myself with more fire and sorrow than I did standing there in the Empty Bottle. I longed to yell at Past Karl's face and break my own jaw. We deserved it.

"Hey, Karl," I said. "Karl? Yo, Bender, what's up?"

Nothing.

I tapped myself on the shoulder. The man before me, myself, Past Karl, did not respond.

I tried to punch my other in the stomach but I felt nothing. Not on my hand or my belly. I tried again. No sensation, no reaction. When I was a child, I wanted to walk into the television. This is what the past looked and felt like. I could take in the colors, smell the faint sweetness of whiskey and cigarettes, and watch as music fans younger and better looking than me took up floor space with the confidence of kings. I could not, however, kick my own ass.

Nor could I take those boots, which I had so loved and now lost, from my old self's feet.

You can't hold onto the past, asshole, I thought as I pressed the heels of my hands to my eyes because I didn't want to be the bastard crying during a shitty band.

The ring of my cell phone pulled me back to the present. I was slurped back to the closet in my bedroom, as if my body were an ice cube sucked through a straw. I was prone on the wooden floor, my face in a cluster of dust bunnies. My head throbbed and I was shivering cold, even though it was warm and sunny and my apartment didn't have air-conditioning and I'd been too lazy to buy a fan.

I told Wayne. He was the only person in my life that I could trust with information regarding the viability of time travel. "You're chosen!" he exclaimed, his blue eyes sparkling so bright over the dark comfort of my bar that my first instinct was to kick him out, lest he ruin what I'd spent years cultivating: a poorly lit drinking hole for the remorseful, aging, and alone.

He went home to his fifteen computers and wrote the software program, an astonishing time-bending navigational system that harnesses the directional pulls of the wormhole and allows you to choose when and where you'd like to land. Two laptops, three generators, and a series of wires now occupy the desk next to my closet. On the laptop screen there is a Google map with a grid over it. You type in the coordinates of where you want to go, physically. A black binder full of laminated sheets, modeled after the ones found in our nation's finer karaoke bars, features a convenient list of bands, venues, and locations that you can choose from. (The binder was my nonscientific music geek contribution to the business. Savvy travelers/music fans will note a heavy bias toward certain indie-oriented clubs, such as my beloved T.T.'s in Cambridge or Cat's Cradle in Carrboro, North Carolina.) If you insist, you can do your own research into the performance history of your favorite band and we'll custom calibrate the controls just for you.

If pressed to explain his scientific understanding of our portal to the past, Wayne would describe Carl Sagan's theory of the wormhole: that it is totally possible to travel from point A to point B on an unseen plane C. "Technically that only works for going into the future, though," Wayne would say. On the fact that point A happened to be the bedroom closet in my apartment on the top floor of a narrow brick building in Wicker Park, Chicago, which also housed a subpar Chinese takeout place called Ming's Panda, Wayne said, "Well, Karl, you just wanted it bad enough." That's Wayne's other theory: the theory of desire. Through my own deep desire, and because of that nasty word *regret,* the universe chose me to be the custodian of a portal to the past.

The number one house rule: the wormhole was only to be used to attend rock concerts of the past. It kept the experience pure and free from the temptation to try to game yourself a better life. Besides, why would we need music if our lives were exactly as we wanted them to be?

Other house rules: no bringing back souvenirs. Do not talk to anyone in the past. Don't touch anything. Do not drink or take drugs. No photographs. No audio recording. No staying in the past longer than the length of the show. No wandering out of the music venue. I know you want to see the old cars and the out-of-style clothes and the date on the cover of the newspaper in the newspaper box and the newspaper box itself, but *no.*

House rules.

I told three old music friends about the portal, and instructed them to keep it on the down-low. I didn't want just anyone off the street coming over to experience this miracle. My indie rock ethics, left over from the nineties, dictated that we keep things small and special. My band, the Axis, was part of an indie scene that attracted clean, artistic children who got good grades, not guys who looked like me—a bulldog-faced pugilist with tattoo sleeves and a broken, badly reset nose. My shoulders were too broad to look good in a cardigan (Axis fans always mistook me for the bouncer), but the twee-kitty cuteness and clubhouse-guarding business model had seeped into my subconscious, so the wormhole was kept quiet and exclusive, the way the Axis's former indie label, Frederica Records, once was.

I warned my patrons that, while in the tunnel, your body U-turns onto the unseen plane—a jolt akin to the spasms of a wooden roller coaster. Most passengers feel like they're going to toss their cookies.

Then you land, with a thud. It hurts. But not for long.

AT LEAST THIRTY interested friends of friends called me or came by the bar to ask a series of questions that always began with "This is a joke right?" and ended with "If you're fucking with me, I will end you." Patrons of my wormhole paid me hundreds, sometimes thousands of dollars to take a trip down memory lane. I explained to them how to come back to the present—you typed a code into your cell phone, which reversed the wormhole's directional pull and slurped you back home. Wayne printed up little cards with the return instructions, just to be safe.

Ahoy, time adventurer!
When the show is over, YOU MUST COME HOME!!!

INSTRUCTIONS

1. Open the Web app.
2. Select RETURN.
3. The DATE, TIME, and LOCATION of your return should automatically appear (example: 06/01/2010 19:30 CDT WESTERN AND MILWAUKEE, CHICAGO IL USA)*
4. Press the red button! ZOOM! You'll be home in no time!

***Do not attempt to alter your return coordinates! Attempts to tamper with the program will result in a $1,000 fine and a lifetime ban!).**

All I had to do was ask, "If you could go back in time and see any band play, what would you choose?" It's a great conversation starter, decent-enough bar banter, something a man more ambitious than me might keep in his pocket for parties full of beautiful strangers. (Especially if asked in such a way as to build a bridge between the lonely islands of age and regret.)

They came back cold and shaken. I gave them what they wanted but thought they couldn't have. Most hugged me. A few kneed me in the groin; a few more threatened to. All of them, to a person, have come back with cheeks wet with tears. When I return from the past, I sit alone with a notebook and write out the lyrics to songs I'd just heard performed. Song lyrics are a particular type of poetry, laying bare your bones and helping you feel something other than sorrow and failure. Song lyrics reminded me that I may be so lucky as to fall in love again someday. Song lyrics are scripture for guys like me and Wayne.

What I don't tell my time travel customers is that the experience is rather short. Time goes by more quickly in the past. An hour is a minute. A minute is a microsecond. You might see the whole show, you might not, but it will be over before the first tear you shed reaches your chin. The experience is only slightly more soul-shaking than watching concert footage on YouTube. The music is strangely softer—at an eardrum-ripping Megadeth show I strained to hear anything besides the bass. Traveling is cold. Damn cold. And you can't bring back souvenirs.

The sorrow you feel when you come back sits deep in your gut. It presses against your head and your heart. Readjusting to the reality of the present hurts like hell; it's a dull, shameful ache that lingers. The world feels different. Your eyes change. Your heart changes. Those same dull walls you've been staring at in the present grow sinister in their sameness. You are left with the horror of yourself. I'm not the only one who has sobbed like a child upon reentry.

I can't help you with that.

ROCK SHOWS I have traveled back in time to see:

Galaxie 500, 1990, Boston
Unrest, 1993, Arlington, VA
Stereolab, 1998, Chicago
Altamont (with too much time spent lingering over an antique Pepsi bottle lying in the dirt next to a heap of wriggling blankets)
The Traveling Wilburys, NYC, 1990
The Cure, 1989, stadium show in New Jersey
Elvis Costello, 1991, NYC (I've been to this one three times)
Miaow/Durutti Column, the Haçienda, Manchester
The Magnetic Fields, first 69 Love Songs show, Knitting Factory, 1999

Shows that Wayne has traveled back in time to see:

The Rat Pack, live at the Sands, 1963
They Might Be Giants in a NYC basement, 1986
The first Sex Pistols show, 1976 (as seen in the film *24 Hour Party People*)
Bruce Springsteen at the Stone Pony, 1975
Uncle Dumpster (Wayne's high school garage band), Sheboygan, Wisconsin, 1991
Some street musician in Madison that Wayne remembered from his college days, 1995

Rock shows that friends/customers seem to like that make me judge them harshly—like, we have access to time travel and you want to see *what*?:

Woodstock (American rock history's most polished turd)
The Rolling Stones' Steel Wheels Tour
Woodstock 1994
The Axis

Popular selections that friends/customers seem to like, whose appeal I completely get:

Beat Happening and Black Flag in Olympia, Washington, 1984
The Smiths, London, 1985
Frank Zappa Halloween show, 1977
The *Johnny Cash Show*, Johnny performing with Glen Campbell (Wichita Lineman), 1969
The Last Waltz, San Francisco, 1976
Rolling Stones in the UK, 1967–69
REM in Athens, 1980–83

I'm a quiet guy. I live in three places: my bar, my apartment, and the cheap Mediterranean place on the corner that keeps me well fed with my daily portion of hummus and chicken shawarma. But Wayne had a car, thousands in the bank, and a hole in his heart, so he did crazy stuff like trading his truck's spare tire for a pet scorpion in the parking lot of a Wisconsin casino, because maybe the scorpion would love him, and he knew that the tire wouldn't. I told him that no part of a scorpion's brain was capable of loving anything, much less the human with the sweaty hand that was holding him nine billion scorpion-feet off the ground, but that he was probably right about the tire. Wayne told me I had no right to speak for tires *or* scorpions.

Wayne recounted to me what he had seen on his trips: the music, the air white and heavy with cigarette smoke, the terrible ways men once wore baseball caps, and the way fluorescent T-shirt paint was abused by our generation once upon a time. Holding court while the jukebox screeched some old Melvins track I'd put in there to make sure only people just like me came into my bar, Wayne melted into Little Boy Wayne, pliant and eager to do another tequila shot and repeat back to me and everyone at the bar his special list of things that made him happy: Lemon bars. Driving to Florida in his pickup truck. Cleaning dirt out from under his nails. Sunflower seeds. Basset hounds. Checking tire pressure. By closing time, Wayne returned to some level of normalcy, but the next night it was the same emotional circus.

I'm not saying I plumbed the depths of his psyche, nor was this the limit of our interactions. I merely allowed myself to act as his unlicensed therapist, an occupational hazard. But we were also buddies. After I told him he wasn't allowed to mop anymore, Wayne would draw monsters in his notebook as I tried to woo the honeys under the reddish neon light of the Pabst sign, with my sparkling wit and straight teeth. I had gotten some cash from an out-of-court settlement of a rights dispute with my band's old manager, who had swindled us. What did I do with that money? I got braces at the age of thirty-four. Wayne liked to leap across the bar to point this out to women. He said it made me seem responsible.

OUR FREQUENT TIME-TRAVELING to rock shows only hastened Wayne's descent into madness. While I was in my office negotiating an online pint glass order, I got a call from Wayne. Wayne's normal telephone greeting makes a bubbly sales manager from the local

Chevy dealer sound sedate, so it didn't immediately register that the slurring, babbling guy on the other end of the call was my friend. I invited him over to my apartment. He clearly needed to talk. Wayne arrived wearing his puffy blue winter coat, even though it was May; he had in his trembling hand a Mad Dog in a paper sack. Apparently the management at his job had threatened him with a layoff.

Wayne threw down his backpack and pushed the mountain of unfolded laundry from my threadbare couch onto the floor so he could lie down. He told me that for the past ten nights he had dreamed that the lower half of his body had been replaced with a circular saw, and that everyone he tried to touch he cut to bits. He talked about what a failure he was, how he was thirty-six and had never really been in love, how all he did was work, give his whole life to a company that treated him like crap, and all for what? A paycheck? Security? He was the most insecure guy he knew.

"I'm a tool, Karl."

"Why are you wearing your coat? Take that off." His coat was zipped up to his chin like a kindergartener about to go out and play in the snow. "It's summer."

"Don't act like I don't know what season it is, Karl."

"What do you want, man? Why the tears? Things are good right now. I sent six people to Woodstock, and I charged them a grand each."

Wayne covered his face with his hands and turned away. "What do you know? You own a cool bar. People actually talk to you. You were in the Axis."

I shook my head. "Please stop talking like that. I'm a has-been from a band that twelve people liked in 1999."

Wayne sat up and uncovered his face as if he'd had an instant revelation. "I've been thinking about my soul. Not in a Christian sense but in a . . . in a soul sense. Where it is and what have I been doing to use it. My soul, you know—meaning that, like, inner essence of goodness and charity. Or whatever."

"Sounds like you're battling your demons. Totally normal."

Wayne wiped his hand across his nose. "I'm weird."

I was inclined to agree. Everyone is weird in their own way. Wayne wore his winter coat in the summer: I liked to eat spoonfuls of mayonnaise sprinkled with Lawry's Seasoned Salt while standing naked inside my refrigerator door. The trick was not to scare others. "Wayne, take off that coat. It's making me nervous."

Wayne pulled his collar up higher around his head so that only his eyes showed. He had an expression of one possessed. I prayed he didn't have a gun on him. Part of me wanted to kick his ass out for bringing me down, but I owed him for all the hard work he'd done on the wormhole. I held his pale hand with the perfectly square fingernails.

"I want to be a superhero," he squeaked.

"Okay. Put on your cape and fly."

Wayne yanked back his hand. "Are you making fun of me?"

"No. Not at all. I really meant put on your cape and fly. Go live your dreams. You deserve great happiness, buddy, and I don't want to see you mopey anymore." I sounded like my mother, who died when I was twenty-three. She was the master of pep talks. I couldn't fight the longing I felt for her every time I tried to talk Wayne down off his proverbial ledge.

"Go live my dreams?"

"Let those corporate dicks lay you off, Wayne. Walk away. We've got plenty of money coming in from the wormhole."

"I don't want to do that, Karl," he said, in a more measured voice.

"Why not?"

"I'll just get another job after that, and everything will be the same. Same corporate slavery. Same unremarkable future. Except the only thing that will be different is that I can go back in time and catch that Echo and the Bunnymen show I missed when I was fifteen because Echo never played Sheboygan."

"Not if you change it. Not if you make a choice to change it, Wayne."

"Not if I change it. Not if I change it." Wayne sat up, dug his knuckles into his eyes, and put his glasses back on. "I've been thinking. I want to try something." Wayne hopped off the couch and pushed past me into my bedroom, over the piles of laundry I'd sorted into darks and lights but had so far avoided dragging down to the basement. "I want to change something. I want to change a lot of things, but this one thing in particular, Karl. I believe the time has come to use the wormhole for heroic purposes."

I knew I wasn't going to like it.

He looked up at me. "December 8, 1980. Central Park West. I'm going."

"John Lennon?"

Wayne nodded his head up and down. "I'm going to be a real superhero."

"You can't change the past," I repeated for the fifty millionth time. My damn mantra. "You can't. You physically cannot change the past."

Wayne hunched over my desk, stabbing at the keyboard with his index fingers. I didn't exactly know what he was capable of with the program he had written. He could change the system entirely and I wouldn't know what he'd done or how to fix it. "What if I just tried?"

"No way, man. No one is allowed to be a time travel vigilante on my watch," I said, though I didn't think he was listening. Wayne had that computer guy gift of hyperfocus, of blocking out the rest of the world without care or apology. I was his friend, his bartender, the guy who held his hand and said nice things to him when he needed to hear them, but the look of determination that had colonized his sweet, boyish face said all I needed to know about how much he was going to take to heart the wisdom of Karl Bender.

"I can do it. I can do something to delay Chapman. Or kill him. Or at least do something. Something to keep him away from John. I can try, can't I?" Wayne wore a maniacal grin and had stopped making eye contact with me.

"You can't take a bullet for John Lennon. Or really mess with Chapman. The past is read-only. You know that."

"I can get around that."

"What?"

"I made out with a girl at the REM show. In 1981. Gosh, she'd be in her fifties now." He composed himself and said, "You can touch people. Talk to them. Kick over a trash can. You just have to get past the first layer."

"No you can't!" I yelled. "Or I can't. How is it that you can touch people in the past and I can't?"

"The exit point is in that other dimension where you can't interact. You just have to penetrate that layer. I thought you wanted the layer so that not having a ticket to the show would be a nonissue."

"How do I do it then? Touch things?"

"I'll tell you when I get back. Look, my soul calls me to correct past wrongs. I'm starting with Lennon. His murder was hugely devastating to a lot of people. At least if I succeed, eighties music won't be half as awful."

"What's a layer, Wayne?" Wayne stared down at his shoes, his mouth shut in defiance. "Wayne?" He remained silent. "Wayne, answer me."

Wayne shook his head. "Forget I said anything."

"No!" I shouted. "What's a layer?"

He shot me a sulky look and then, as if he were preparing to travel, walked back out to the living room and picked up his backpack and put his arms through the straps. I felt the crux of our relationship—Wayne's needing me—rip away like a Velcro shoe fastener. "Fuck you, Bender."

I walked over to Wayne, who flinched when I got up close. "Oh, stop it. I'm not going to hurt you."

"Maybe you are," he said. Wayne dashed back into my bedroom and threw himself on the bed. I followed behind him.

"Wayne, seriously, dude. Why John Lennon? What's that going to solve?"

"Lennon was a great peacemaker. He's, like, he's . . . he's the one guy who really could, you know . . . bring the happiness and love out of our hearts. And he had a great creative partnership with the woman he loved. He gave a lot to his fans. To the world."

I wanted to pat his head in a maternal fashion, but I also wanted to pound his ass and tell him to knock it off. I'd never had a friend like Wayne before, one who was kind and sweet and super smart and who I could trust completely, but who was sometimes the thirty-six-year-old equivalent of a cranky toddler.

"That's my wormhole too, damn it. Just because it's in your apartment doesn't mean it's not mine." Wayne's hands shook, even though they were balled into fists, but his eyes were in some crazy hyperfocus mode. If I tried to talk him out of it, he would override me. Not with physical strength, but with intent. I guess he just wanted it bad enough.

A cluster of colored wires sat anchored to the floor with duct tape, coming out of floorboards into the two laptops that sat perched on my old wooden desk. He rolled off the bed and crawled on his hands and knees to my closet and grabbed a fistful of those wires and looked me straight in the eye. "I'm going to 1980. I'm going and you're sending me, or I pull these wires out and smash these computers and then I go home and smash my head against the wall. I mean it."

I made a move toward him.

"Don't, Karl." He tugged on his handful of wires. "I'm getting my way."

"How about, instead of messing with the damn wormhole, you rededicate your life to the spreading of peace and love, or make an album of peace songs, or whatever else John Lennon would have done."

The wires remained firmly in Wayne's fist. He wore a backpack full of supplies: flashlight, water bottle, granola bars, extra cell phone, and most importantly, a solar cell phone charger, since zapping back to the present drains the hell out of your battery.

He sniffed a few times and looked me square in the eye. "No."

I weighed my options. I could jump him, but I didn't want to hurt the guy. Plus, he'd take those wires with him, the whole deal would be over, and I'd be cut off forever from the drug that was time travel. I wasn't yet willing to give up the special, sexy rush that was a trip backwards.

"Wayne, did you interact with people in the past? Wayne? I need to know. I need you to tell me what a layer is, buddy. I need you to tell me that you really can mess with the past. Can you?"

Wayne flipped me the bird, then took his cell phone out of the pocket of his puffy coat and pointed it at me.

"Central Park. December 8, 1980," he said, a little quake in his voice. His face was red and flushed. "Do it. Do it or I wreck this thing and I never set foot in your bar ever again."

"Why Lennon?"

Wayne's mouth fell open, and as if it were bad breath, I was hit with a cloud of Wayne's disappointment in me. "Damn, Karl," he said, looking away. "If you have to keep asking, you're, like, not the guy I thought you were."

I sat down at the computer and stared at the wormhole interface that Wayne had made. It looked like Pong. In the Chron POE (point of entry) field, I typed 08 DEC 1980, and entered 72nd and Central Park West, Manhattan, in the field for Geog POE. I typed slowly, looking up at Wayne to let him know that things were going to be very bad between us, regardless of whether or not he succeeded in saving Lennon. Vigilante shit angered me. Okay, say Wayne saves John Lennon, and then what? We're obligated to kill Hitler, free the slaves, reverse the 2000 election, and punch about fifty million grade-school bullies in the nuts. I prefer to limit my moral obligations to not banging married women and donating money to the Red Cross. The wormhole was already fraught with moral quandaries, and here I was, going against my gut, giving the toddler his way.

Wayne wiped the tears from his cheeks. He jumped up and down like it was his birthday. "Call me in an hour, Karlito. I think this is a benevolent act, I really do. All of your albums over there, they're going to catch fire! You watch!"

I watched. I pushed the button. And in an instant, Wayne went through the floor.

Thirty minutes later, my album collection remained intact.

Twenty minutes after that, a text message from Wayne popped up on my phone: *THIS IS WRONG. WHERE AM I? NOTHING BUT TREES AND SNOW.*

Then: *THERE ARE NO BUILDINGS OR CARS. THIS IS NOT NYC.*

Then: *CHECK THE COMPUTER!*

I like to admit it when I screw up. I find identifying one's faults to be an admirable trait. Once, on a tour, in Providence, I forgot to load our brand-new amp into the van after a gig. We were in New Haven by the time I realized what I had done. Milo, the lead singer who had fronted the money for the amp, responded with a left hook to my face. He then tried to snap my neck like a twig after we raced back to Providence, only to find that someone had stolen the amp.

I looked at the computer screen: CHRON POE: 08 DEC 980.

Fuck.

I had left off the number one in 1980. I had shuttled my friend one thousand and thirty years into the past. For a moment all I felt was admiration that the system Wayne had set up could be so exact.

Nine hundred and eighty. A full five hundred years before the first boatload of Dutch colonists landed on the Island of Mannahatta. There is no recorded North American history for the year 980. It would be another one hundred years before Vikings arrived in Newfoundland.

Then I came to. I dialed Wayne's number, hoping that would bring him back to the present, knowing it wouldn't. Reentry requires an electrical power source. He would need to be in a place with many electromagnetic fields, such as a rock club with lights and amps and neon beer signs. Without electromagnetic fields, reentry was impossible. It was a flaw that Wayne was working on eliminating, but science and safety take time to develop while, apparently, saving John Lennon's life thirty years after the fact simply couldn't have waited another second.

I texted him: *I SENT YOU TO THE YEAR 980.*

Minutes later, the response: *ARE YOU KIDDING?*

I typed in the reversal code. Error code. Nothing. I tried again. I said a prayer. I cried. I punched the desk until my knuckles turned purple.

I CANCELED MY four o'clock appointment with my bar-back Clyde and his twenty-something friends, who wanted to see Nirvana play

Olympia in 1991. I went to the bar. I poured myself a shot of whiskey. I mopped the ladies room. I swapped out an empty keg. I made idle chatter with a dude named Keith who wanted to know where he could get some seed for his bird feeder.

My mother died of cancer when I was a hate-spewing shithead of twenty-three, and I remember very clearly sitting around the Bender familial manse in West Hartford, after the doctors had sent my sister and me home because my mother's suffering was over, watching Brooke lie facedown on the couch in her ham-pink nurse's scrubs, asking her repeatedly if she was still breathing, thinking about how much of my life depended on my sister's lungs taking in air, because without her there wouldn't be anyone permanently responsible for giving a rat's ass about me ever again. Wayne cared about me the way Brooke did in the days after our mom died, needy but sweet, and motivated by losing a parent before we were old enough to comprehend just how barren and raw our mother's early departure would leave me and Brooke in the hardest moments of our adult lives.

Once, I'd offered to set up Wayne with Brooke, now an operating room nurse in Orlando. Both are kind souls and a bit high-strung, and Brooke had been unlucky in love to the tune of one ex serving time for postal fraud and another ex who disappeared with his AA sponsor's old lady a month before his and Brooke's paid-for Disney wedding. Wayne thought that Florida was too far away for a relationship. Brooke said that any man who spent time in my bar was probably an alcoholic lowlife and therefore not suitable marriage material. I told Brooke that Wayne had a Little Mermaid soap dispenser in his bathroom. She still refused. This hurt my feelings.

Due to the bending of time and space, cell satellites are in the sky even in the year 980, so yes, Wayne's phone worked, as long as his phone had power.

HEY SHITHEAD, he texted, *IT'S WINTER HERE AND THERE ARE NO BUILDINGS. I'VE GOT FROSTBITE ON MY SCROTUM AND IT'S YOUR FAULT!*

And: *YOU'RE LUCKY I WAS A BOY SCOUT. I BUILT MYSELF A HUT OUT OF DIRT AND STICKS. AND AT LEAST I HAVE MY COAT.*

And: *I GUESS I'LL JUST INVENT ELECTRICITY. NO PROBLEM. OH, RIGHT, NO CONDUCTIVE MATERIAL.*

And: *RACCOON! IT'S WHAT'S FOR DINNER!*

And finally: *YOU'RE TOO DUMB TO FIX THIS YOURSELF. GO FIND AN ASTROPHYSICIST.*

2

HOW DO YOU find yourself an astrophysicist? You order one online.

My bar is called the Dictator's Club, and in spite of its can-do attitude and bitchin' Wednesday night dollar drafts special, it did not attract Chicago's astrophysics community. I wasn't really in the right neighborhood for that. I didn't know any science people, save Wayne—just a lawyer, a chiropractor, two dental hygienists, and a guy who owned a really creepy reptiles-only pet store. No one with an academic understanding of the space-time continuum.

When a regular dude dials up the physics department at the University of Chicago and asks who he should speak to about the viability of time travel, admitting that he has no academic credentials and demanding to be taken seriously, he gets hung up on.

Each of the PhD candidates in astrophysics at Northwestern was pictured on the departmental Web site in poorly lit photos taken in the artistic tradition of the department of motor vehicles.

No way in hell would this overwhelmingly serious, fashion-backward, sloppily bearded bunch of dudes believe me when I explained my situation to them, and if they did, they'd steal my operation and have me killed.

The Web site showed two female PhD students in astrophysics: a woman from China with a tight black schoolmarm bun who stared blankly at the camera, a look that indicated that she'd never heard of Fugazi. And then, this girl: a kindred soul; a young, unsmiling woman who had streaks of blue Manic Panic in her otherwise black bangs, the only one who showed up for picture day in Buddy Holly glasses and a Melvins T-shirt, giving the camera a perfect Courtney Love snarl. *Lena R. Geduldig, BS, Physics, University of Montana, 2002. Areas of expertise: cosmology, string theory.* You could tell she was as ferocious as she was smart, and that she wasn't above biting you if the occasion called for it. I liked this girl and knew that she was part of my big cosmic family, someone I'd have in my bar every night, someone I'd try to protect from the hurt and the sorrow of continuous spins around the sun.

The page listed her office hours. I waited until Wednesday from ten a.m. to noon to place my call.

"This is Lena Geduldig." She had a deep voice, slightly hoarse.

"Hi. My name is Karl Bender. I, um . . ." I should have prepared a speech. My voice quivered, like I was afraid of Punk Rock Science Lady.

"Are you one of my students?"

"No. Just a regular guy. I just, have a problem that requires an astrophysicist."

"Are you worried that an asteroid is going to take out North America? Because you have nothing to worry about, at least not until 2029."

"No. I'm a bartender and a musician but I need some physics help. Could you meet me for a drink so we could talk about this?

I don't feel comfortable talking about it over the phone. It's a serious problem and I'm willing to pay you for your time."

I started to panic. I was placing trust in a person because she was wearing a Melvins T-shirt, because her bangs were blue, and because she seemed like the kind of chick who could use a trip back in time to see a band. She was a real scientist who could realistically take over my wormhole, or destroy it, or report me to some scientific police agency, even if she did hold dear some punk, fuck-the-cops politics, which I couldn't be sure of from just a picture.

She was silent for a bit. "That sounds ominous. You say you're a bartender?"

"I don't mean to sound ominous. I just need some help and you seem, based on your photo on the Northwestern Web site—"

"Based on that shitty picture you want to talk to me?"

"I like the picture."

"Why? I look disgusting."

"It's not disgusting at all. You look like the only person in your department with a personality."

"Wow. A personality. Thanks for noticing, dude. No one has paid me a compliment like that in a while."

"Absolutely. And you obviously have great taste in music."

"Oh god. The Melvins shirt? Right. Physics and bands. The only two things men want to talk to me about."

"Yeah, sorry. Um . . . meet me at my bar? Drinks on me."

"You're not going to ask me your question over the phone? I have to drag my ass out to some unknown corner of Chicago to meet some strange man who found my punk-ass physics bitch picture on the Northwestern Web site? How is this not shady?"

"I swear it's not shady. I'm sorry if it seems that way. I'd go to Evanston to meet with you but I have to work every night this week, and this is urgent. If you get here and I or my bar freak you out, I'll pay for you to take a taxi home." Then I added, "The Dictator's Club. Bucktown."

"You own the Dictator's Club?"

"You know it?"

"Uh . . . yeah, kind of." Her statement lingered unacknowledged for a few seconds too long. I guessed she didn't think too highly of my bar.

"Blue Line, right?" she asked, and I felt slightly, vaguely relieved. "I guess I can be out there around six."

"Blue Line to Western. Thank you, Lena. I look forward to working with you."

"I carry pepper spray," she said, and hung up.

Lena Geduldig had already been camped out at one of my tables for an hour before I arrived at the Dick to meet her. Beneath the Old Style neon and the velvet Elvis Costello painting that my friend Susannah made for my thirty-eighth birthday, sat the girl from the Northwestern physics department Web site. Two empty pint glasses, a laptop, a stack of books and papers, and behind that, the wizened face of the smartest girl I'd ever had the pleasure of ordering from the Internet. Lena Geduldig looked like she'd learned to cover up her big brainy-brain with a considerable amount of urban costumery: magenta-streaked hair pulled into pigtails that jutted from the back of her head, green and white striped kneesocks, and a black Hüsker Dü T-shirt with the neck cut off, revealing the red and black swirls of an indecipherable tattoo drawn between her collarbone and her heavy breasts. Lena was a thick girl, with a mound of belly pressing up against the table and plump calves beneath where her homemade-looking skull-and-crossbones skirt ended. Her dark brown eyes were hidden behind her Buddy Holly glasses, and even though she was probably around thirty, she was still into black nail polish and writing notes on the back of her hand in different colors of ink. Lena Geduldig, PhD candidate in astrophysics, looked up from her laptop and said my name.

"Yeah, that's me."

"Is that your real name?" she asked.

I am accustomed to the females of the species smiling at me when they meet me for the first time, schooled as they are in flirting as a means of gaining approval, but Lena Geduldig did no such thing. She maintained her baseline frown. Number of shits given by Lena: zero.

"It is."

Lena snorted. "I thought maybe it was a pseudonym. Like you're hiding something. It seems too perfect. Like, if I were writing a sci-fi novel about a guy who could time travel, I'd never name the guy Karl Bender. It's too much like Carl Sagan and the robot from *Futurama*."

"It's my real name." I usually want to smack people who like to pun off my name. But Lena Geduldig, in her stripy socks and her pigtails, complete with choppy toddler bangs, was probably one of those girls who play at being tough to cover up the fact that they're about to cry.

"Let me ask you, Karl: Do you let teenagers drink at your bar? You've got what appears to be a minor sitting over there by the jukebox." Lena Geduldig pointed to a girl with a long black ponytail, wearing a white lab coat made of a shiny white papery Tyvek-like material. The girl was fiddling around with something on her wrist.

"That's weird," I said, and as I was about to walk over to speak to the too-young-to-be-in-my-bar girl, she looked up at me, yelled "Sorry," and disappeared.

"Did she just disappear? What the hell?" I asked.

"That was weird," Lena said.

"I don't let teenagers drink here."

"Your bar is weird. Why do you keep it so dark?" Lena asked, and that kind of hurt my feelings. The Dictator's Club rejects abject illumination. It's lit only with the orange glow of various beer neons and the regulation exit signs. The restroom walls are a gnarled poem of sex slogans scrawled in drunk Sharpie. The jukebox is curated by yours truly, featuring Iggy, Bruce, some Elvis (Costello, not the other one), Melvins, Siouxsie, Pixies, Kate Bush. Eighties Kate Bush. The Cure in the winter, Sebadoh in the fall, Unrest in the spring, the Replacements if I want to make the honeys cry. Wilco, only because this is Chicago, and the Clash, only because I am not a complete failure in life. My bar was in no way weird. My bar was a temple. I told Lena this, and she made a huffy snort out of her nose.

"Speaking of, your bartender? Clyde? He loves you. He foamed at the mouth about how cool you are. He also told me that you were in the Axis? I'd heard a rumor that a guy from the Axis owned a bar in Chicago, and I guess this means it's true. I loved the Axis. I had all your albums. *Dreams of Complicated Sorrow. Look, Mom, I Found a Ditch.* And *Big, Bigger Love*? I drove all the way to Portland from Missoula, Montana, to see you guys play that album in its entirety. Milo Kildare. Shit. *Big, Bigger Love* is flippin' genius. 'Pin Cushion' was my personal early-twenties anthem."

"I hear that a lot," I told her.

I admit that I hired Clyde because on his application he wrote, "I seriously love the Axis. Not kissing your ass, just saying." Clyde told me he played my old band regularly on his college radio show, years after effete front man Milo Kildare and I mothballed our instruments and sold the tour van to a similar act that hadn't been worn down like a pencil eraser over years of exhaustion, lost wages, and petty late-night arguments over whether Milo should be allowed to put a clothesline up in the van to dry his socks and underwear after he washed them in a rest stop men's room sink, or whether Milo had the right to force me to wax my chest, because he found the tufts of fur that poke upward from the collar of my T-shirt "distracting." It should be mentioned here that Milo wore cravats and deliberately high-water jeans and had a black ink tattoo of a cheese grater on his wrist, which he'd rub on my face whenever I said something he didn't want to hear. (*"I'm grating your face, Bendo!"*) Clyde was maybe thirteen years old when Milo and I parted company: me for the cold, damp peace of Chicago and the Dictator's Club; Milo for Portland, Oregon, where he designs Web sites and treats raising his kids like just another thing that's no fun without an audience. His wife, Jodie, e-mails me pictures of little Edgar and Viola running around in the frilly steampunk costumes she and Milo design and sell at the farmers' market. I haven't spoken to Milo since the last time he breezed through Chicago on tour with his now-defunct Japanese-y freak-folk act, which was five years ago. I called to tell him I couldn't make the show. Our exchange went exactly like this:

KARL: *Hey, Milo, it's Karl.*
MILO: *You coming to my show tonight?*
KARL: *Sorry, dude, I couldn't find anyone to cover me at the bar tonight, but if you want to come by for drinks afterwards, I'd love to see you.*
MILO: *[*Long pause*] If God appeared before you and touched your cheek, you'd, what, say you had to work? [*Hang up*]*

Lena sang Milo's lyrics in full voice, banging out the introductory guitar riff on the table: "This is the start of a revolution! I'm the pin and you're my cushion! Soft hips soft lips beneath my fingertips! Round like I found you. Round like I want you. Round how I love you. Don't let them teach you, just let me reach you, don't let them teach you, so much to love. This is the start of a revolution, shake that belly proud. . . ."

Of course she was a Milo fan. Every feminist chick that went to college in the nineties loved Milo. Those girls who shook their bellies proud in his direction when he stormed the crowd during one of his performances were our primary fan base during the later years.

"That one was all Milo. I had nothing to do with that one."

"Milo rubbed his crotch on the microphone stand during that show so much, I bet his dick was always chafed. That, and I'm sure he slept with every plus-sized girl in the western United States. I bet you have some stories."

I tried not to look disappointed that my astrophysicist wanted to wax nostalgic about Milo Kildare's chafed dick. Milo had many fans, and they were all big-boned, educated, fashionably "alternative," brunette, wrote long feminist screeds on the Internet about things that angered them, and looked like they were about to kick your ass or burst into tears or both.

"Can I get you another drink?"

"Sure. This was Goose Island something. Clyde picked it. He said it was on the house."

"If you help me you can drink at my bar for free for the rest of your life."

Lena slammed her laptop shut. It had a yellow Teen-Beat Records sticker stuck on the front. "What do you need from the wonderful world of astrophysics? Asteroids? Black holes? String theory? I'm a string theory girl, which is more mathematics than anything. I'm not really, like, a NASA-type physicist. I just write formulas that my PI tells me to do over because they suck."

I took a deep breath and leaned across the table, lowering my voice to share my secret. "Do you believe in the possibility of time travel?"

Lena snorted. "No. Sorry. Can't happen. Thanks for the beer, though."

"What about wormholes?"

She raised her eyebrows at me, making sure I got the message that she thought I was an idiot. "What about wormholes?"

"What do you know about wormholes?"

"Theoretical stuff. The Einstein–Rosen Bridge?"

"Exactly."

"Oh god. Really?" She made that snarl face, like in her picture. "Let me guess. You're writing a novel?"

"No. I'm not writing a novel. I'm talking about a real wormhole. A portal to the past. A highway, if you will, to the rock shows of yesterday." I braced myself for a blasting.

"Sounds sexy. Sci-fi sexy."

"It is."

Lena took a sheet of paper from the stack on the table and began to sketch a diagram with her purple pen. "Theoretically, we can time travel. To the future. Not backwards. It would involve launching yourself into space, your body not aging very much, and landing back down on Earth in the future. Theoretically. No one has actually accomplished this. This is the basic formula, which I know looks like a bunch of lines and figures, but there it is." She turned around the sheet of paper to show me her lines and figures, and a drawing that looked like a funnel.

"But that's not a wormhole."

"It's a theoretical wormhole, and wormholes are only theory anyway. One could theoretically build an artificial negative-mass black hole and use it for time travel, but that involves matter with negative mass with the power to curve space-time like a

Pringles potato chip. How much do you know about Euclidian geometry?"

"Uh, nothing?"

"I mean, if you can travel through time and then come back to the present, that pretty much kills Schwarzchild's topology, and that leads me to some questionable rethinkings of the laws of quantum gravity. Hmm. Frankly, I think time-traveling to the future is stupid, because when you come back all your friends will be old or dead and you'll have missed out on a lot. I mean, even if it's crappy, it's still your life. Maybe medicine in the future will improve. But the environment will be shot to shit. I'd say stay right where you are."

"I have a wormhole," I said. "In my apartment."

I could tell by the way she cocked her eyebrows at me that Lena was used to talking about physics with people she deemed to be beneath her level of intelligence. "My years of scientific training tell me you don't."

"Well. You'd be wrong, then. Isn't science, like, constantly changing?"

"No." Her tone was snotty. "I don't even know where to start with that."

"What I mean is, don't new things get proven? Isn't science a constant quest for the truth about the world?"

Lena picked up her stack of papers from the table and started to put them in her bag, an old, beat-up army surplus model covered in band patches.

She pointed her index finger around my bar and raised her voice. "Everything around us? You, me, this bar, Chicago? Is temporary. It's not like you can hit rewind and all the old cars and houses are suddenly new, and dead people come back to life. It doesn't exist anywhere in the universe. It's dead matter. It's all gone."

"You're not going to like this, but you're wrong."

"I'm not, but okay. Let's say I'm wrong. Where did you go in your wormhole?"

"1990."

"How did you know it was 1990? How do you know you actually, physically, went back in time?" Lena's voice grew louder and her cheeks grew redder. I almost felt bad for involving her.

"I fell through the floor of my bedroom closet and landed at a show at T.T. the Bear's Place in Cambridge, Massachusetts. I knew it was 1990 from the posters on the wall. The cars, too. When was the last time you saw a Pinto, an AMC Gremlin, and three really old, angular Subarus parked next to each other on the street?"

"So you fell through your floor and ended up in a magical parking lot with some ugly cars from the seventies. Anything else?"

"The passage. It was freezing cold, with blinding lights the whole time."

"How long did it take for you to get to the magical parking lot?"

"About a minute."

"You know, there's a salvage lot on the West Side. You can see it from the Green Line train. Maybe you were there. Certainly there is a place that still exists on earth that you just, you know, happened to be at."

"I wasn't in Chicago. I saw Galaxie 500 play a show. It was at T.T. the Bear's Place in Cambridge, Massachusetts, in 1990."

"I love Galaxie 500. Did they play 'Tugboat'?"

"Yeah."

Lena blushed. It was nice to see her drop her guard for a bit. "I really love Galaxie 500."

I gave Lena a thumbs up and said I loved Galaxie, too. "Okay, so let me ask you. Purely hypothetical. It's a game I like to play with people I've just met. If you could go back in time and see any band perform, who would you pick?"

"'Hypothetical' meaning I don't get to go for a ride in your wormhole?"

"Okay. Yes. You really do get to go back in time and see whatever band you want."

I racked my mind for a guess as to whom Lena would want to see. She looked like she would pull a fast one and pick someone unexpected, like Merle Haggard or Tupac Shakur. She did know Galaxie 500, even though she was probably a little on the young side to remember them during their time. She wore a Hüsker Dü shirt and had a Fugazi patch on her bag. Her attire and demeanor suggested an appreciation for Sleater-Kinney and other Pacific Northwest riot grrrl bands, but that she might also be more into hard-core stuff, judging from her Melvins T-shirt in that photograph on the Northwestern Web site.

"Thinking Fellers Union Local 282." She didn't even have to think about it, was so bursting with the need to say it. Thinking Fellers. It was on the tip of her tongue.

Didn't see that one coming.

"Not the Smiths?"

She clicked her tongue at me. "Do I look like I give a shit about the Smiths?"

"No. You appear to have lived a full, productive life without any help from Morrissey."

"Damn right I have."

Thinking Fellers. Early nineties San Francisco weirdo band, spoken of in the same sentence as Ed's Redeeming Qualities. Clearly she deejayed college radio.

"Did you deejay college radio?" I asked.

"No."

"So how do you know the Thinking Fellers?"

"Why do you think only college radio deejays know the Thinking

Fellers?" Lena Geduldig was excellent at making an old bartender feel like a complete idiot. I decided to never tell her that I dropped out of college.

"I don't." Talking to Lena felt like carrying ten boxes of records up ten flights of stairs. "Well, yeah. Okay. You win, sister."

She took a long swig from her glass of beer. "The college radio station in the bumblefuck town in Montana where I grew up used to play the Thinking Fellers. When I was a kid, I used to call the deejays there and ask them to play They Might Be Giants. The one guy, Mark, he was sick of TMBG, so he told me to listen to the Thinking Fellers instead. I liked them."

"I see."

"You're a rock 'n' roll kind of guy. Not all bookish and vintage-clad like the standard Axis fan. Sleeve tattoos. Goatee. I remember you, kind of. You had long hair. You clearly have an opinion about a lot of bands."

"I do. But opinions are like assholes."

"Full of shit?"

We made eye contact, and I saw in Lena's eyes a kindness that wasn't there before. She really did have a soft center, like a pillow or a powdery dinner roll. I liked her eyes, big and brown, with clumps of mascara clinging to the tips of her eyelashes. The grumpy girl was smiling. At me.

"Are you sure your little trip back in time to the magic parking lot wasn't a memory lapse or a dream? Something with you brain's memory center? Psychotropic drugs?"

"This may surprise you, but I've never done any drug beyond pot. And I'm positive I was really there. I saw myself. In the crowd. And it smelled weird. Like burning tires or something. That's the smell of the accelerator burning."

"Do you just travel to rock shows you've seen?"

"I've gone to Altamont. I wasn't even born yet."

"You went to Altamont?"

"You sound skeptical."

"A good scientist is always skeptical. I'm a good scientist." She stood up and grabbed her bag. "I want to see Thinking Fellers. San Francisco, 1993. Take me to your wormhole."

I TOOK HER back to my place, praying it didn't stink when I opened the door, which it did. A cloud of Karl Bender BO/Ming's Panda stank wafted into our nostrils, but Lena said nothing. Normally I cleaned up a bit before having strangers come and ride the wormhole. I cringed as Lena stepped over a pair of my worn white briefs, yellowed crotch sunny-side up.

"I like your apartment," Lena said. "It's cozy." Lena pointed at my floor-to-ceiling bookshelf of vinyl records. "Wow."

"Sorry about the mess."

"I bet you eat a lot of Ming's Panda."

"I avoid it like the plague. Their dumpsters reek and their egg rolls may contain dead people."

"Does the fireplace work?"

I glanced over at my fireplace, which I often forgot was there. It contained the requisite bouquet of Nuestra Señora de Guadalupe candles from the Mexican grocery down the street, only lit on occasions when a lady is present and I endeavor to create a mood. "No. So, where in San Francisco do you want your entry point to be? I have to figure out the coordinates—"

"Corner of Divisadero and Hayes."

"Sounds like you've been there before."

"Many times, when I went to Stanford. Just not to see the Thinking Fellers. They were a bit before my time. I'd go up to the city a fair bit for arts and culture. It's called the Independent now. Not the Kennel Club, as it would have been in 1993."

"Let me see your cell phone."

"My cell phone? Why do you need my cell phone?"

"You need to have your cell phone for reentry. If you have an iPhone I can install a special app designed by my friend Wayne. You dial my number and I bring you back to the present."

"I just have this old one." She held out a flimsy pink flip phone. A dinosaur. The casing was scratched and a plastic Hello Kitty charm dangled from the bottom.

"I don't know if that'll work for this. Wayne's pretty sensitive about technical specs. You can take one of mine." I handed her my iPhone. "Just send a text to this number when you're finished. Hold the phone in one hand and press your other hand to an electrically charged object—an amp, a streetlamp, the electric hand dryer in the restroom. Whatever you can find. The wormhole is cold. When you arrive you will experience a pretty shuddering physical drop. Sort of like you fell off the roof of a bus."

"Okay."

"It goes away pretty quickly, though."

"Okay."

"No interaction with anyone. Even if you find that you can communicate, don't."

She made a face. "Why can't I interact with anyone? What's the point of time traveling if you can't talk to people?"

"It's dangerous. House rules, Lena. Definitely do not go blabbing around to people that you're from the future. People will just think you're high."

"I don't care what people think."

"I care, Lena. No souvenirs. No T-shirts. No bringing back an old soda can or magazine for nostalgia value. Nothing can come back with you."

"What if I get there and I'm naked?"

"You won't be naked. Did you read *The Time Traveler's Wife*? Everyone who's read that book thinks they're going to land in the past naked."

"So my clothes travel, too?"

"Yes."

"How is that possible?"

"You tell me, Dr. Science Lady."

I MADE VERY sure I typed in 1993 and not 993 before sending Lena through the wormhole. Then I gave the floor a quick sweep, changed my sheets, and Googled the living hell out of Lena Geduldig.

Lena R. Geduldig, BS, Physics, University of Montana, 2002.

Lena R. Geduldig, Butte High School Class of 1996 ten-year reunion. (She did not attend).

Lena Geduldig, Capo, Evanston Knitting Mafia.

Attended Steve McCormick and Mariah Wilkes's wedding on April 11, 2009, in Berkeley.

Non-Northwestern e-mail: l.diggy@hmail.com.

Her father appeared to be Dr. David Geduldig, professor of geology at Montana Tech. A grizzled hippie with manic eyes and huge, disfiguring glasses, Dr. David Geduldig possessed the kind of long, shaggy, salt-and-pepper beard that a family of voles could use as a condominium.

Her middle name: Rose.

Date of birth: December 13, 1978.

The control panel beeped. Back came Lena.

She crawled out of the closet. "Can I lie on your bed? I have to rest."

"Sure."

Lena flopped onto my clean bed, took off her glasses, and rubbed her face with her hands. Her breathing was labored, and her head was damp with sweat.

"That was exhausting."

"Yes."

"And exhilarating." Her bottom teeth were crooked. "Oh my god."

"Take your time. When you're ready we can talk about my problem and how you can help."

"Oh my god. That was amazing!" Lena yelled. Because I am a filthy old man, I felt like I was getting the soundtrack of what it must be like to have sex with her. I looked away politely, allowing her to feel what she felt, without my invasive eyes tracking the movement of her breasts as she rolled back and forth on a surface where I often masturbate.

"Yep."

"It was really 1993. The hair. And the band. Well, the band was sloppy. I'm not going to lie to you. They totally tripped up on 'Narlus Spectre.' But being back in 1993. Oh my god, wormholes do exist."

"Please don't tell anyone at your school," I said.

"What?"

"I need you to keep this a secret."

She looked at me like I had twelve heads. "A secret? Are you insane? Proving the existence and functionality of the Einstein–Rosen Bridge? I'm already on my PI's shit list. Bringing in some huge breakthrough like a portal to the past would save my career and make me—us, obviously—a ton of money."

"Lena, please. Please keep it to yourself. At least for a little while longer. I need you to keep it quiet until we complete the mission I'm about to hire you for."

She sat up and looked at me. Looked through me, really.

"I'm paying you for your services and to keep your yap shut about this to your science people."

"This is insane," was all she said. "I don't think you understand the gravity of this situation."

"Want a drink? I've got Coke, and water and bourbon, too, if you want."

"Water would be great. Not as awesome as the existence of time travel. But for now, water sounds really nice."

It appeared that Lena wasn't going to leave my bed anytime soon. I got her a glass of water, which she drank in one gulp.

She handed me back the glass.

"Can I trust you not to blab about this to your department?"

"Give me a minute to regroup," she said. Sweat collected around her eyebrows. Lena sat on the edge of the bed and used her fingernail to pick at her already-chipped black nail polish. "So what do you need from me? With regards to your wormhole? I should warn you that I'm not the shiniest star in the Northwestern physics galaxy. I'm kind of screwed with the department, actually."

"I need you for a lifesaving mission."

"What does that mean?"

"My friend Wayne. He's the one that rigged up all the software and wires and programs in order to send people to where they want to go. We set it up as a business. We sell time travel trips to rock concerts. We were exploring other types of entertainment until Wayne went missing. I have one guy who loves Dorothy Hamill. So rock shows and the occasional sports event. Anyway, something bad happened."

She sat up. "Yeah?"

"I sent him to 980. He wanted to stop John Lennon from being assassinated, and when I typed in all the information on the computer I left off the one in 1980. So he's in 980. And there's no electricity there, so we're having trouble getting him back to the present."

"How do you know he's in 980?" Lena asked, curling into a fetal position.

"I forgot to type in the one. Manhattan was just a big forest. He can text. The satellites are still in the sky and the towers still function. Don't ask me how that works. I get texts from his number. He describes what it's like in 980. Just trees and snow.."

"You can't know for sure that he's in 980."

"Hey, I got you to San Francisco in 1993, didn't I? Right on time for the Thinking Fellers."

She stood up and smoothed her skirt down. "I'm just going to go ahead and suspend my disbelief and, I guess, believe you, even though I'm a scientist and we're not really into believing stuff without proof."

"Good."

"I can't ask anyone in my department about this?"

"Right."

She bit her lip. "If it's just a matter of his having access to an electrical power source, you could throw a generator down the wormhole down to 980 and jolt him back that way. The problem is, the end of the wormhole in 980 won't be in the exact spot where your friend was expelled."

"Okay."

"There is no way a wormhole is static. It can move inches or feet or miles. It could disappear. You can't go backwards. Forwards is possible only based on a theoretical model. String theory is just a theory, after all. Also, are you actually sure he's in 980? I mean, within the space-time continuum, the calendar is pretty arbitrary."

I nodded.

She flopped back on the bed. "I never got to see Elliott Smith," she said.

"He was great."

"No shit he was great."

"Are you asking for something, Dr. Lena?"

She smiled at me. "I'm not a doctor, and yes. I want to see Elliott."

"It takes two hours for all the computer stuff to reset."

"Will you come with me? It would be more fun to go with someone, I think."

"Yeah, I could do that. I mean, I'm a little nervous traveling without someone back home at the controls, but we can do it."

Lena looked at me with expectant eyes. I couldn't tell if these were eyes of interest of a sexual nature, hoping that I'd give her a proper shag, or if she was lonely and I was the first person she'd talked to in a while who wasn't a jerk. She seemed to need something from me.

I was sweating—that funky stress sweat that smells like old cheese.

She pointed at my left arm and yelled, "Oh hey! Your tattoo."

"Which one?"

"'The moon is a lightbulb breaking.'" She touched her finger above my elbow, where the words snaked around an image of a broken lightbulb. She turned her back and lifted up her shirt. Across the small of her back was the same line from the same song by Elliott Smith, the same dead singer/songwriter, who we both obviously cherished enough to have his words seared into our bodies.

"We're the same."

"I suppose we are."

"Not every day you find someone with the same tattoo. I mean, not like they're identical designs or anything. And a song lyric, not some dumb tattoo that everyone has and thinks is edgy"

"It just means we're both really cool."

Lena blushed, lifting her hand to her cheek. I found myself liking this girl, if not in a sexy, romantic way, then at least in an ally-in-this-cruel-world way. I moved to place my big, clumsy hand on her shoulder and cure her hurts with the twin blessings of time travel and rock and roll.

"So, just to be clear. You're going to work on a plan to retrieve Wayne?"

"Yeah, I'll add that to the top of my list of stuff to do. Right now, school is kind of . . . It's uh . . ." Lena stuck her tongue out. "I have to turn in my dissertation by the end of August, right? So, not to get into the blah-blah of a bunch of stuff you don't understand, but one of my so-called colleagues stole a bunch of my research and is about to publish it, and they believe him because he went to Caltech and has a penis, and I'm just the punk rock bitch who graduated from a state school, so, like, the last seven years of grad school are pretty much down the crapper for me. I can't turn in my thesis because it got stolen and I can't do another one in three months, so I'm hosed."

"Hey, if you get Wayne back by the end of the week, I've got two thousand bucks for you."

She sat down on the bed again. "I'll figure out something. I might fail a few times along the way. That's what we scientists do. Fail."

"Do me a favor and don't fail."

She looked away and said, "I fail a lot, Karl. Just warning you."

Lena sighed and I sighed and we sat in each other's presence without talking. I negotiated the inherent risk of trust—handing this stranger the keys to my wormhole. At the age of forty, I would honor the Latin phrase I had tattooed on my knuckles when I was a hopeful man of twenty-three, *AMOR FATI,* and love my fate. I would trust that Lena was here to help.

She seemed hesitant to leave.

"Do you need money for the train or anything?"

Lena shook her head and headed toward the door. "No, I've got a monthly card."

"Sorry. Not trying to—"

"The moon is a lightbulb breaking," said Lena with childlike excitement over Elliott Smith, moons, and lightbulbs, and for that, I was grateful. "We're the same."

3

THE NEXT MORNING I rose early from my slumbers, hoping to find in my in-box a lengthy, instructive missive on Wayne retrieval from my fellow lightbulb breaker, Lena Geduldig. Instead, I found an e-mail from my landlord. I do not claim to be psychic, but believe me when I say I felt this notice slithering down from the gilded pedestal on which its sender had situated himself.

> Dear Mr. Bender,
>
> It has been brought to my attention that your apartment has been overloading the circuit breakers in the building that envelops your apartment. Complaints have been lodged by your upstairs neighbor who shall not be named due to privacy. There have also been complaints of noise, spefically a loud noise that hurts the ears, described by this tenant as like a

motorcycle. Please call my office immediately. You should be conscious of good neighborliness. Also stop the noise. You've been warned. Do not escalate this situation or you will face eviction.

Your friend,

Sahlil Gupta
Your landlord
Gupta Properties
Serving Chicago with class since 2006

Sahlil Gupta thought that because he collected a rent check from me once a month and occasionally sent over his cousin/incompetent plumber to look at my toilet when it didn't flush, that we were friends and therefore he could drink all night for free at my bar. One night, a year ago, he had draped his lank body over one of my barstools like an old, filthy sweatshirt, leered at the women, inserted himself into the conversations of others, and complained loudly that my bar is too far from his large two-story high-rise condo on Lake Shore, for which he paid two point five million dollars, and that he is only thirty, which is young to own so much expensive property. He signed all of his professional e-mails with "Your friend," like a third grader with a box of supermarket Valentines.

The second e-mail, opened during the morning nod to responsibility called breakfast, caused me to spill a full mug of OJ on my lap.

At first I couldn't open it. It had arrived via an e-mail protocol that I'd never heard of—.vpx-post-a. It took a few tries before the e-mail popped open on my screen. Embedded in the e-mail was a photo of me. I was wearing square-framed glasses of an unfamiliar design, holding up a picture of what looked like a bride and groom posing, each with a lighter in their hand. The man's arms were a blue-green blob of faded tattoos, and the half smile/half scowl on his face was my own.

The e-mail read:

> Hello from the post-a world, asshole. You like water? You'll love 2031. Congrats on meeting lena geduldig. You like her? She's the best thing that will ever happen to your sad, sorry life. Don't lose lena. That is my advice to my younger self. You will avoid a lot of loneliness and wasted time if you stay with her. Do what you have to do. Signed, yourself at 61. March 22, 2031. P.S. Meat is over post-a. Go eat 100 burgers right now.

I got up and ran to the bathroom and rested my face on the cold toilet seat, expecting to heave. I admired the brown barnacles of filth clinging to the underside of the toilet rim for a spell, realizing that I would neither throw up nor have another peaceful moment in my life, ever again. Me at sixty-one was the last person I wanted to hear from, and that included my dirty old man of a dad.

"She's the best thing that will ever happen to your life"? In 2031, I would still think of my life as sad and sorry? Well, that was disappointing.

I rang my girl in Evanston.

"Figured anything out yet?"

"Karl?" she asked.

"Working hard, I hope? Lena? It's been another whole day. Wayne could be dead, for all I know."

"Hold on. I'm in the library. Give me a minute." I heard a muffled airy noise, like she'd held her phone up to the blowing wind. Then she came back on the line. "Have you heard from Wayne?"

"Yes, and he's pissed. He's subsisting on walnuts and raccoon meat."

"You know what was really plentiful in Atlantic waters a thousand years ago? Eel. He should eat eel."

I picked up my toilet brush and scraped at the barnacles. "Lena, I'm hoping that we can get Wayne back to the present sooner rather than later, so . . ."

"When can I see Elliott Smith play? I never got to see him play when he was alive. I don't think he ever played Montana."

"I'm afraid the wormhole is unavailable for concertgoing for the time being. Until you figure something out, the wormhole may only be used to retrieve Wayne."

"We need to take another trip so that I better understand the velocity and relative time dilation through space-time. I have some mathematical equations I'm working on. I want to see Elliott."

"Nope. Not happening."

"Excuse me?" she asked.

"Work first, Elliott later."

"Look, I'm going to be honest with you. You can't know that Wayne is in the year 980. Any date you type into that system of yours is arbitrary. I'm pretty sure that time did not move at the same pace in 980 as it does today. The Earth's axis has shifted a lot over the last millennium and there's no way we can count on there being a twenty-four-hour day in 980. It could be 981 or 994 or 1237 wherever Wayne is right now."

"Okay."

Lena exhaled loudly. "Second, as I mentioned, your wormhole could have shifted. As far as we know, there is no way to affix one end of an Einstein–Rosen Bridge to any single, fixed point. I don't know how you've been keeping your wormhole in your closet, but I need to examine it further, because as it stands, it's already defying everything we physicists know about time and space. There is no way to verify that Wayne is on Manhattan Island. He could be in Antarctica or he could be down the street in Chicago and bullshitting you. We can proceed assuming he is where you say he is, but again, I cannot know that for certain. So the problem I'm dealing with is how to apply the metrics by which I understand all this stuff and make them go backwards. Synchronizing the clocks will be ridiculously difficult, if not impossible. But I'm willing to try."

"Thank you. Do whatever you need to do.

"I need a trip and I want to see Elliott."

"Fine. Come by at seven. We'll go see Elliott."

"We?"

"Well, yeah. Wanna go on a time travel date with me?" I made a fist and bit down hard on my knuckles, realizing too late that I'd just put the hand that had touched the toilet brush in my mouth.

"A date? Like a *date* date? I thought I was your employee."

"Well, yeah. You are my employee. I mean, is that cool?"

"Is that *cool*?" she said, a crack in her voice. "I mean, that strikes me as unprofessional. But it's not like other people are knocking my door down. I don't know. We'll see on the date thing. Your need for immediate gratification where getting Wayne back is concerned doubled with this out-of-the-blue date request is freaking me out. Ease up on that. Girls like me hate getting bossed around. See you later." The phone went dead.

Way to woo the honeys, Rico Suave. No wonder I hadn't had a real girlfriend since the nineties.

Also: Was that a yes?

I cleaned my apartment with unusual fervor. Washed sheets, put laundry away, scrubbed the tan streaks of piss off the rim of the toilet. I hid my bottle of happy pills in a drawer in the bathroom and threw an unopened box of Q-tips over said evidence in case Lena was a bathroom snooper. I was a bathroom snooper. I actually hoped that Lena was a bathroom snooper, too, because we'd have that in common, wanting to know what prescription drugs are zapping the brains of the ones we love, and if they use a good brand of deodorant.

Other than music, I feared that she and I shared very little. Music isn't enough. Disappointment looms large when you spend an evening leaning in toward a pretty woman, engaged in a fierce discussion of the success of New Order post Ian Curtis's suicide, and then figure out you can't talk about anything else but bands. Bands! Bands! More bands! My ex-girlfriend Meredith liked country. *Country.* How much Emmylou Harris I listened to for that Meredith McCabe.

Meredith had lived beneath the pool table in an anarchist squat in Cambridge. Her sole possessions at the time we were together (1990 to 1996) were a sleeping bag, a toothbrush, and a mayonnaise jar full of broken jewelry she'd hoped to fix and sell from a blanket in Harvard Square. Meredith dumped me in 1996 to move in with a woman she'd met in the shower line at the Michigan Womyn's Music Festival. Not a single worthy lady had revealed herself to me since. Meredith remained the one for whom my heart would not heal. With her, my life was golden. I had muscles.

We were standing outside the Middle East on Mass Ave when Meredith kissed my cheek good-bye. The wind coming off the bay that afternoon was as cold and cruel as Ms. McCabe, and when I staggered into the nearest drinking establishment to warm my body and regain some composure, I tripped over some guy's feet, face-planted into the contents of an ashtray someone had spilled, and split open my right big toe kicking a hole in the bottom wood part of the bar, for which I was asked to pay four hundred dollars. As I confirmed via a time travel trip back to that November day to rewatch the breakup, the weather was really that cold and I did kick a rather impressive hole in that bar. At the time, I'd felt that Meredith was worth such trouble and destruction.

Lena arrived at 6:50 p.m. I'd put on a black necktie for the occasion. I wore my newest jeans—crisp ones that had never been splashed with beer or bleachy mop broth. I tucked in my shirt, which was pale blue oxford cloth, purchased at a real store within the past five years. It was clean and free of pit stains.

"Hello," she said, winded from the stairs. We hugged awkwardly, she trying not to touch my body with her breasts. Though Lena was dressed in a rather plain black top and red knee-length skirt, my eyes were drawn to her calves and feet: weathered purple Doc Martens boots that were appropriate if time traveling back to the nineties. Still, she was smiling. She was pleasant. She was here to help.

"Nice boots," I said.

With great pride, she lifted up her left foot to put it on display. "My God, Karl, do you realize what it took for a teenager with no credit card in Butte, Montana, to acquire these boots in 1995? Before Internet commerce? A girl in Seattle I knew because she ran a zine called the *Canadian Penny* bought them and shipped them to me and I had my father reimburse her with a check. A check! Of course, all the cowboy assholes at my high school thought they were ugly and called me a freak. I love these boots."

"Quite a story there."

"Yes." She sighed. Over the years, I've learned that women who sigh like this in the presence of a man are horny, and they're trying to let you know. I considered the possibility of taking Miss Lena to bed after our return from our trip to 1997 to see Elliott Smith, but I thought better of it. Lena might have been horny, but it wasn't my place to assume she was horny for me. Further inspection of Lena indicated not horniness but garden-variety suspicion.

She stood in my kitchen with her arms folded in front of her, her holey black cardigan pulled taut across her chest.

"Can I get you a drink?"

"Water, I guess. Hey, so you're coming with this time? Some sort of date bullshit?"

Damn, she was harsh. "Yes. I mean, you should also be doing your calculations. Calculations first, date bullshit second." I couldn't tell if I was flirting or not. Probably not.

"Hey, can we show Elliott our 'St. Ides Heaven' tattoos? And beg him not to kill himself?"

I shook my head. "No talking to Elliott. You'll really be pissing me off if you do that."

"Wouldn't it be better if he wasn't dead?"

"That attitude is what got Wayne marooned in 980."

"Not wanting Elliott to kill himself is an attitude?"

I didn't want to fight with Lena, but I wasn't going to let her mess with Elliott Smith, either. This was a quiet enterprise, this time travel thing, and its purpose was nostalgia. I liked to think that I was closer to a drug dealer than to a carny, but neither of those occupations garnered any modicum of respect.

"Have you heard from Wayne?" Lena asked.

Wayne's texts had grown disjointed and unintelligible. I worried that he was starving to death, or freezing to death, or had lost a finger, or had gone completely loco in the *cabeza,* but he would have told me if anything bad had happened, or stopped texting if he was injured or dead.

I MET PEOPLE. CONTACT MADE. DID NOT FIGHT OR KILL ME. VERY SMALL. MONOBROWED WOMEN IN COLORFUL DRESSES, MEN SMALLER THAN WOMEN, MORE TIMID, TOO. THEY HAVE DOGS.

ALL OF MY SKIN IS ITCHY. I KEEP THINKING ABOUT THE TUBE OF LOTION IN MY TRUCK BACK HOME AND HOW I'D MURDER MY BEST FRIEND KARL BENDER WHO CAN'T USE NUMBERS PROPERLY TO HAVE SOME LOTION.

ATE A FISH. I WOULD CALL IT SUSHI-GRADE.

THIS IS LIKE BEING IN SOLITARY CONFINEMENT. MY BRAIN HURTS, KARL. THERE IS NO ONE TO TALK TO AND I'M SCARED.

I KNOW YOU DON'T LIKE FISH BUT THIS IS THE BEST FISH. IT DOESN'T EVEN TASTE LIKE FISH. IT TASTES LIKE TRUTH AND BEAUTY.

SO MUCH FISH. I ATE A LOT OF FISH STICKS AS A KID AND NOW I'M GOBSMACKED THAT HUMANITY WOULD EVER BATTER-FRY THESE NATURAL WONDERS.

KIND OF LIKE EATING A TRANSLUCENT, SLIGHTLY SALTY BIT OF WONDER.

FUCK YOU, YOU DUMB LOSER. I THINK I LEFT MY OVEN ON. MAYBE I'LL JUST SHARPEN THIS STICK AND STAB IT THROUGH MY BRAIN.

YOU DON'T EVEN HAVE TO COOK THIS FISH. SO GOOD.

HAVE YOU EVER DANCED NAKED IN THE MOONLIGHT? REALLY ANSWER THAT QUESTION. SINCERELY. THINK

ABOUT DOING IT TONIGHT. DRIVE UP TO WISCONSIN AND FIND A MEADOW. AND A MOON. THERE ARE TWO MOONS IN THE SKY HERE. HOW DID WE LOSE A MOON IN 1,000 YEARS?

I'M COLD BUT I'VE GOT ALL THIS FISH.

I'd assured Wayne that Lena and I were working furiously to get him back, that he was much missed by everyone, and that his empty barstool was a constant reminder that something was wrong at the Dick. The truth was, I missed Wayne in the same hopeless way I missed Meredith: muddy with the fear over the possibility that I'd never see him again, and that it was all my fault. But mostly, I was worried about Future Me and this message about Lena and "the post-A world."

Post-A?

Also, how was this going to work with Lena, exactly? I wasn't even sure she liked men. She did seem to like me, though, what with the sighing and the not wanting to leave my side when our time together found its natural end point. But still, she was a girl who wore all of her hurts like fresh tattoos, who built walls around her heart and her body, who had long ago abandoned girlish predilections like flirting or caring about her appearance. Since I'd declared our outing a date, she couldn't even look me in the eye. She stood over the computers in the bedroom, tapping at the keys, glazed-eyed, shifting her weight to one foot and then the other. I noticed how thin and worn the gummy soles of Lena's purple Doc boots had become. I saw the golden glint the sun made as its rays illuminated her arm hair. I admired the generous curves of her breasts and belly, the arch of her calves in their torn black tights. Crusty edges made a girl more beautiful. Meredith was all bloody lips, missing teeth, and ghosts in her eyes that my love and kisses sometimes chased away. When they did, I loved and cherished Meredith beyond what I ever felt myself capable of, for which I had absolutely no point of reference in my life.

I was raised by a man and woman whose marital rage peeled the paper off the walls of their bland suburban split-level. I feared that my relations with women would forever be marked by Steve and Melinda Bender and their failed pairing, his cheating, her chilling stoicism, and his draining the joint bank account and fleeing to Florida while she lay dying in a hospice unit that reeked of urine and medical-grade cleaning fluids. They belonged to that last generation of Americans who viewed divorce as a greater failure than daily misery. Seven months, from cancer diagnosis to death, I had never seen my mother happier—in a hospital gown, with me and my sister at her side, knowing that her husband wouldn't be wherever she was headed.

I had never accompanied someone on a time travel trip before. Nostalgia is, and should be, a solo endeavor.

"Where are we going?" Lena asked.

"Boston."

"How about Portland?"

"Boston," I repeated.

She sighed. "Elliott's best shows were in Portland."

"We're going to Boston."

"Didn't you live in Boston in the nineties?"

"In the late nineties, I was touring so much with the Axis, I didn't live anywhere."

"Yeah, but the Axis was a Boston band, even if you weren't living there. So we're going to visit your old haunts? Old you, maybe?"

I didn't answer. I stared at the computer screen, or past it at the greenish paint on the wall behind it, programming our trip to Boston, because I'd only ever been to Portland to play Axis shows and the city held no nostalgia for me, but Boston, city of college, of youth, of pain, of Meredith and T.T.'s, was the toy box of my longed-for past. I didn't want to go to Portland because fuck Portland. This was my wormhole, damn it. Boohoo, big baby. Boston or nothing. Boston or I take my ball and go home. To Boston. Go Sox.

"I think you have seen your old self," Lena said. "The corners of your lips are curling under. You're lying. I can tell when someone's lying."

"I'm not lying."

That knocked the smile off her face. "You need me more than I need you."

"Way to start a date, Lena."

She picked her messenger bag up off the floor and hoisted it over her head, like she was going to leave and I'd never see her again. "Are you this much of a dick to all the women you date, or just me?"

"You pick the artist, I pick the show. Fair's fair."

She looked at me with her left eyebrow arched. "Fair? Really? I'm the physicist here."

"It's my wormhole. You wouldn't even know about it if I hadn't contacted you."

"You're being an asshole," Lena said, and part of me loved her for not being afraid to say it to my face.

On April 29, 1997, I was in a tour van with Milo, Trina, and Sam, nowhere near Boston, though I can't remember exactly where we were that night. We were popular in Athens and Chapel Hill, but Milo's then crush/now wife, Jodie, lived in Portland, and so we played a lot of shows there, mostly in the dark, piss-and-beer-smelling Reed College student union, though at some point we graduated up to playing actual clubs. That said, the Elliott Smith show in Cambridge would be packed with old friends, old band-mates, and probably my old bartender, Jake Crowley, my Boston-era ad hoc therapist and the man who mentored me when I bought the Dictator's Club. Meredith and I used to talk about asking Jake to officiate our wedding. We'd get married in his bar, family expectation be damned, and have bands play all night long while we went out to the van to have sex whenever we got bored talking to people. Instead of gifts, we'd ask guests to donate money to build libraries in Nicaragua. Then, for our honeymoon, we'd go down to Nicaragua and build those libraries.

LENA AND I landed with a thud on the pavement of Mass Ave, right in front of the Middle East.

Welcome home, baby boy.

"That was some crazy harsh pull. I might barf," Lena said.

Around the corner came Jake Crowley. Nowadays, Jake is as plump as the guy who carves the ham at the Polish buffet, and his male-pattern toilet seat of hair has turned the color of cigarette ash, but here, Jake, his body lean beneath his black pompadour, sauntered past us and into the club. No amount of effort stopped my lower lip from quivering. Wayne had never explained the whole layer thing to me. I took a swipe at a *Boston Phoenix* newspaper box. My hand made no contact. I could see Lena, and she could see me, blubbering like a goddamn baby.

"Can you see me?" I asked, waving my arms around like a sea creature.

Lena nodded her head. "Why did you want to come here when you knew it would make you sad?"

"Because I want to be sad, Lena. I like being sad. You like being sad. Elliott Smith loved being sad so much he wrote the soundtrack to our sad lives and then he died so we could all be even more sad."

"Hot damn, dude. Calm down."

I shouldn't be doing this, I thought. *I should destroy the wormhole, let 1997 stay in 1997.*

Once Wayne was back, I promised myself. I would yank out the wires, pour cement on the wood floor, take an ax and chop the drywall into puffs of dust.

Lena scanned the landscape. "So we can go to your old city but not mine. I see how it is." She reached down and opened the *Boston Phoenix* newspaper box with no problem.

"How did you do that?"

"Do what?" She held the newspaper in her hand, flipping it open. "I just want to see what other bands are playing. Galaxie was over by '97, right? Luna, maybe? Ooh, remember Atom and His Package?"

"How is it that you're holding on to that paper?" I took a swipe at the paper, but my hand went through it. It was all just air to me.

Lena leafed through the *Phoenix* as the pages waved in the wind. "I didn't do anything special. I can interact with the past. No big deal." She gave the newspaper box a kick.

My hands failed to meet the handle of the metal newspaper box. I walked through an old Tercel. I took a swing at a woman wearing cat eye sunglasses. I couldn't feel cold, couldn't smell the exhaust of the passing MBTA bus.

And yet, Lena. Lena flipped through the newspaper. A guy on the sidewalk dodged her and said, "Excuse me." She existed. But not me.

"This is fucked up," I said, swiping at Lena's newspaper.

Lena grabbed my arm and then stopped a couple walking a dog. Lena could touch me, but I couldn't touch her. "Excuse me, but do you see a man with a ton of tattoos and a gray goatee standing next to me, right here?"

"What? There's a man there?" the woman asked.

"He's having a bit of an invisibility problem today." Lena laughed and pointed at me while the couple looked through me, confused.

"Good luck with that," the guy holding on to the dog leash said.

"Thank you," she yelled at the couple as they crossed Mass Ave. "And please vote for Al Gore in 2000."

"Lena."

Lena reached out and ran her hand across the top of my head. "I don't get this. I can see and touch you. Why not anyone else?"

"It's starting to really piss me off."

She bit her lip in that thinky way. "You know what it is? Why you can't interact? I think you, like, freak out midway through the portal and it puts you physically outside this dimension. Like there's a plastic bubble around the past and you're peeking inside instead of experiencing it. You're so hung up on treating the past like a jigsaw puzzle you can't bear to take apart and put away that you, like, psych yourself out of arriving in the past completely."

I considered what she said. As I pass through the icy-cold tunnel, I am admittedly a little fearful, the same way I am on a roller coaster or in a taxi piloted by a driver obviously flying high on crank. I do not love the past. I fear it, now that it has been returned to me.

"Are you afraid of anything when you pass through the tunnel?" I asked.

"I'm so busy running numbers through my head, trying to figure out how the time-space slip is happening, I'm not thinking of anything but science."

Lucky science girl, blessed with a brain unencumbered with matters of the human heart. Her travel was pure: just for the music, or for the science, not for the baggage. "I want to go for a walk," I said, charging forward so as to not give Lena the chance to protest.

"We are *not* missing Elliott," she yelled from behind me.

I was three strides ahead of her and I was not going to slow down. "There are two opening acts."

"Don't I need a ticket? If people can see me? You can just mosey right on in, but I can't. I have an Illinois ID card that expires in 2016. How am I going to explain that?"

On a very familiar street corner, I began to notice how faulty my memory had grown. There were the old cars, sure, and I relished seeing old landmarks I held dear—the J.P. Licks, where Meredith would order Oreo ice cream with Oreo topping, turning her tongue a plaguelike Oreo black. The white-walled Ethiopian restaurant with the spongy bread and shocking audacity with marrowbones. The rainbow-colored flyers stuck like feathers to posts and bulletin boards. But my eyes weren't the same and I wanted to spray them with Windex and wipe away what I'd seen that made everything so different and sad.

"Did you bring cash?" Lena asked. "For the door? I don't have any cash."

I mumbled something affirmative.

Lena dug through her wallet, a purple sparkly number decorated with a white skull and crossbones. "What if they look at the serial numbers on the cash? What year is your cash from? Does your cash even exist here? I have some quarters in my wallet, but they're the kind with the states. Those didn't come out until '99. Look, Utah." Lena held out a handful of coins. "That's a later state. And California."

"Don't worry about the quarters."

"Karl," she said. "They haven't even announced the state quarter program yet. It started in 1999. You're not even listening to me."

Lena yelled from behind for me to slow down, as I bounded even further ahead of her. I knew I was being an asshole, ignoring her, but I had to see something that was just a few blocks ahead.

Lena continued her tirade about the state quarter program and about how she was wearing a bra made of some space-age bra material that didn't exist in 1997. I did not slow down. I turned the corner on Pearl Street, not telling Lena what I was doing, where I was going, admitting I had an agenda, not caring if she could catch up with me or not, not caring if I saw Lena Geduldig ever again. It was with the intent of a bullet that I sped toward Berkman House, Meredith's old anarchist squat. In 1997, she was living in Washington, DC, with Shower Lady, but the house as I remembered it—the old wooden porch bending from neglect, the smell of yellow curried lentils and unwashed bodies—would still be as I remembered.

"Karl, would you please slow down? You're scaring me."

Lena. Who was this chick? She didn't know me and I didn't know her and I wasn't sure I wanted to know her. *Don't lose Lena.* I wanted to see Berkman House. But what would I see when I got there, on this day in the past, after I'd quit Boston in a haze of anger and sorrow over getting dumped? Meredith's squat friends all cold-shouldered me after that. Then the Axis got famous. For years I looked for her in the crowd, even though, under all those lights, the audience is nothing but a sea of black.

"Holy shit," I said as I stopped in front of that dilapidated house. My stomach lurched as I looked up past the busted wooden railing of the porch.

Meredith was there, on the porch, sitting on the louse-ridden couch that mildewed to a shiny, living green every summer, engaged in some intense and personal lady chatter with her friend and fellow squatter Kate, who I am certain was responsible for infecting Meredith and, by extension, me with crabs the summer of 1993, since that bitch had no boundaries with regards to bath towels, or anything else. The two women sat facing each other, gesticulating wildly, lit cigarettes between their fingers, engaging in that alienating lady-on-lady conversational practice, which to my ears meant they were talking about me.

"That's my girlfriend. Ex-girlfriend," I whispered to Lena. "Meredith."

"The redhead in the tank top?" she said.

"Shh. Yeah."

"Not cool, Karl. Not cool."

I knew that, of course. But in the moment I just didn't care. I was pretty sure I was going to lose it, though. Not because Meredith was right in front of me, a jewel of beauty in a dirty white men's undershirt that showed off her upper arms, lean and strong from boxing. Because here's the horrible truth: If I really wanted to see Meredith again, in the present, I could. There is no reason in this world why I couldn't find a reason to go to California, call her, and catch up over tacos and beer. But I couldn't. And it's not just because she's married and has her own life, which is normal and natural, and if she's happy now, then I'm happy for her. It's just that the Meredith of today isn't the young and vibrant goddess of beauty and virility that I idolize and hold fast to my heart. The Meredith of today is another man's wife. She's a little girl's mother. She has more to her name than a sleeping bag and a jar of broken jewelry.

"Wow. You're still in love with her. Your face is turning a hundred shades of red."

Was it the crying? Or could Lena smell the musky shame of undead love emanating from my body?

"You're shaking."

"Damn right I'm shaking."

She put her hand on my invisible-to-everyone-but-Lena shoulder. "Want me to talk to her?"

I flinched. "No. Don't you dare!" I glanced up at Meredith

chatting away, her hands flying around, the smoke from her cigarette making gauzy trails around her face. I remembered every single ring on her fingers. Seven total. The onyx one, which she wore on her right middle finger, I'd bought from a street vendor in Harvard Square, with the intent of proposing, but I ended up giving it to her as a birthday present instead because in 1994 I was a bigger coward than I am now. She was still wearing it. What did that mean? Did she still have the ring? Why did I still care?

"Sorry. I just . . ." I had no excuses. This was a dick move, taking Lena to Berkman. I hadn't thought Meredith would be sitting on the porch. I'd only gone to Berkman House to be with her essence, the way normal people visit cemeteries.

I'd made a mistake, though, dragging Lena along.

Lena looked up at the Berkman porch and said, "Let's just end this right now. Let's rip off the Band-Aid, shall we?" Lena walked toward the front steps of the house. Nine steps total, and each one sounded the cry of ailing wood and nails. There was no way they wouldn't notice Lena.

I reached out to restrain Lena. I tried to grab at one of the magenta pigtails jutting out from the back of her head. My hand slipped through her hair like it was air.

"Lena. Don't," I said, but she had already bounded up to the top of the steps to the Berkman House porch.

Meredith and Kate looked up at my smiling, pigtailed physicist.

"Are you Meredith?" She pointed at my redheaded spark plug, so beautiful, sitting cross-legged on that slimy sofa.

"Who's asking?" Kate said, rude as I remembered.

"My name is Lena Geduldig. I have some terrible news about Karl Bender. You know Karl, right?"

"Who are you?" Meredith's face betrayed no sign of, say, being worried about my health or safety.

She looked down at me and then said, as if she were reciting lines, "I'm Lena Geduldig. I was dating Karl for a while, but we broke up because he had this really bad habit of calling me Meredith."

Meredith laughed, snorting cigarette smoke out of her nose.

"Nobody likes to be called the wrong name during sex," Lena said. "After the fifth time it happened, I had to break up with him, because his obsession with you was so off-putting. And he wasn't even sorry. He just kept doing it."

"I didn't know Karl was dating anyone."

"He's not anymore. He's single. Extremely single. I guess he's on tour with the Axis, but when he was in Boston he was calling me Meredith all day long. 'Meredith, I mean, Lena, give me a hand job. Meredith, er, Lena, tie my shoes. Meredith, I mean, Lena, don't break up with me, Meredith. Why don't you just change your name to Meredith? It would make things easier.'"

"Are you serious?" Kate asked.

Lena nodded. "I tried to get him to go to therapy but he refused. Anyway, he had all these pictures of you in his apartment, so I recognized you. I just wanted to say no hard feelings, and if you've still got any affection left for the guy, I'm sure he'd take you back in a second."

"She's not interested," Kate said.

If I weren't a time travel ghost with no discernible arms, legs, free will, or body mass, I would have dragged Lena from that creaky porch.

"He'd give his left nut for you," Lena said, and then snorted one of those loud laugh-snorts. "And the right one."

Meredith's eyebrows started doing that arch thing, that one that foretold that she was about to let you have it. "Who are you, you weird girl? You're acting really weird. Is this a prank?"

"No." Lena was clutching her midsection, trying not to double over. "I swear this is all true."

Meredith arched her eyebrows. "Karl called you Meredith? How did you meet him?"

Lena was a hundred shades of purple and appeared to be on the verge of cardiac arrest. If I didn't hate her so much at that moment, I would have suggested a trip to the emergency room. "Okay, I'm from the future. He's my friend. In 2010, you should call him. Or you can call me. Here's my number. In 2010, you'll keep your telephone in your pocket."

Lena scribbled something on the back of a flyer she'd plucked from a 1997 lamppost and handed it to Meredith, who took it as if Lena were handing her a dead puppy.

"Is there something wrong with you?" Meredith asked. "Do you need help?"

"I'm telling the truth," Lena said, but Meredith had already shut her out, and Lena could see that pleading with her would get her nothing. Meredith, I recalled, didn't think about the future much. She was all about what was happening in the moment. My heart hurt watching her like this, not being able to touch her. I could only Internet stalk her and wonder, late at night, if at the age of forty-three she still rolled joints with her toes.

"We're going to see Elliott Smith play at T.T.'s now. You should go too. He'll be dead in six years."

Meredith stood up and put her hand on Lena's shoulder. I'd forgotten how tiny Meredith was. "I hope you get the help you need. You kind of hurt my feelings, you know. It felt like you were making fun of me. Not cool."

Kate yelled, "Karl is such a dick it's not even funny, babe. Steer clear."

Lena skipped down the steps, actually making them creak

beneath her feet, as I followed her. I found enough resolve deep within me not to smack the back of her head. Which I couldn't do anyway.

"You're permanently on my shit list, Geduldig. You know that?"

"Ooh, nobody ever calls me Geduldig." Lena skipped ahead of me like a schoolgirl. "No one can pronounce it, even though it's really easy if you just spend a minute looking at it."

"Please turn around and listen while I am yelling at you. I hired you for a job. To get Wayne back. Not to fuck with my past and make fun of me."

Lena kept walking in front of me, backwards, nearly running into an upturned trash can lying in the sidewalk. "You're the one who called this a date, and then you took me to see your ex-girlfriend, you rude, disrespectful ass-munch."

"You do not—do not—go around telling people you're from the future. You do not interact with people in the past. I explained this to you. Why do you insist on ignoring me?"

"If you wake up tomorrow morning and realize that you got back together with Meredith back in '97, then what? Or what if she calls you tomorrow and says, 'Hey Karl! I've spent the last decade dreaming about you, I still love you—' "

"She won't, and it's not up to you."

"Wait a minute—"

"You're being a nosy bitch and you're overstepping—way, way, way overstepping—your bounds."

Lena stopped cold on the sidewalk. A dude on a bike swerved to avoid hitting her. She raised her finger to my face, an arrow of hostility aimed directly at the dumb part of my brain. "Fuck you, Karl. Fuck. You. Don't you ever, ever call me a bitch."

The weight of my error pressed on me like a cinder block to the head. "I'm sorry."

"Or 'lady.' I hate that. So condescending," she said. Her eyes narrowed. "I honestly don't need any more men in my life wanting something from me and then treating me like shit when they don't get what they think they deserve. Good luck finding yourself another physicist. I promise you, exactly zero of my colleagues will give you the time of day."

"Okay, I'm sorry. You upset me and I reacted. I'm just . . . Let's just go to the show."

She stopped me dead on the sidewalk, planted herself, and told me what was what. "See, there's this pattern in my life, Karl, and I'm feeling pretty confident that what it's going to take for me to eradicate it is to become a nun, except that I'm Jewish and I've got more important things to do than sit in a cloister just so insecure men like you don't have the chance to use me as some sort of emotional cum rag."

"I said I'm sorry." Tears pressed at my eyelids. I really was sorry, but saying so repeatedly felt fake and weird.

"*Sorry* is just a word that reminds me how little respect I get in this life." Lena turned her back to me. "Maybe you feel bad, but I'm not here to console you or anyone else."

Lena walked back toward Mass Ave. We didn't speak, except for when Lena pointed to a glass-topped coffee table on the curb and asked if she thought we could bring it back to 2010. When we got to T.T.'s, Lena, chronologically age eighteen, ducked and pushed past the doorman without paying or flashing an ID, and I followed behind her, her ghost. A group of women in denim skirts, holding plastic cups of beer, passed right through my body and I didn't feel a thing.

For the first time in my life, T.T.'s in 1997 was about the last place I wanted to be. I wanted to go home to my bar, but Lena was hell-bent on seeing Elliott, and who could blame her? Who back home in the year 2010 wouldn't open a vein to sit in this holy cavern and watch a man create so much beauty out of nothing?

Lena leaned and pushed her way to the front of the stage as Elliott sat down on a wooden chair, his gaze downward. I admired the softness of Elliott's face, the quiet sincerity with which he placed his heart into his music. Men didn't sing like Elliott, all soft and open. I didn't play like that. Milo didn't either. Just Elliott. My mind fluttered with recognition when I saw that tattoo of Ferdinand the Bull he had on his right bicep. I looked down at my own breaking lightbulb tattoo and tried not to cry for the man while he was in front of me, still alive. He opened with "Needle in the Hay." His lips hid behind the silvery bulb of his microphone as he sang, eyes focused downward.

I watched Lena, too. Mostly the back of her head, the stillness of her pigtails. How hard Lena fought to stand dead center in front of Elliott. How hard Lena fought to be a woman in the sciences, to just get through her day. I tried to think of ways to convey how sorry I was for blowing up at her, to tell her how much I admired her.

I walked through the bodies of the crowd, up to where Lena stood.

"Can I hold your hand? I really want to hold someone's hand right now. This is a date, right?" I said.

I held out the hologram of my hand. She looked at my hand like it was garbage and turned her back. "Lena?" I said, my voice small. But once Elliott took another swipe at his guitar, Lena became unreachable. Her back was to me and I stood and waited for her to see me, stupidly competing with Elliott Smith for her attention. I watched her face melt into a mixture of happiness—the unusual privilege of coming back to this—and sadness, because she knows how all of this ended. Because she understood the value we assigned to things once they are gone forever.

Lena didn't want me. I was just a ghost who didn't pay the cover, so I wandered to the back of the club, where all the douche bags who didn't know how lucky they were to be in this place at this moment were talking over Elliott, like anything they had to say meant more than the man and his music. The two men beside me were engaged in a heated discussion about whether one of the guys should get rid of his Bowflex exercise machine. ("It takes up a lot of space," he said, and I was like, *"Elliott Smith is playing twenty feet in front of your stupid face."*) I waited for a calm to settle over me, the calm that I imagined would be felt by a king whose every whim and wish is granted without question, but it never came. I only felt the emptiness of a man long in mourning, waking from the trance of sorrow only to wonder what it was he missed so badly.

Elliott played a jittery set for less than an hour. He glanced shyly at the crowd as he retreated backstage with his guitar tucked under his arm. Then Lena, black mascara tears making the Nile delta on both cheeks, found me. Red-faced, she just shook her head from side to side and told me to take her home.

I saw Meredith in the crowd just before Lena and I were sucked through the floor of T.T.'s. I looked away, typed the digits into my phone, and grabbed Lena's hand, happy to be returning home, happy to be holding Lena's hand. Shivering upon reentry to the present, I apologized like my life depended on it, which it did. I sank to my knees and pressed my cheek to Lena's belly.

"You're an asshole," she said, shaking her leg to remove me from her person, and I agreed with her with all my heart, but what does a man gain when he admits to being an asshole? Nothing, Lena reminded me, and I told her I was grateful for this, and she told me that she was just one person, someone who wanted to understand the velocity of stars, not someone charged to correct the asshole behavior of assholes. Then she said she had to go to the bathroom, ran down the hall, and threw up in my bathtub.

After I applied sponge and Pine-Sol to the bathroom, leaving the stench of vomit plus pine cleaner plus Ming's Panda oily chicken plus wormhole accelerator to linger in my apartment, I watched as Lena brushed her teeth with a blob of my toothpaste on her finger.

"Sorry about the barf," she said.

"It hurts to come back."

"It hurts to be there."

"You have to be somewhere," I said.

"Right now, I'd like to be nowhere."

"Can you be right here?" I said, holding out my arms.

She hung back, shaking her head. "You can't do this, Karl. You can't use me and then throw me away when I'm not who you want."

"I want you. I don't want to lose you. I want to hold you. Please."

She didn't move. She just stared. I couldn't tell if I was scaring her. I didn't want to.

"If the answer is no, that's cool," I said. "Just say no. I still want to be your friend, even if the answer is no."

She covered her mouth with her hand. She didn't run back to the bathroom. She just stood there, her finger coated with white bubbles of Crest, not moving away, not moving toward me, not saying no.

"I'm not going to hurt you, and I'm not full of shit. I'm sorry about the Meredith thing. I'm sorry I called you a bitch. That was wrong and it will never happen again and I feel like a giant piece of shit about it. This is why I have my rule against using the wormhole for stuff other than shows. It turns me into a big, raw nerve. I promise you, my aim is true."

Lena looked at my face, then the door. "You know this is a point of no return, right? If we do this? By 'do this,' I mean date. You're never allowed to hurt me."

"I never want to hurt you."

She examined me like I was a difficult problem she needed to solve. "Should I rinse my mouth out first?"

I went in for a mouthful of toothpaste. The kiss burned a little. My mouth filled with minty bubbles and Lena's tongue. I wasn't lying when I said my aim was true. *Don't lose Lena.* Only a fool doesn't listen to his future self.

4

I RECEIVED A long e-mail from Wayne:

> The native tribe I have hooked up with has names. I wrote them down with ash on a leaf. Would it be wrong to teach them written English? They are long and complicated names, names that contort the tongue in new and stretchy ways. They gave me a name that sounds like Honnakuit. It probably means "tall pasty white guy." They are not armed and seem to be very concerned with one another. They sit very close to each other in a circle to eat. They all have long hair, even the men, and spend a lot of time doing each other's hair. I mean updos held together with tree sap and strips of cloth. They weave cloth. They are very small stature-wise, but they do a lot of singing and have musical instru-

ments. Lots of drums. Some stringed instruments, not really guitar-like, but maybe along the lines of a round ukulele. They would make an excellent band. NPR would do a story about them.

I eat with them: fish cooked over fire and mushrooms and nuts mixed together to form a paste. We eat berries when we find them. I help the women mostly, tearing the skin off of fish and plucking their bones out with the tips of my fingers. The women hunt. Mostly squirrel and raccoon but the occasional moose-like animal happens by and BLAMMO. Arrow to the heart. They are excellent bow-and-arrowers. Everything is shared. I wish they had computers, not because they need technology but because I want to be able to fix something for them, to show them my worth. I have no talents here. The only thing I know how to fix is a computer. They have math and birth control and it appears that no one is married. No couples, but lots of babies and children. They smile a lot. I like them. The oldest woman of the tribe gave me a big piece of leather.

I wish you could smell the air here. It smells of dirt and flowers and is so clean. I could just lay in the grass and breathe all day. It's not winter anymore. The thaw came and my tribe jumped naked into what I guess is the East River. No body shame and full of joy. They were confused about why I wore tight white cotton around my manhood, and I realized that if everyone else was naked, I was supposed to be naked, too. I took off my clothes and jumped in. This experience made me see my penis differently—just a silly knob of flesh, neither shameful nor powerful. Why was I circumcised? I can't ask my mom that, she'll get mad, but the people here, they noticed and said something. I don't know what they said in words, but one of the women made me a little foreskin out of brown cloth for me to wear on my poor, exposed peen. A little sleeve to keep my man part safe. That sounds weird, right, but it was an act of kindness. Part of my body isn't right and they fixed it. Why are we walking around with cold, unprotected dicks, Karl? Mine's wearing a love jacket and it doesn't make me horny at all.

You know what really stands out to me, buddy? These people—they don't hate or compete. They just do. They find food, they eat, they share everything, and they all seem to love each other in this really magical, uncomplicated way. The women are in charge, and it's weird—when one of the older women gave me a few bits of fish she'd cooked in the fire, she touched her cheek to mine and pressed my mouth to her mouth, as if to transfer her love to me. My own mother never did that. That would have been dirty kissing, but this wasn't dirty. It was pure.

I miss you and the bar and my mom, but I don't miss Chicago or my job, which I've probably been fired from. I don't even think about it at all. The sunsets are too beautiful here.

Please say hello to Lena and give her my best.

HONNAKUIT aka Wayne A. DeMint

My riot grrrl worker bee was working furiously on math problems that would allow for Wayne's reentry without the propulsion of an electromagnetic field, on top of her own doctorate and teaching the twelve or so students who actually showed up for her summer session of Intro to Cosmology, and all Wayne could say is "Give her my best"?

She doesn't want your best, Honnakuit. She wants to get your ass back here.

Wayne:

FWIW, I've been giving your wormhole dough to Lena for her diligent work on getting you back to 2010. Since you got lost, I've been hesitant to send folks on trips, but Lena's been an enormous help. People at the bar keep asking about you, and I don't know what to tell them.

You would love Lena. Get back here so you can meet her. She's super smart and has great taste in music. We went to see Elliott Smith last night. 1997! She's totally your new best friend. And my new girlfriend! Lena. She's amazing. Super smart in a tough-girl punk rock package. I have no idea what she sees in me but I'm going to go with it for now. You two have tons in common and would be best friends. Seriously, she is special.

Not much else is new, other than your new best friend/my girlfriend Lena. Still working on getting you back, buddy. I miss you. The whole bar misses you. You're missing a fantastic summer in Chicago, man! Come back!

—KJB

I would not call him Honnakuit when he got back. That is what we in the drinking industry call bullshit.

I also got another, far more disturbing e-mail. Worse than having your friend in 980 tell you his new name is Honnakuit:

Dear Karl,

Strange thing—I was cleaning out some stuff in the garage to make room for my daughter's baby things and I found a note that a girl gave me one afternoon thirteen years ago, when I was in Cambridge visiting Kate Voss (remember her?). It was the year after I moved to DC. Kate and I were sitting on the old porch on that nasty couch that gave me rashes all the time and this crazy woman with pink pigtails approached and said she was from the future and knew you in the year 2010 and that you were still in love with me. And then she told me Elliott Smith would die in six years.

I blew it off at the time—so much crazy shit happened in 1997—but when I heard the news about Elliott and looked at the calendar and saw that that girl was right, I couldn't get her—or you—off my mind for some time.

I've been thinking about that girl a lot lately. Lena Guldig. Do you know her? I know it's weird, but I swear to you I am not making it up. Anyway, I just wanted to give you a little shout and find out how things are by you. Definitely not trying to find out if you're still in love with me. I think about our shared past a lot and realize you probably wouldn't be in love with me now. I'm a total sell-out, got a kid, have a real job. Time does crazy shit, right, Bender?

I don't mean to put you in a weird position. I just want to tell you this story and tell you I am well. As you probably know, I had a kid a few years ago. Saoirse (pronounced Seer-sha—I went turbo-Irish on the name) turns four this August and keeps me very busy. I take it you're still in Chicago, still running the bar, still breaking hearts with that guitar of yours? I picked up a copy of *Dreams of Complicated Sorrow* in a used CD bin not too long ago. It still sounds great.

Hope you are well and happy, and do let me know if you make it out to the Bay Area. I would love to see you.

Obligatory picture of the rugrat attached. Being a mom turns you into a cheeseball.

All best,

Meredith McCabe

P.S. They tore down Berkman a few years ago to build condos. Fuck that.

I closed my laptop before further bad news could come through the tubes at me. This is why you don't talk to people in the past when you travel, *Lena*. You change the future, you mess with the right now, and that is trouble.

Meredith.

She was the fifth of nine kids from an Irish family in Southie. She had a purple scar across her forehead from the time her father was out on parole and had slashed her face for losing the keys to his old Firebird. And she had four older brothers, brutal, bug-eyed bastards who slapped her around for good measure. Meredith left home at sixteen and lived on the streets until she took up with the anarchists. She was unbelievably breathtaking, a rose blooming from a pile of shit, her strength collided with her beauty and took away my words and my will.

"Fight me," is what Meredith McCabe said to me after an hour of beers and idle chatter about bands and lefty politics, digging her dirty feet into my thighs as I sat beside her on one of Berkman's crusty couches. I'd had three shots of whiskey and more than my fair allotment of oatmeal cookies that one of the Berkman residents had brought home from his job at the cooperative bakery. I admit, I noticed her the moment I walked in: the way she seemed to be in charge of the entire joint, passing around a jumbo bag of stale barbecue potato chips, making sure everyone got to take a handful.

"Excuse me?" I said.

"I'm training to be a boxer. Fight me. You look like a tough guy. Square jaw. Head like a toaster. Let's fight."

I examined her sinewy arms. Rock-hard muscle peeked out from beneath the apricot freckle constellations that swirled about her flesh. She had a rose-colored, jagged scar up the length of the underside of her right forearm.

The people who had overheard her gauntlet-toss began to hoot and holler, demanding the satisfaction of seeing the new dude get his ass kicked, and so she dragged me off of the filthy couch to the patch of burned, spray-painted grass out back. A murmur erupted among the crowd, and soon she and I were at the center of a circle of cheering punks. She raised her fists at me.

"Don't hold back because I'm a woman."

"I'm sure you can take me," I offered.

"Stop talking. Punch me. In the face. I see you hesitating. I have four older brothers. Do you think any of them have a problem hitting me in the face? Do it!"

My flimsy fist brushed her chin. Meredith returned with a sock in the gut. Not a regulation move, I'm sure, but then this goddess-pugilist felled me with a left hook to the chin. A stream of blood from the torn flesh inside my cheek trickled onto my white T-shirt. I lay there on the scratchy grass and gazed skyward as Meredith McCabe collected a series of high fives.

Someone handed me an old T-shirt to collect the blood spurting from my mouth. And then Meredith, holding a towel full of ice to her knuckles, sat beside me and said, "I hope you're not mad at me. It doesn't mean anything."

"It was an honor," I mumbled. The bleeding, as I recall, didn't want to stop.

"I'm going to kiss your cheek."

She leaned in and gave it a painful kiss. "There. That should heal it. I hope I didn't hurt you too bad."

"Nah, it's fine."

"I hurt people."

"Good to know."

"Hey, do you have a bed?"

"What?"

"A bed? Like a real bed? You live in some sort of apartment, right? I'm sore, not just from fighting, but from sleeping on a wood floor every night. If you have a bed large enough to share, do you mind?"

You might judge such an inquiry to be sexual, or ridiculously romantic, but the way she asked it, very matter-of-factly, didn't indicate to me that there would be quid pro quo booty attached to this request. The next day, after eleven hours of restful sleep, with our arms and legs tangled like hair, our genitals safely tucked in our respective underpants, Meredith took a long shower and used one of my clean towels. (I don't remember how, at age twenty-one, living in that sticky Somerville rattrap with Milo and two other guys, I had clean towels, unless my mother had been by my apartment and had done my laundry for me.) I made her maple-flavored instant oatmeal in a mug stolen from the Tufts dining hall, for which she kissed me on the tip of my still-throbbing nose and told me I was sweet.

Lesson number one, dudes: being a gentleman got me laid five days later, when, on a mattress that technically belonged to everyone in Berkman House, I had sex for the first time with a woman I loved. Knowing the difference between basic friction and making love to a woman whose every cell fascinated me and whose company I considered an undeserved privilege, I felt myself metaphorically leaping over some invisible wall, from stupid kid to Man of the World. The experience filled me with fervor, such that I saw for the first time how religious men before me had fought so hard to ruin the holiness of sex for everyone else.

Fourteen years.

Fourteen years of one-night stands, of female friends needing a postbreakup hookup, and three "girlfriends" I didn't miss, once they wised up and left. I hadn't seen God since 1996.

LENA ARRIVED AT my place at nine in the morning, her arms weighed down with two paper shopping bags.

"What's all this?"

"Flashlights. We're going to send Wayne some flashlights. Hopefully he'll locate the flashlights and turn them on, thereby creating the appropriate electromagnetic field. At that point we'll reverse the charge and, faster than you can say, 'Frostbite on my scrotum,' Wayne comes home."

Lena had re-dyed the ends of her hair to an Easter grass greenish yellow. I wondered if she went out of the way to make herself less attractive. An ancient memory of my mother, a cigarette between two thin fingers, nails painted beige, leaning back in her red velour La-Z-Boy and remarking upon the singleness of one of my overweight cousins: "She'd be so beautiful if she only lost that wide bottom." But Lena *was* beautiful—she had perfect, porcelain skin and a rather intriguing bump in the middle of her nose, rosy cheeks, and a rack that would have made Tom Waits pull out his harmonica. I loved looking at her and drinking her in.

"Here's the receipt for the flashlights," she said, digging it out of her bag. "Add it to my check."

"Wayne sent me an e-mail. He met up with a native tribe. They've adopted him and given him a name."

Her eyebrows shot up. "Wow. I want to be adopted by a native tribe. Pre-European infiltration. They're probably amazing."

"He'll probably die of cholera if we don't get him home quick. He's already got itchy critters living in his body hair."

Lena frowned. "Most of the people in the world have bugs, or at least an intestinal parasite or something. Americans are the clean-freaks of the world."

"I like cleanliness. I had crabs once. That woman on the couch with Meredith? She infected the whole house with crabs. We spent days sitting around in our underwear covered in this strong, stinky ointment. I had to shave my entire body, which was not sexy."

"I bet that was fun for you, Karl," she said. "I bet that's one of your favorite memories."

Wow. She had called me out something wicked.

"It's hard to be a person," I said.

Lena looked at me like I was the biggest loser. "Maybe we should stop talking about Meredith."

Lena, sliding two chunky batteries into the chamber of one of the flashlights, looked up into my face and said, "I know. Human beings just make trouble for themselves. That's why I like science. Although science is studied in service to humanity, I find it satisfying in that you don't really have to talk to anyone."

Lena hooked two flashlights together with a pair of metal hooks and placed them on the floor of my closet. "Text Wayne. Tell him I'm sending over the flashlights. There are ten flashlights total. The first two are going to January 1, 981, to the corner of Seventieth and Central Park West, approximately."

"He's not answering. He's been fishing. I don't know where he's been fishing."

"Okay, ask him where he thinks he is, in terms of modern Manhattan landmarks."

Wayne's response:

> NOT TODAY. THERE'S BEEN A BIRTH IN THE TRIBE AND WE'RE HAVING A FEAST. I HAVE MANY FISH TO CLEAN. MY KNIFE IS MADE OF BONE.
>
> I CAN'T BLOW OFF THIS CEREMONY. THAT'S A DOUCHE MOVE, ESPECIALLY SINCE THESE NICE PEOPLE HAVE BEEN TAKING CARE OF ME.
>
> FLASHLIGHTS AREN'T GOING TO WORK. YOU NEED MORE ELECTRONS. BUT GO AHEAD AND SEND THEM. I'LL TRY. IF NOT, THEN THE TRIBE CAN USE THEM AT NIGHT. WE DON'T EVEN HAVE CANDLES. JUST CAMPFIRE. WHEN IT'S DARK, EVERYONE SLEEPS. VERY NATURAL!

I asked again for his address and told Wayne that his mother had filed a missing person report with the Chicago PD.

> MAYBE BATTERY PARK? I'VE BEEN WALKING A LOT. WE'RE ON THE COAST NOW. THE WATER IS SO BEAUTIFUL! NO SNOW, BTW. IT'S SPRING.

Lena typed in the coordinates for Battery Park and the flashlights fell through the wormhole, a puff of steam and a stream of yellow light in their wake.

She shuffled her feet around on my wooden floor and I lay back on my bed. She looked at me. I looked at her. I gave her a thumbs up.

"So I guess we just hang out now?" she asked.

"Something like that. Help yourself to a drink in the kitchen."

Lena, her squarish feet in mismatched socks, padded down the hall to my tiny kitchen. I heard the clink of all the condiments in my refrigerator door. I liked Lena digging through my fridge. The familiarity of it.

"Hey Lena," I called from down the narrow hallway that connects my bedroom to the rest of the apartment. I realized that I used the exact same tone of voice I once did to get my mother's attention. That juvenile, slightly whiny, "Hey Mom!" that hadn't crossed my lips in the seventeen years since the funeral.

"Hey what?" she said, coming back into the room. She had found a Faygo lemon-lime soda in the bowels of my fridge.

"I think I bought that, like, six years ago."

"Tastes fine to me."

"Look at these texts from Wayne."

She took my iPhone. "Huh. I wonder what they use to carve bone into a fish knife. I assume they do not have any metallurgical processes."

"I don't think he wants to come back."

"That seems reasonable. What does he have to come back to?"

"The bar." I spat. "He practically drinks for free!" It was true. Wayne hadn't pulled his wallet from the back pocket of his khakis in my presence in months.

"Free beer. Yay. What does he really have to come back to?"

"The bar."

She shrugged and took another sip of Faygo. "I like your bar, but it's generally not a consideration for me when I make an inventory of my reasons to live."

"He has friends, he has a mother who dotes on him. He's frickin' loaded! Even before the wormhole he had tons of cash."

"Calm down."

"Don't tell me to calm down," I fought the urge to slap that

Faygo out of Lena's hand, but I have an unspoken agreement with my sixty-one-year-old self.

"Don't tell me to not tell you to calm down."

We sat on the couch and I explained to her about my bar, which was the same thing as my life, and how, even though I poured drinks for people all day and had earned the business of a few regulars who were good people who shared their lives with me, I hadn't had a good guy buddy since Milo, before indie fame turned him into an arrogant turd. That I hadn't realized how much I missed having a friend to talk to about stuff, eating dinner at a table, across from another person, instead of standing up next to the cash register while occasionally turning back to the bar to serve a drink. These were all perks of life I thought were only the province of girlfriends, and for whatever reason, I hadn't found the right person in so many years, but along came someone who actually cared about me. Wayne drove me to a smoking cessation program out in the suburbs, waited around for three hours for me, and then remained silent the whole ride home afterward as I proclaimed smoking to be the greatest of human endeavors, that my own mother had smoked a pack and a half a day and didn't mind dying of cancer at fifty-two because she got to enjoy all those tasty, morality-enhancing cigarettes, and that quitting was for cowards. He stopped at a 7-Eleven for me, so I could buy more cigarettes, even though he was disappointed. He said he was hoping I'd stick to quitting because he didn't want me to die young like my mother.

Then the doorbell rang. I opened the door without looking, because I thought it was Clyde arriving early for his trip to see 1963 Miles Davis at the Green Mill, and because the peephole in my front door sat at belly button level, and who wants to bend over and look at someone else's belly button when they're arguing with a physicist?

"Karl Bender, my friend!"

I stuck out my tongue at him. "Sahlil."

Sahlil leaned himself casually against my doorjamb, elbow up, his armpit at my face level, like we were totally chill buddyroos and his unannounced arrival at my doorstep was a normal, bro-like thing. Sahlil, a skinny, slight motherfucker in a pink oxford shirt tucked into khakis belted two inches below his nipples, should not call me his friend.

"What do you want?"

"Just came by to see my good friend Karl. Like this new shirt? Karuna bought it in New York City at a very expensive shirt salon. Very intricate stitching. Look at these cuffs! French cuffs." He held out a bony arm. I averted my eyes. I would not give into any form of power exchange with this guy.

"How is Karuna?" I had long ago vowed to seduce Sahlil's orthodontist wife. Tragic, beautiful Karuna, she of the shiny curtain of black hair and deep, kind eyes, doomed to forever gaze upon Sahlil and suppress her gag reflex whenever he issued yet another boastful claim. I imagined flicking my tongue into Karuna's warm, velvety bush as she bucked against my chin, proving that, while Sahlil owned real estate, I owned natural, unpretentious skills in the oral arts.

Sahlil puffed up his chest, as if offended that I'd said his wife's name out loud. "Karuna is very busy. Her practice is skyrocketing. We're both very successful. Do you know what a power couple is? We're a power couple."

I patted Sahlil on the back in order to push him back out the door, but he didn't take the hint. "Great, dude. Hey, I'm super busy, so you'll have to leave now. Thanks for dropping by. See ya." I blocked his entrance into my place with my body, but Sahlil, who weighed maybe 120, managed to slither around me and get into my apartment, like a raccoon trying to get something out of a trash can.

Sahlil held his arms out to me. "Buddy, let's chat."

"I have a guest." I gestured toward Lena as she peered out from the kitchen.

Sahlil leered down the hallway at Lena. "You can keep your johnson in your pants for a little while longer. We must speak immediately." Sahlil pushed me aside and took quick little steps to my couch. He made a big show of dusting imaginary germs and filth off the cushion and then looking at his hand, as if my ancient couch could infect him with a flesh-eating disease.

Lena walked over and Sahlil looked her up and down. "You're not one of the girls I see Mr. Bender flirting with at his Dictator's Club," he said. Lena offered her hand. He limply shook it, never taking his eyes off of me. "At Karl's bar, he has a different girlfriend for every night of the week. He has girlfriends like how normal men have socks."

"I make no claim on Karl's johnson," she said.

Sahlil laughed. "I'm a self-made millionaire, happily married. It is funny to me to see women hurling themselves Karl, a man who rents. Normal women want wealth."

Lena arched her eyebrows. "No, man. Renting is what's normal. And you know, dude, people don't really go around saying that they're self-made millionaires."

"What's the use of being a millionaire if you don't tell people? My father's not a millionaire. Only a doctor. In New Jersey. Six figures, no matter how you arrange them, are not seven figures."

"What do you want, Sahlil?" I asked.

"You didn't respond to my letter about the large quantity of electricity you are using. My secretary has received many complaints from the lady upstairs and from the Ming's Panda family."

"I pay my electrical bill on time and in full. I don't see how my use affects other tenants."

"It does. It makes their lights blink. They've been complaining about loud, booming noises. Also, I received a telephone call. A big, important telephone call from a very famous entertainment conglomerate that makes films and music. They want to buy this building."

"What?"

"An entertainment conglomerate wants to buy this building. Now, Mr. Bender, I'm sure you know, of my real estate holdings, this building is not my finest. In fact, this building is my lowest-quality building, and you have lived here for ten years, longer than this building has been a part of the Gupta Properties portfolio. But it was my first building, that I purchased with cash only a year after my graduation from Princeton, and so I have much love for it." Sahlil walked up to my never-used fireplace and ran his finger across the mantelpiece, where I'd propped up record albums with beautiful cover art.

"Okay," I said.

Sahlil leaned forward. "Now, why would this very large entertainment conglomerate want to buy this dingy old apartment building in Chicago? Hmm?"

I felt a burning sensation in the pit of my stomach, mentally scanning my list of clients to sniff out the rat. "I have no idea."

Sahlil licked his lips. "Oh, I think you do."

"Do you want me to read your mind?"

Sahlil issued a villain's cackle. "I bought this building for half a million in 2004. They are offering me two million. It's appraised at seven twenty. No way is this building worth more than eight hundred, tops. Why would they want it so badly, Mr. Bender? It makes no sense."

"You're right, man."

"I have put very little into the maintenance of this shameful building."

"That's true. My dishwasher has never worked and I've asked you to fix it multiple times."

"And yet: two million. For a building with terrible apartments and a greasy Chinese place. There must be something special about this building. Your apartment in particular."

I forced my fists into my pockets. "Okay, Sahlil. What is it? Tell me. Out with it. I'm tired of you. You're a shitty landlord, my dishwasher doesn't work, I freeze my balls off every winter because you're too cheap to get the boiler looked at. . . ."

Sahlil continued to grin at me like I was his lunch. "Take me to your closet, Mr. Bender."

"There's a closet right there," I said, pointing to my hall closet, crammed with coats and boxes of vinyl I hadn't listened to since the Clinton years. Sahlil was getting up in my business so bad that I would have gladly stuffed him in there, locked the door, and bricked him in, Poe style.

"You have a gold mine in your closet, I am told."

"I demand you leave, Mr. Gupta."

Sahlil pushed past me and scurried into my bedroom. "Look at your lease, Bender. You can't ask me to leave. With all that extra money you've been making, it's a shame you don't hire a woman to clean your apartment. Look at the dust piles around the perimeter of this room."

"Hey, Mr. Landlord, Karl told you to stay out of there," Lena said, following after him. "Hands off my computers!"

Sahlil ran his hands over the collection of laptops and wires. "Generators on the floor. Do you keep these generators for illegal activity? Perhaps an illegal time machine? Rock concerts in the past, perhaps?"

I balled my hand into a fist, preparing to punch Sahlil's lights out, and the lights of the rat fink who squealed to my landlord.

Lena said, "No, and that's really stupid."

Sahlil's face relaxed into this really creepy look that made me pity Karuna even more. "You know who I love? I am telling you a huge secret. I love Freddie Mercury." He emitted a long exhale, uncomfortably postcoital, and then he raised his big brown eyes to mine, like a naughty child checking to see if his mother still loves him.

"Freddie's the shit, man," I said.

"I'm not gay, but I very much love Freddie."

I eyed my solid ash Louisville Slugger. Slamming the shit out of Sahlil's egg-shaped noggin would soothe me like a baby with a warm bottle, and I had more than a hunch that Karuna might appreciate Sahlil's early death. There was probably a healthy insurance policy in place. Karuna would find a better man.

"Sahlil, I know we've just met, but you are a truly ridiculous person." Lena told him straight to his face. She was enjoying herself. "You brag like a naked emperor, and then you come out with 'I'm not gay, but I love Freddie Mercury.' Freddie Mercury is a gay icon, for crying out loud."

Sahlil looked at me like I had the IQ of a dead chicken. "I know that. He had the voice of an angel. But I'm not gay. I just love Freddie."

"It's okay if you're gay," Lena said. "I'm bisexual. I had a girlfriend for two years in college, and I still date women. You just gotta love, Sahlil. Love hard, man. Love like no one cares about your bank account."

Sahlil said, "I'm only thirty, so I was unable to see a Queen concert in the 1970s."

"Yeah," I said. "Wouldn't it be great if that were possible."

"Can the shit, Bender!"

Lena muffled a laugh with her hand.

Sahlil grabbed me by the collar. "Take me to your time machine! I want to see Freddie Mercury. I know you have a time machine. You have taken others to Woodstock. To Rolling Stones concerts long ago! One of your customers informed this conglomerate and then they contacted me, the landlord. They've made a handsome offer on my building. I should be making money off of this. I own this building, which means I own your time machine."

I shoved Sahlil off of me. He fell backward on my bed. "What? Who the hell rat finked on me?"

"Savvy business people have their ear to the door," Sahlil said. "Something you wouldn't know, with your two-bit dive bar full of lowlifes and the most foul men's room I've ever had the displeasure to use. This is going to be huge. Do you know how many billions of dollars they're going to make off your time machine? I should definitely sell the building for more than two mil."

Lena watched me closely to make sure I wouldn't box the shit out of Sahlil's stupid head.

"Who did this?" I asked. "Who takes the time out of their busy day to contact a major corporation to tell them that they have a chance to steal something from an independent business owner? Do normal people, like, call Walmart to tell them to ass-fuck the local general store in some small town? What the hell?"

"It's a wormhole, not a machine," Lena said. "And shame on you for trying to sell it, Sahlil. You're a greedy shit."

Sahlil pointed his finger half a centimeter from the tip of Lena's nose and said, "I'm not a naked emperor. I'm a businessman."

Lena laughed.

Sahlil Gupta was not a man who could handle mockery. He took a step toward Lena. "Stop laughing. You take that laugh back."

I took a step toward Sahlil. "Stay away from my girlfriend, Sahlil. I mean it."

"This is my building," he said.

Lena said, "If I take it back, then you don't get to see Freddie. And we have you killed for threatening to evict Karl."

Sahlil was really throwing around that index finger of his. He waved that finger in my face and said, "She just made a threat. Your bisexual girlfriend made a murder threat. I'm calling the police. I will not have unsafe people as tenants." Sahlil dug his phone out of his khakis and began to dial.

My hands were bigger and stronger than Sahlil's. They're pretty much fleshy frying pans with calloused fingertips and a black dot on the right thumb, where I'd had the tattooed *M* for Meredith covered up on the advice of a previous therapist. I took Sahlil's little chopsticks into my beefy mitts, crushed his bony chicken fingers, phone and all, and whispered low into his ear, "Look, dude, I don't want any trouble, but you fuck with my wormhole, you fuck with me."

"Do not threaten me, Karl," he whimpered.

"Then don't threaten me." I gripped his hand harder, waiting to hear his toothpick of a pinky crack.

"You're hurting me," he whispered. I pressed my thumb into the soft spot between his thumb and index finger.

"You're hurting me, man," I said. "Don't come into my home and threaten me in front of my lady friend. I don't come to your fancy condo on Lake Shore and make you look like less of a man in front of Karuna."

"Ownership is nine-tenths—"

I spoke low and measured, directly into his ear. "Nine-tenths of nothing, Gupta. You should be scared of me. You've got money; I've got brute strength, a functioning wormhole, and nothing to lose. Fuck with me, and I'll destroy you. Are we clear?" Part of me hated playing the thug. Part of me hoped this show of bravado turned Lena on. Part of me wanted to give Sahlil some pain.

He squealed like a little pig. "I'm still going to call the cops."

"And they're going to do what, exactly?" I lingered a bit with my nose near the top of Sahlil's head, my hand still clenched around his, so I could smell his fear. I clutched his hand a little harder, even though the grip was beginning to hurt me. The wormhole was all I had in this world. Wormhole, bar, and Lena.

Lena tapped me on the shoulder. "Let's send him. London, 1978, probably?"

I released Sahlil's hand, which he immediately cradled to his chest. "I'll look it up. Sit down, cowboy. You look tense."

Sahlil shook out his throbbing hand. "Can I get some ice?"

"No. Sit down. Sit down and shut up." I pointed at the bed. Lena sat at the computer and began to type in coordinates.

"You want to see Freddie Mercury, huh?" Lena said, like a helpful travel agent. "London, Lyceum Ballroom, December 13, 1979. Hey, that was my first birthday. Happy birthday, baby Lena."

"You have no idea how grateful I am," Sahlil blathered. He asked again for ice and I told him to stuff it.

Lena arched an eyebrow at me. "Yeah, everyone's grateful. Go stand your millionaire ass in the closet, Sahlil. It's awfully cold during passage, and it hurts when you land. Kiss Freddie for me. On the lips. Oops, forgot, you're not gay. London, 1979. Have fun!"

"Thank you," Sahlil said as he fell through the floor.

Lena leaned back in the desk chair and laughed. "Wow. I knew you were a bartender, but I had no idea you were a thuggish, threatening bartender who would crush a skinny rich guy's hand and sling all sorts of aggressive thug talk at him. What a scummy motherfucker you are."

If I hadn't been so pissed off, I would have taken Lena's observation of my bravado as indication to take her in a manly fashion. "That dishwasher has never worked and I've lived here for ten years, and I've asked him at least fifty times to replace it or fix it and he sends over his incompetent cousin who stands there and says there's nothing wrong with it, while it shoots water all over the floor.

And who would tip off some giant corporation about the wormhole? Really? The same guy who, in the nineties, thought it was a good idea for major labels to sign every white dude who sounded like a wounded horse channeling Eddie Vedder?"

A look of horror crossed Lena's face. "Shit. I didn't tell him how to come back. I guess we could leave him there. Evade the whole situation."

"That's my wormhole. And Wayne's." I resisted the urge to kick my couch.

Lena was annoyingly calm. She'd told me that her pills kept her from feeling things strongly one way or another, that every emotion she experienced was smothered by a pillow made of SSRIs, and that she at times missed rage, sorrow, and rainbow-unicorns-out-the-butt joy. "Well. Sahlil didn't ask about how to return. If he's so smart, he would have asked. I guess that's one less millionaire we have to worry about."

"I don't want to see him again. Sahlil, that is. That sleazeball trying to get his grimy hands on my wormhole. But we can't have another missing persons case."

"*Another* missing persons case? There's one on Wayne?"

"Wayne's mother reported him missing to the cops."

"Shit. So we can't leave your landlord in London in 1979?"

"His wife is super hot," I said.

"Thanks, Karl. I appreciate hearing that from your mouth. All two hundred and twenty pounds of me loved hearing that."

"Sorry." Something told me that Lena had never in her life heard herself described as hot. Maybe luscious or cute, but probably not hot. I, for the record, found her hot and I told her so.

"I'll come back tomorrow and fish out Sahlil," she said. "But he's spending the night in London. I have to teach my stupid class now. Tell Wayne I'll have coordinates for him in the morning and to say his goodbyes to 980."

Lena hugged me good-bye, planting a kiss on my lips and making me promise I'd take her to the all-you-can-eat Polish buffet out in the suburbs after she got Wayne back. She looked away as she mumbled something about wanting to hug the fat man in a stained white coat who sliced ham beneath a red heat lamp. She snuck a last quick kiss on my cheek before she ran down my stairs and up the street toward the train stop.

I picked up my phone to call Clyde and see if any of his friends were the stinkpots who ratted me out to the fuzz, but instead of dialing, I looked at my closet. The wires, the tape, the computers, the inky smudges on the walls. The wormhole was a weapon.

TEXT TO WAYNE: *WAYNE? IT'S KARL. PLEASE TEXT YOUR MOM. THE COPS CAME TO THE BAR AND ASKED ME QUESTIONS. PLEASE TELL THEM YOU'RE OK. ALSO, LENA NEEDS YOU TO BE IN A CERTAIN PLACE ON THE ISLAND TOMORROW MORNING. WE NEED TO SYNC WATCHES.*

Wayne's response: *I MADE A BOAT. I AM PROUD OF MY BOAT! I CARVED IT WITH MY VERY OWN HANDS.*

5

LENA FOUND MY other army boot in the kitchen, under the sink, when she went looking for dish soap to clean the charred remnants of accelerator exhaust off my walls. I had no idea how the boot ended up there, with the cleanser and the dehydrated sponges. I didn't care. I had my boot back. I hugged it and hugged her and thanked her and got a little too sappy for her taste. The boot was immediately returned to my foot, red laces tied tight and proud. I felt recharged.

Lena had her own pair of past-boots, but she said her relationship to them was different, that she didn't look at them and feel happy or proud of the person she was when she wore them. Boot-wanting teen Lena was a mess, she said, and her dad probably only bought her two-hundred-dollar purple Doc Martens because her mom had died and there was a window of time, between the death and the stepmom, where her dad gave her everything she wanted:

the boots, a robust CD and vinyl collection, Harvard summer school, and a black cat that she named Ian in honor of Ians Curtis, McCulloch, and MacKaye.

"You were in Boston the summer of 1993?" I asked hopefully, and then remembered that she would've been fourteen and I would've been twenty-three.

My boots were Boston and Meredith and power and vision and clarity, though I needed to rein this in in front of Lena, lest we approach a level of intimacy that I wasn't ready to enter. What I was ready for was a trip to the Black Cat of 1995 Washington, DC, to thrash to the cleansing joy that was Fugazi. Lena wanted to stay in 2010 and lay out in the sun on my roof, above Wicker Park's screeching traffic and the rising odor of grease, lamenting the slanted pitch of her own building's roof, and its close proximity to the tracks of the Purple Line train, the rumble and noise and the peering eyes of passengers gazing upon the hillocks of her body as it received its disappointing share of bastard Midwestern sun.

On the roof, after I had listened to her blather about science this and accelerator that, Lena squealed like a schoolgirl as she revealed to me her teenage crush on Ian MacKaye. "*Sassy* magazine used to write about him," she noted, and I imagined young Lena's head on her pillow in her bedroom in Butte, Montana, surrounded by stuffed animals and physics texts, *Steady Diet of Nothing* blasting on her stereo speakers. "Ian was a little more down to earth than Henry Rollins, but still tough. And less manic than Mark Robinson from Unrest, though I loved everything Teen-Beat put out in the nineties. And while we're on the subject of DC indie rock, I really looked up to Jenny Toomey from Tsunami as a kid, and then I met her at a show and she made me feel about two inches tall."

"The Axis opened for Fugazi once. In DC. A long time ago."

I expected a girlish demand for details, descriptions of the contours of Ian MacKaye's cheekbones, or some sort of affirmation that they weren't a bunch of pricks. But Lena didn't react. I suppose she'd moved on from MacKaye and the wonders of ethical punk rock. She had science. And me.

"What does 'a long time ago' even mean to you, Karl?"

I hadn't thought about that, like, ever. "What does it mean? I don't know. Time is so arbitrary. A long time for a forty-year-old man is different from that of a child, or a carton of milk."

I stripped down to my boxers and rolled out a towel for myself. Lena wore a granny-style black bathing suit with a skirt. Her skin was the color of pale milk. I surveyed her body, her tattoos. Beneath the sun for the first time in ages was the Edward Gorey *Doubtful Guest* tattoo on her left thigh, the purple scar gouged deep into her shin ("Bike accident back in Missoula," she explained), the roll of belly fat that flattened when she lay down, the two stripes of black hair in her armpits, and the red bumps where the razor made a pass at her snatch. A purple and black constellation of planets and stars tattooed around her right thigh. A string of letters and numbers composing a formula tattooed around her upper left bicep. The spidery red and black swirls that crawled from breast to shoulder, and the old-school tattoo-style letter *G* surrounded by stars on her ankle. I wanted to bury my face in her body, but she was being a bit standoffish about physical things, and so I stayed on my towel.

"It smells gross up here," she opined, smearing sunscreen on her stars and planets.

"Ming doesn't clean up after his panda."

"I don't eat chicken. It's gross. Factory farming and everything. I still eat beef—I grew up in cattle country. Cows are delicious. I never liked chicken. Then Hana the Stepmonster showed up and started cooking chicken fifteen times a week. She knew I didn't like it. Making me eat chicken became just one more thing that psycho bitch could do to make me look like an ungrateful child to my father. She was always trying to make a case to send me to live with my grandparents in Skokie, even though I got straight A's and spent all my time after school with the debate club or making extra money tutoring."

"Sorry," I said, hoping that simple word would acknowledge that particular pain brought by a woman who drew sorrow out of a young girl with stepmotherly claws.

Lena slid a pair of purple sunglasses on her face. "I was on the swim team, too. I may be chubby but I'm a good swimmer."

"I was on the swim team for a while, but then joining the pot smoking team took precedence, so I quit."

"Do you have a stepmonster?"

"No. My dad was remarried for a couple of years after my mom died, to a cocktail waitress who was still technically married to some other guy, but eventually she got smart and bolted."

She squirted some sunscreen on *The Doubtful Guest* and rubbed it in. "Lucky you. What's the band you're most embarrassed about loving?"

"Don't have one."

Lena paused before sunscreening up her constellations. "Nothing you're embarrassed about? You don't love ABBA or anything like that? Rick Springfield? Extreme?"

"Nah. Bad music doesn't even register on my radar."

"It has to. How can you know what's good if you don't recognize what's bad?"

"Okay, fine. Who's yours?"

Lena looked excited to tell me. "I have many. I'll confess one: Art Garfunkel. Solo. Post Simon breakup. I think we can all agree that Simon had the writing talent, but Garfunkel had the underappreciated vocal talent."

"I'm not agreeing to anything."

"Garfunkel was a force."

"Garfunkel was a force to hit the Stop button on the tape deck, like—"

I almost said, "Like the Karl Bender of the Axis." That would be true. I was Garfunkel to Milo Kildare's Simon. It wasn't just about charm and swivel hips with Milo. He had an ear. He had a vibe that was just as surreal as it was sexual, projecting retro rock sensibilities with a quirky nineties aesthetic that allowed him to turn on women simply by wearing a checkered bow tie and rubbing his crotch on stationary objects. I was just a guitar monkey playing by rote, ripping off my betters. There's a reason people still talk about Milo Kildare. Axis fans don't even seek out my bar very much anymore, and when the rare one does, they just ask me about Milo.

"I was Garfunkel once," I said, as if she should pity me for not being the front man with the velvet cock and the fans.

Lena made a Bronx cheer at me and chucked the sunscreen tube at my stomach. "No you weren't. And even if you were, there's nothing wrong with being Garfunkel. He has a great voice."

"Milo had a great voice."

"Are you comparing yourself to Milo? Please don't do that," she said, with a look in her eye that was so sweet and caring that I wanted to stab myself in the chest with the business end of that tube of sunscreen. Hard plastic on sternum.

I always compare myself to Milo.

"No."

"You should just be happy being Karl," she said, and I kissed her hard on the mouth. "Karl gets to date Lena Fucking Geduldig, and how awesome is that?"

"Pretty dang awesome," I agreed, and kissed her some more.

"Wayne never found your flashlights," I told her after the smooching, changing the subject while changing my kisses from mouth ones to forehead ones. Lena's hair smelled like fruity shampoo. Talking about Garfunkel made me itchy, and I didn't want to scratch off all my sunscreen. I squirted a big blob in my hand and smushed it on my face, knowing that it would get stuck in my stubble and look gross. "Or, if he did, he's lying about it."

"Honestly, babe, the more time passes, the more it's obvious he doesn't want to come back. He says he doesn't even know where in Manhattan he is anymore. And he's always going on about his fish and his boat."

"Hand me the sunscreen," I said. "This conversation is making me sweat it all out. My ink cannot bake." Lena handed me the tube and I smoothed some over my broken lightbulb. "What if we sent Barry Manilow back to 980? To hound Wayne into coming home? Maybe we could drop a Casio keyboard back in time for him? A little "Copacabana" on repeat and Honnakuit will be running back to the Dictator's Club for dear life."

Lena nodded. "You really miss him, don't you?"

"Yes. It's weird. I'd never really had a guy friend until Wayne. Like a good guy friend. I mean, Milo, I guess, before the falling out."

Lena moved her foot over to mine, to hold it. We were holding feet like cautious lovers in a storybook about secrets. I liked it, especially when she brought her other foot over to rub the top of mine, making nurturing circles with her big toe. I took her hand in mine and held it to my chest.

"It's been years since I've had a good female friend," she said. "The last time I had a close girlfriend was Linnea, my girlfriend-girlfriend at the University of Montana. I don't connect with many women, sadly."

We made out a bit, soaking up the sun and each other. Lena let me cop a feel under the top of her bathing suit and I thrilled to the fact that my giant gorilla hands weren't big enough to hold one of her breasts.

I pressed my lips against her right ear and whispered, "How do you feel about removing that suit up here?"

She pushed me off. "I want to see Garfunkel."

My mouth remained open, like a goddamn drawbridge. I was trying to be sexy. "Fugazi. I am offering you Fugazi. And rooftop sex."

Lena laughed and said, "Garfunkel. It's my turn to pick."

"You picked Elliott."

"Well, duh, Karl. We have the same Elliott tattoo. We had to," she said, and I smiled to myself because I liked to think that Lena and I shared a great cosmic connection and that the greater purpose of the wormhole was to bring us together.

We packed up our urban beach environment, got dressed, and flushed ourselves into the beyond, like excrement to the sewer that was a Garfunkel solo concert.

I didn't watch Lena program the trip. I trusted she knew where we were going. I assumed a Las Vegas casino, or worse, a casino somewhere other than Las Vegas. At best, Central Park, where we'd be bodies lost in a crowd of thousands and barely able to hear a thing.

We landed in a puff of dust. I looked around. Mountains of a certain shade of green and brown. The sun in a certain part of the sky. Not Vegas. The buildings were small and brick and the cars were mostly trucks.

"This is Montana, isn't it?" I've never been anywhere so mountainous. "Mountainy" is a better term, for the tininess of the buildings and people seemed to be amplified by the enormity of the mountains off in the yonder. Also, the old cars with Montana license plates. I slammed my hand against the hood of an old Dodge truck to make sure I could touch things in Butte, and I was relieved to feel the hot metal and the dust residue left on my fingertips. Montana. A slow breezeless landscape of quiet. I wanted to leave.

Lena, walking ahead of me, backwards up a steep sidewalk, threw her hands up as if to show me all the wonder that surrounded us. "Welcome to Butte. You know what Lenny Bruce says about a Jew in Butte, Montana?"

I instinctively reached into my shirt pocket for a cigarette. "Yes. I know the joke. Garfunkel played Butte?"

"Yes, Garfunkel played Butte."

Lena was the child of Jews from Chicago, academics willing to live in a far-flung place for a job. She was raised in this scrubby Western town, small and unexpectedly Victorian, with a single giant camel's hump mountain presiding over the scenery. I immediately thought of the word *gulch* and envisioned the blue-headed cowboy Muppet on *Sesame Street* pushing through swinging saloon doors looking for an alphabet-based Muppet fight. I could feel the temperature of the wind. I expected it would be dry, based on the brown scenery, like a city built on toast crumbs.

"What was it like growing up here, Miss Jew from Butte?"

Lena, walking a few steps ahead of me, turned around and shot me a look that said that the report from her Jew from Butte childhood wasn't good. "School was always crappy, but it would have been crappy anywhere. At home, well . . . Until my mother died and the stepmonster showed up, my parents weren't religious. I was rather pissed when my dad quit eating pork, to tell you the truth. I had some good teachers at Butte High. I wanted to go to boarding school most of the time, but mostly because I hated my stepmom and wanted to wear a schoolgirl uniform. There used to be a really great bookstore, too, but it closed."

"Did you have a lot of dust in your hair all the time?"

She stopped and made a face. "Do you really think it's that dusty here? It's not. It rains and snows a lot."

"It's like another planet, with all the mountains," I said. "Mars-like."

"Montana is nothing like Mars. Give me a break."

I didn't expect the Jew from Butte to defend her homeland, but she did. I followed her up a hill, past low-slung houses, all with hulking American cars parked in their driveways. Pickup trucks with Bush–Quayle stickers stuck to their asses, some with gun racks, some without, were parked in driveways beside Oldsmobiles and the occasional rusty Pinto with a Montana Tech sticker in the back window.

"What year is this?"

"1988."

"Are we going to your house?"

"Garfunkel did not play at my house."

"Garfunkel didn't play Butte, Montana," I wanted to say.

"Are you fucking with me? Lena? Lena, I'm talking to you."

She kept on walking two paces ahead of me, just as I had with her, that day in Cambridge when I forced Lena to tail me all the way to Berkman House just to see Meredith on the old mossy sofa.

"We better not be on some sort of personal field trip," I said.

She whipped around, looking to fight, her eyes narrow and cold. "Shut up, Bender."

Lena's Converse-clad feet scurried across a huge parking lot, past some low, scrubby bushes, up to the pathway of a pink and brown Victorian house surrounded by playground equipment, blue plastic trash cans, dry grass, and a blue and green hand-painted sign that indicated that this was in no way a theater, club, or concert venue.

"Silver Bow Montessori School?"

I followed behind Lena as she flung open the front door. "They always kept the door unlocked," she explained, somewhat dazed. "Oh, God. That smell. Old paint."

"You're in there, aren't you? In 1988 you were, what, nine? Your nine-year-old self is in there."

She wouldn't even turn around to look at me. "Yeah, and your twentysomething-year-old self is in every time travel trip you've ever taken, even if it was a show you didn't actually go to. You hear your young self in the music."

I followed Lena up a flight of stairs. The walls were covered in children's crayon drawings and cheerful posters explaining good manners and parts of speech.

"You know, I really hate this shit. This is a misuse of the wormhole, damn it."

"You set this precedent, remember? You dragged me to see your old girlfriend on what you later called a date. I get to go to Butte in 1988."

"Lena . . ." She was probably never going to let that go.

She turned and pressed her hand to my mouth. "Shh. We're just in time."

At the top of the stairs and around a corner, in a room with a low ceiling and a cluster of child-sized tables and red plastic chairs, stood three lines of children, the tall ones in back, the short ones in front, all a bunch of awkward nose pickers who couldn't stand still for shit. At the piano, a balding man in a suit began to play a lilting tune that I remembered in the furthest reaches of my memory. I picked out nine-year-old Lena immediately, in the middle row, chubby cheeked and jack-o'-lantern toothed, clearly not the most confident child in the room. She was dressed in a shiny lavender dress that fell off her shoulders, her braided pigtails coiled around the sides of her head, Princess Leia style, and she had on those terrible big-framed glasses that overwhelmed her face in a way that a 2010 parent would call child abuse.

A big-boned woman with dark, curly hair, wearing a long denim skirt and similarly insectlike glasses, raised her hands, a pencil serving as a conductor's baton. The children began to sing, off key and in unison.

"Garfunkel, eh? You seriously wanted to see yourself sing that song as a kid?"

Lena wasn't crying so much as she was erupting, like a volcano, quiet and hot, and I worried she wasn't breathing. Lena steadied herself on one of those plastic red chairs.

"What's wrong with you?" I demanded.

"That's my mom. The teacher," she forced out in a whisper. She pointed at the woman in the long denim skirt. I saw the resemblance. She was taller than adult Lena, but the roundness of her face, the salt-and-pepper curls, and the gentle, dopey way her lips curled indicated a genetic link to my girl. Lena's mom. That was Lena's mom.

"We came here to see your mom?"

That was rude, and it made her sob harder. She gasped loudly, and then I noticed little Lena, midsong, stop and look at the strange, crying lady standing several feet away. Sensing who she was, little Lena began to cry, too. Only little Lena kept singing. Gasping for air, tears bubbling over behind the giant glasses.

Lena's mother turned around to see the adult daughter she'd never know. The children's chorus grew sloppy without her direction.

"Excuse me?" Lena's mom said softly, her face registering some level of recognition. "Do I know you?" She turned back to look at her child, and then back at the adult woman whose face was lumpy and red with tears.

"Yes," Lena said. Her voice cracked and her face had turned suddenly pale. With shoulders quaking she said, "I'm Lena."

Lena's mom whipped around to look at her nine-year-old in the lavender dress and then back to see the red-faced thirtysomething iteration of her daughter.

"Excuse me? I'm sorry. I don't understand what you mean," Lena's mom said.

Lena hesitated a bit, almost looking like she was going to go to her mom for a hug, but instead she turned and ran out the door, stumbling down the stairs. I followed, catching her in my arms before she tumbled to the ground in front of the school like a dropped sack of groceries.

Lena's body heaved, struggling for breath. "I just wanted to see her. I wanted to sing "Woyaya" with her one more time. One more time. I miss her so much. Everything in my life turned to shit after she died."

"How old were you when she died?"

"Fourteen." She sobbed. "She had cancer."

"I was twenty-three. Cancer, too."

Lena sniffed loudly and pressed her head to my chest. It felt good to be touched in the past.

"Moms aren't supposed to die," I said, thinking of Melinda Brooks Bender and what I might find her up to in some accessible past.

We held each other for a long time. Lena left a snail trail of cry-snot on the front of my shirt. We staggered outside into the sunlight. Lena lifted her head and pointed to a gray Honda Accord of an early 1980s vintage, parked just outside the front door to Silver Bow Montessori. "That's her car."

We pressed our noses to the windows and looked inside, like it was a box of sunken treasure. Lena's mom's red-framed sunglasses, eighties style, with enormous lenses, rested on the dashboard. On the backseat sat a pile of unreturned library books, mostly Judy Blume novels and science how-tos, and stuck to the left-hand corner of the back window was a purple Northwestern decal and a

Montana Tech parking sticker. A red shoebox of cassette tapes lay on the floor on the passenger side. It looked like any other mom-type car to me, but this was Lena's childhood chariot. Those were Lena's books, and that was Lena's backseat, where she once sat with a book in her lap, staring at the back of her mother's head and out the window at Butte, Montana, and though she hadn't seen it in years, it was as if it had never gone away.

"Are you an only child?" I asked.

"The little girl in there singing is, but I'm not. Dad and Hana have a daughter. Rachel."

Lena continued to stare into her mom's car. "I remember riding around in the backseat of this car. She played that song, "Woyaya," a lot on the radio. And we'd sing it. And she'd tell me that I was going to be really happy and successful someday. And she died and now I'm miserable and a failure at everything."

"Hey, you're not a failure," I said, grabbing her back into a hug.

I could feel Lena's body shudder. "My dad turned into an idiot and married the first opportunist bitch that came along. I had to leave Stanford. The only grad school I got into was Northwestern, and that was only because my parents are alums. If she'd lived, I would have had a completely different life, Karl. Really."

All I could do was hold her and tell her I was glad I got to know her. She sobbed and said she wasn't that great. I disagreed. I liked her spirit. I hugged her some more, let her cough into my chest. She went limp in my arms and I told her that I was sorry, that I cared about her, that she deserved all good things. She sobbed and asked why, if she deserved all good things, the universe kept giving her all the bad ones.

Lena tried to wipe her tears and snot off the front of my shirt. "Really, all the bad things that can happen to a woman have happened to me. I get all the bad, Karl."

"Please let me be the good," I said, and I meant it.

After our trip to 1988 Butte, we returned to the roof of my building. We re-spread the beach towels, reapplied our sunscreen, and talked some more about Fugazi, about bands—not about her mother or Butte or what we had just seen. With her forearm across her eyes to block the sun, she told me hadn't been back to the state of Montana since 2002, the year she graduated from college. She'd seen her father twice since then: at her uncle's funeral in 2004, and four years later, when he was in Chicago for a conference. He had met her for dinner and spent the entire meal talking about Rachel, now thirteen. "He's brilliant at science and dumb as shit about people," she explained, her head on my chest.

"I'm sorry."

"I want to go back in time and kill her. Hana."

"Lena, no."

"It would be the perfect crime. Kill her and then, *poof*, back to the present."

"What if you kill her and then your father marries some other bimbo who makes your life hell?"

Lena pushed some tears off her cheek. "He might have married someone nice if Hana hadn't shown up. He just doesn't think. Couldn't take my mom to a good doctor. Couldn't see how he married a monster. He's a nice guy but he doesn't see people for what they are. I'm just . . . I'm just talking. It helps to talk. I'm not going to kill anyone. I think about it a lot, though. If I could just go back in time and get rid of Hana. But then I'd be getting rid of my sister, and I don't want that, really. I have a list of people I'd like to kill, but I won't do it."

Her eyes were mashed shut because of the sun, her head still pressed to my chest. and I kissed the top of her head.

She hooked her arms around my neck and plowed in for more. Lena, an amateur in the amorous arts. Lena, a head full of formulas I can't even comprehend, her clumsy lips warm with the taste of banana lip gloss, her breasts pushing against my chest. Kissing a girl like Lena was dangerous, I knew. I was signing a contract not to be a total dickhead. She wasn't a write-off. She wouldn't disappear after I swept up for the night and locked the door.

How many women had I kissed, expecting them to disappear?

"Say something nice about me," Lena demanded, punching me lightly in the gut.

"You're really smart."

"Whatever. I know that. You think I've haven't heard that one before?"

"Your eyes are gorgeous."

She punched me again. "Say I'm better than Meredith."

"What?"

"Say you like me better. And mean it. I know you don't, but dude, you've got to move on. Just say the words."

"I am. I'm moving on. I haven't seen Meredith in over ten years, Lena. I like you."

"I like you."

"I really like you. You're pure magic."

"Thank you. You're cute and weird and funny and have a noticeable spot of low self-esteem, which I find makes you more trustworthy. I like your tattoos. You've got Snoopy, and *amor fati* knuckle rockers, and a bloody heart. And a lightbulb breaking. A range of inky themes. You must contain multitudes."

"I try."

"I still work for you, you know." She kissed me again. "I saw Fugazi play in Seattle a long time ago. I think that was enough. I'm not young anymore. I don't even really remember what their politics were. Whatever they were, they didn't stick."

She was thirty-one. Nine years fewer on this dirt heap than me. She never experienced the seventies without diapers on her butt.

Lena sat up and looked into my eyes. She caught me sneaking a peek down her swimsuit.

"Karl, have you ever looked at Art Garfunkel's Wikipedia page? The guy wrote a book of poetry, and acted in films, and won all sorts of awards. He was even cantor of his own bar mitzvah. He's done way more than you and me combined. Being Garfunkel is nothing to be ashamed of. I saw Milo's solo thing a few years ago. He's just a big rip-off of Elvis Costello. You, Karl? You have cred."

"Take off that bathing suit," I commanded, thinking of that old Fleetwood Mac lyric about doing your stuff in the tall grass. Only we were on a tar roof in Chicago, nowhere near any grass. After paying me a compliment like that, there was only one way to show gratitude.

"No," she said, her hand shooting up to the top of her bathing suit. "Not up here."

I suggested we go down to the apartment, then, and Lena mumbled something about needing to go to the bathroom. She wrapped her towel around her, pressing it to her body with her armpits.

Did Lena not know what she was missing? I consoled myself with trumped-up ideas of my own capabilities as a lover of great skill and imagination. Hell, did Karuna not know what she was missing?

Oh shit.

Sahlil.

6

"DAMN YOU, KARL. You shit of a man."

We found Sahlil lying in my bed, wrapped up to his chin in my not-very-clean sheets. We'd left him in 1979 London for a little over a day, and I could tell by the look on his face that he had enjoyed his visit yet was choosing to be confrontational. I wanted to be lying in my bed, either above, below, or behind Lena, who, upon seeing Sahlil, ducked into the bathroom and locked the door.

"Did you see Freddie Mercury?" I asked.

He shook his head excitedly. "I did. Yes."

"Great, Sahlil. I need you to get out of my bed, man. The ride is over."

Sahlil made a sound like a wounded animal. He grabbed at the bottom of my shirt, his too-long fingernails scratching my belly. "You have brought me to my knees, Karl."

I pulled his hands off of me. "Not my fault you didn't consider the emotional dangers of time travel. Lena and I have these little information cards we hand out before sending people on trips, but you were being impatient, so you get what you get."

He stood up. Sahlil reeked of motor oil and BO. There was a flat purple splotch (a hickey?) on the side of his neck, and a trickle of blood on the collar of his shirt.

He looked at the bloodstain on his collar with a combination of derision and excitement. "Karuna will probably think I have been with a whore. I haven't. I was with the most beautiful man who ever lived."

"What the hell?" It seemed reasonable that someone would use the wormhole to go back in time to hook up with a dead rock star; however, not being much of a gambling man, I wouldn't have put money on it being my landlord. But there it was, on his face. All over his face in every way.

"I can't go home to my wife," he said.

A big, goofy laugh flew out of my mouth. "Freddie Mercury, huh? You're welcome. Now get out."

Sahlil jumped up, taking with him a white streamer of bed sheets. "You do this. You give people their deepest hopes and prayers. You show them life as a beautiful thing and you suck them back to the hell they have made for themselves. And now I'm torn apart inside."

"What happened? Not the brutal, graphic play-by-play, please."

Sahlil swooned. "Freddie and I locked eyes from across a pub after the show at the Lyceum. It was meant to be. We talked all night long."

"Great."

Sahlil sat on my couch, dropping his head into his hands. "I can't sell the building."

"No, you can't."

"I have to be with Freddie."

"You have a wife and a business here in Chicago in 2010. If you want to leave all that, well, don't look to me to help you"

He put his head in his hands. "I'm a fool."

"I'm sorry, Sahlil. I'm a bartender, and I can tell when people can't hold their liquor, and clearly you can't hold your time travel. Also, I cannot in good conscience aid and abet adultery."

"It wasn't adultery," Sahlil said.

"I'm just going to tell you right now, dude. If you leave Karuna, I'm going after her."

"Hey," Lena said. "I heard that."

Sahlil chortled. He wiped a blob of snot from his nose with the back of his hand and wiped it on his khakis. "You are not wealthy enough to earn Karuna's love."

"Right."

"You're broke-ass enough to earn mine, I guess," yelled Lena from the bathroom.

I thought Sahlil was leaving, but he kept his feet firmly planted on the floor beside my bed. "May I go to sleep on your couch? I am tired. Overwhelmed."

I sighed. "I've got a lady here, man."

"Please? I have nowhere else to go." His hands shook as he took a handkerchief out of his pocket and used it to wipe his nose.

"Fine. Just get out when you wake up, okay? I've got to go to work in a few hours. Take a shower while you're at it, too. You look like hell. There's a clean towel in there, under the sink."

Frightened and depleted, he turned his back to me and lay down on my couch. He removed one shoe and then another and asked for a glass of water.

"You will send me back? Tomorrow? After I talk to Karuna?"

I poured Sahlil a glass of water from the kitchen tap. He took it with his trembling hand and drank the whole glass in one shot.

"Maybe. No promises. I will end you if you so much as talk to those conglomerate people. Are we clear?"

Sahlil nodded. "Aye aye, captain."

Lena came out of the bedroom, "Hey, Sahlil. How did you get back here? I mean, we forgot to tell you the code for reentry, but here you are, back safe and sound."

Sahlil looked away. "It was like . . . It was . . . Love. Love forced me back."

"Any scientific procedure?" Lena continued. "Did you reverse the pull? Did you use your phone to reverse the pull? I need to know. To make the portal safer. Would you mind telling me specifically how you got back?"

He shook his head. "I will sleep and go to see Karuna. Tell her everything. Karuna will be a very wealthy woman. And then you send me back there. To be with Freddie. Forever. And I will die with him when the time comes." Sahlil lay down on the couch, already outfitted with blankets and a pillow. He pulled the blanket up over his head.

"How do you mean, love forced you back? I'm looking for something scientific."

He shook his head. "I have a lot of money, and I thought that's who I was, but now I know who I am. I know a lot. I should be grateful. I will pay you a lot to send me back to Freddie in a few days." Sahlil shut his eyes.

Lena and stood I over Sahlil, watching his eyelids flutter. "How did he get back here?" I asked.

"The force of love."

"The force of love?"

"I tried to get him to tell me in scientific terms. He just said love. But love has no mass. I don't believe it for a second."

"He's in love," I said.

"I guess Wayne doesn't love you. Or he'd be back by now."

From Wayne: I PHOTOGRAPHED A RAINBOW. LOOK HOW CLOSE AND BRIGHT THE RAINBOW IS. WE HAVE TO USE DRUGS TO SEE THE WORLD THE WAY IT WAS IN 980.

I told Wayne I loved him and asked him to please come home.

> I LOVE YOU TOO! MEN KISS MEN HERE. I COULD KISS EVERYONE IN THE TRIBE AND IT WOULD BE LIKE SHAKING THEIR HAND. WHITE PEOPLE RUINED KISSING. AND SEX. AND THE ENVIRONMENT.

I ENVIED WAYNE'S new, uncomplicated lifestyle so much that I decided to further complicate my own complicated lifestyle. I had someone to settle a score with. That good-looking old man with his hard-to-open e-mails.

I made it to age sixty-one, at least. I should have gone out for a hundred cheeseburgers to celebrate.

7

I HAD NEVER traveled to the future. There wasn't even a setting for it on the control panel.

But I'd been wondering about a few things, and I wanted to speak to a certain sixty-one-year-old man named Karl Bender. Tell him what I thought of his harassing messages.

My eyes had seen the past again and again, with tears of love sloshing across my poorly shaven cheeks, but the future was a dry, fearsome spectacle, a box of broken secrets too painful to assemble. It was the slowness of the delivery of age, of disappointment, that made it tolerable. Swallowing a full twenty years all at once was another thing. I prepared my throat for the giant pill.

I scrawled a note to Lena on the back of an old envelope and laid it across the controls: *Went to Seattle, 2031. Be back by dinner. Love, KB.*

I programmed the computers and fell forward, through a portal so hot I thought my clothes were going to melt onto my skin. It felt good when I landed in a river of tepid, brown water, which just happened to be the land beneath what once had been Interstate 5 in Seattle.

Yes, Future Karl, I see what you mean about water. I landed with a splash. Thick chunks of I don't know what (soggy clumps of old toilet paper?) clung to my body as I hoisted myself onto a cement platform that appeared to be some kind of sidewalk. A broken city of buildings cracked in half, and the intrusion of water had turned future Seattle into Venice, complete with gondolas and eerie signage ordering citizens to "Boil water before drinking. There might be fecal deposits in your water. Don't forget to put floaters on your pet."

There were no streets to loiter upon, no sidewalks and storefronts, no bars or coffee shops or anything suggesting the calming commerce that I take for granted in my here and now. The fronts of buildings and houses had all been wrapped in thick green and blue plastics, dirty brown lines on the plastic, indicating where the waterline had receded. People lived in makeshift aquariums, and it occurred to me that you could drown in your bed if the plastic tore or if an earthquake hit and ripped the walls of your house down again.

I was afraid to ask what had happened to poor, sweet Seattle, a city I adored, mostly due to the strong Axis fan base that existed there back in the day. Something had happened to Seattle, though. Something profound and frightening. There were hardly any people about. One boat floated by, but the boats all seemed to be owned by the military. A woman with a bullhorn shouted at me to get inside, now.

Wait, what?

"You can see me?" I shouted at the woman.

She was wearing a bright green plastic suit with a helmet that covered her face. "Sir, we are ordering everyone indoors. There has been a sewage explosion in the area. Get inside now."

The water was up to my knees, oddly warm as it soaked through my jeans. The air smelled of sulfur and burning wood. I felt okay, though. I knew where I was going. I had the address, or at least the number of the house. Lena and I lived in building 6641.

Hello, Post-A Cascade Zone 1. You reek of dried fruit and flaming shit and you look like a horrible B movie set.

Building 6641 was wrapped in bright green latex, like a giant condom over an old brick apartment building. The lucky ducks on the top floors had windows that looked over the watery city. I walked along the floating plastic sidewalk, which required sea legs I did not have, until I found building 6641.

The door opened. It was more of a suctiony porthole than a door, and it was lined with a bright orange rubber gasket. A teenage boy in yellow plastic pants walked out and I rushed past him and into the building. It looked like any other old apartment building: dark wood stairs, white walls flecked with black mold. Plastic-wrapped signage, instructing tenants to boil their water, lined the walls.

The names on our future mailbox: K. Bender/L. Geduldig/G. Park. Maybe I was a committer after all. Maybe our marriage had slowed to something dull and unremarkable, or we simply lived together because we were unable to afford rent in the watery postapocalypse. Or maybe I was just a dumb old codger and Lena didn't mind buttoning my pants for me.

Who was G. Park?

I jimmied open the door and let myself into our future apartment. Slobs we would be, in our dotage. Coffee cups half filled with milk and mud sat around the house, as did newspapers, each one housed in a plastic wrapper. I was glad to see that paper still existed. I felt joy in seeing the familiar things that still existed in the year 2031: flat-screen televisions, crackers that came in boxes, sodas that came in cans, sticks of butter wrapped in waxy paper. Lena's and my future bed had some sort of plastic breathing dome over it—probably a safety precaution here in Waterworld—but still, a normal bed with normal pink cotton sheets, tangled and unmade. Our future apartment had small, white, blinking boxes attached to the walls, whose purpose I did not know—nor did I care to. Better to be surprised. Also, better save my money. They looked expensive.

On the bedroom wall, wrapped in wispy sheets of plastic, a photo of me and Lena. Bride and groom, me looking like a walrus in a top hat, her dressed in bright pink satin and lace, more soft and beautiful than the razor-blade science goddess I knew. The photo was taken in bad lighting, and she and I were holding what appeared to be cigarette lighters next to our faces. Older, chunkier, wrinklier, but happy and in love.

Don't lose Lena.

If my future was this, watery and damp, under gray skies, with Lena by my side, then I welcomed it. Think of the hours spent in a plastic dome, underneath blankets, laughing and sleeping and pressing strange blinky-box buttons on my wall, that I had to look forward to.

A computer screen the size of a cereal box, stuck to the wall, scrolled with what I assumed was news. Or internal documents. Or something that has something to do with sixty-one-year-old me.

POST-A SPIRAL

CASCADE ZONE 1

29 MARCH 2031 14:05PPAT

From GLORY PARK (@gloworm13): ARE YOU HOME MOM? Garfield High Post-A Teen Requisition Team. Get KARL OR DAD to transpay for req trip to SOUTH CALIFORNIA, pleez. BELLA AND MOLLY AND ALL SIX EMMAS ARE GOING SO WHY NOT GLORY?

From GLORY PARK (@gloworm13): GARFIELD HIGH CLASS OF 2031 POST-A COMMENCEMENT EXERCISES 08 JUN 31 NO RUBBER SUITING IN THE TENT SHOW SOME RESPECT Mr. Yun sed the ceremony might be down in Cascade Z 3 if the water thing cannot be fixed so gross.

From GLORY PARK (@gloworm13): Mom in Capitol Zone 4 until 02 JUN DO NOT MISS GRADUATION MOM

From LENA GEDULDIG (@theycallherdrworm): Line up for algae paste+*crackers no later than 8am KARL.*

From GLORY PARK (@gloworm13): Line up for PEANUT PASTE afterwards KARL DON'T BE A DICKBAR DO IT luv GLORY.

From GLORY PARK (@gloworm13): DAD and MADISON are in Siberia looking at the giant hole. *MADISON (@mhchenpark)* TAKE PICTURES PLEEZ DAD *(@parklife76)* please chat me NOW away from the SPIRAL because of REQ WORK.

From KARL J. BENDER (@benderisboring): I scooped dead dogs out of a drain pipe today, Glory. I'm coming home and going to bed. I'll get your peanut paste tomorrow. I really need you to be nice to me right now.

From GLORY PARK (@gloworm13): KARL, I am always nice to you!

From GLORY PARK (@gloworm13): FIND SOME CHOCOLATE PLEEZ

The front door opened and in walked a tall, lanky teenager with slightly Asian eyes wearing a white plastic bonnet that matched her white Post-A Teen Corps Cascade Zone One jacket. When she pulled it off, a long, black ponytail fell down her back. She wore Buddy Holly glasses, apparently still the height of hipster style twenty years hence, and white knee-high rubber boots studded with red and blue rhinestones.

"Hey Karl. Just came home to get my—" This teenager examined my face for a bit, then looked a little scared. "Karl?" she yelled down the hallway. "What the hell happened to your face?"

"I'm not here to . . ."

"You're not here to what? I thought you were down in zone two with the Kildares."

"You know Milo?"

"Don't have time for your stupid questions, Karl. I just came back to get water cans. You never signed my thing for Teen Corps." The girl held out her arm at me. On her wrist was an orange plastic box, strapped on like a watch. It was a small, square computer screen. "Can I get a thumbprint, please?"

"I'm sorry, I don't know what you're asking."

She gave me a teenagery weird look. "Oh, flips, hold on. I have to shut the door or else the water will come in." She closed the door, pressing a button to the side of doorjamb that made a suction sound when activated. Then she looked at me. Really looked at me. "Karl, is there something you want to tell me?" I didn't respond. We just stared at each other.

Then I nodded yes. "I'm confused."

The girl gave me a worried look. "Oh, wow, you were in the water?"

"What is this stuff?" I asked, plucking a wad of toilet paper stuff off me.

"Ew. Don't touch it. And don't drop it on the floor." She ran to the kitchen and returned with her hands in rubber gloves and picked up what I'd instinctively dropped. She rushed the handful of white stuff to a metal box by the door, dropped it in, and pressed a button on top of the metal box.

I was curious. "What is it? Animal, vegetable, or mineral?"

She said, "It's birds, Younger Karl. Birds that fly into the pumping system and get pulped. Sorry." I felt myself begin to retch and then the girl said, "But you traveled forward, so obviously you want to know things. Please don't vom-bomb the floor."

"Hey, I've seen you before. At my bar in Chicago, sitting next to the jukebox. Who are you?"

"Glory," she said, and flashed me a smile. Her teeth were brown and rotten beneath her bleedy-looking gums. "Glory Rhiannon Park."

The girl waved her hands over her bracelet. "Hello?" a female voice emanated from the girl's wrist thing. Her wrist thing appeared to be a telephone.

"We have a little Karl situation here. No, he's fine. Is he down in zone two or is he here? Zone two? That's what I thought." Although she didn't have to hold the wrist thing to her ear, apparently only she could hear the other person on the line.

The girl said, "Karl, aka you, is in Cascade Zone Two right now, helping out with drying all the books that got sloshed when the Willamette River overflowed. With Eddie and Vi Kildare and your friend Milo, the famous guy." She smiled with her mouth open, but quickly closed it after she saw my reaction. I felt so bad for the girl, who was far too young to have a mouthful of rotten teeth.

"Wait—this is the home of Karl Bender and Lena Geduldig, right?"

"Maybe it is. Maybe it's not. It's definitely my home. Or one of them, at least."

"And you are?"

"Glory. I told you my name already. You know me."

"Why were you in my bar? In 2010."

"Pretty neat, huh, since I was born in 2013."

"So you can time travel?"

She walked into the kitchen and came back with two metal cans shaped like bullets, which she placed in the pockets of her jacket. "We just call it traveling, nowadays. The current preferred leisure activity of the rich and of the lucky daughters of the physicists who developed it. I mean, since the asteroid, we're not allowed to do it for fun anymore, but I have my ways of getting around the government."

"Wow. So. Daughter of a physicist? We have a kid?"

"Physicists. Three of them, in fact. I'm a good kid," the girl offered. Glory. *Miss Glory,* I recalled from an earlier e-mail from sixty-something me.

"I hear you're an excellent kid," I offered, trying to seem cool.

"I am. I'm a drywall leader at Teen Corps, and that's a big deal. I can drywall like a fiend."

"Park?" I asked. "What kind of name is that?"

"It's Korean," Glory said. "My real dad's Korean American."

"You have a 'real dad'?"

She shot me a sassy grin. "Don't you?"

"Who are you?" I demanded, wanting to hear her say it. To confirm it. To let me know who's kid she was. And wasn't.

"I told you. Glory. You're Karl. You're in zone two today, so you must be Karl who owned the bar in Chicago. He's told us some stories. No more alcohol since the asteroid, can you believe it? No more distilleries. Grain can only be used for food."

"Asteroid? What happened?"

"Dr. Lena said not to give you any information," Glory said, swiping her finger around above her wrist. "But. There was an asteroid. Siberia, April 27, 2029, and everything in Washington

State is still effed up. Oh, sorry, Post-A Cascade Zone One. We don't have states anymore. The coastline shifted. We're technically an island nation now. 'We' meaning Seattle, the great city of my birth. Ex-Seattle, zone one, that is. If it weren't for all the pumping, the whole city would be under the bay. That's why there's so much water around here. And hunks of bird pulp. I have to go."

"What?"

"You don't have to leave. I mean, I have to report to my work site for a fun evening of drywall dance party, but you can hang out. Just don't drink all of our water or our Medical Malt. Mom's doctor has her on the Medical Malt ever since the whole dealie with the parasites. You can get parasites from touching bird pulp, by the way. Do you have any food from the past on you?" she asked. "Preferably food that hasn't touched bird pulp? Chocolate, maybe? All the chocolate is gone. Look, if you come back, bring me some chocolate, okay?"

"What? Okay. What happened to chocolate?"

"It's gone. Everything's really expensive, except for rice and algae paste. Hey, I'm going to Florida for college in the fall." She pulled open the front door and waited for me to walk out of it. "Gainesville's not so bad, post-A-wise. Pretty much intact, which is why UF is so hard to get into now. Dad and Mad pulled some strings, though. We're in the thick of this asteroid mess for at least another six years."

I reached into my jacket pocket and produced a tin of Altoids, half gone, taking one for myself, to get the vom-bomb flavor out of my mouth.

"Oh my god! Altoids! Thank you!" She grabbed the tin out of my hand and cradled it to her chest. "Come back and bring me food, okay?"

"If you can time travel, or travel, sorry . . . how far backwards have you been?"

"In time? All the way back to the dinosaurs, and all the way forward to the sludge. We don't have much time left here, anyway. All my drywalling will end up being for nothing."

This girl seemed so airy and nonchalant, like she was so over it, like the most miraculous thing to ever happen in this natural history of the universe was like the band that was cool two years ago but that only lame poseurs talked about now.

"When you say 'back to the dinosaurs,' what year, exactly?"

The girl acted like the question was so commonplace as to be boring. "I don't know. I have to go to drywalling now."

"You're not going to tell me?"

Glory shot me a look. "I don't have to tell you anything, you time hobo."

"You wouldn't travel if it weren't for me."

"Go home, Time Hobo."

"Okay, I will."

She examined my face, looking like she didn't like what she saw. "You do that, you big hobo."

"Tell Lena . . . Tell Lena I love her. In 2010, I love her."

Glory gave me that classic teenage "You're weird" look. "I can't tell her that."

"Why not?"

She blinked in that teenage way that indicated that she thought I was stupid. "Because in 2010 she was married to my dad."

"What? She's not married—" My phone rang. I didn't have time to ask more questions. I fell through the floor and all that water, backwards, with that nauseous feeling of knowing things I shouldn't, unable to give them back to their rightful owners.

HEY LENA, ARE YOU MARRIED TO A GUY WITH THE LAST NAME PARK? I texted.

NO. ARE YOU GOOGLING ME OR SOMETHING?

NO. I JUST. I MET SOMEONE.

FUCK YOU VERY MUCH FOR BREAKING UP WITH ME BY TEXT.

NO! NOT LIKE THAT! I MET SOMEONE WHO SAID YOU WERE MARRIED. YOU KNOW WHAT? NEVER MIND. I'M SORRY. NO, I AM NOT BREAKING UP WITH YOU.

I'M GRADING PAPERS. THEY'RE TERRIBLE. BE NICE TO ME OR LEAVE ME ALONE. I MEAN IT.

SORRY. COME OVER TONIGHT?

MY HUSBAND AND I HAVE PLANS. HA HA.

SO YOU ARE MARRIED?

OMG, PARANOID BARTENDER. STOP.

8

CLYDE OUTDID HIMSELF for Rockabilly Night at the Dictator's Club. The event promised to draw in a more prosperous, overdressed crowd. Taking the stage at 10:30 was his new, as-of-press-time unnamed rockabilly band, with his lithe and luminous girlfriend, Chloe, as the singer, and a fedora-wearing goon with a fat, stubble-coated chin, on upright bass. Clyde's ginger-colored hair was swept into a pompadour so slick with pomade that goo rolled down his temples into his sideburns. He had cleaned the place from top to bottom, leaving bucket of black mop water and a trash can full of grimy paper towels. He had wiped off all the chairs and installed Christmas lights above the stage he and two of his friends had built and painted bright red. The bathrooms no longer reeked of piss.

"Nice work, Vaseline Face," I said, as he swept the floor in his fancy duds. I didn't know anyone in Chicago who owned cowboy boots, but there was Clyde, rocking some black ostrich numbers with red stitching. Since returning from the post-A future, I'd been extremely nice to every person who crossed my path. I was comforted by knowing that I'd be married to Lena but distraught over the pulped birds and Glory Park. I always imagined I'd be kid free.

"Thanks. Maybe we'll get some clientele other than your friends and those teamster guys."

"Don't dis the teamsters. Teamsters need to drink."

I had been letting the Dictator's Club go. This happens when I am a man obsessed. Unless my obsession was a woman and why an okay-looking bartender such as myself wasn't dating one, in which case I made sure the ladies' room was clean and well stocked, and even put a plastic canister of free tampons on the back of the toilet. Free tampons! What a female-friendly thing for a barkeep to do. Ladies noticed the details, the details that affirmed menstruation as a mysterious power that only females were holy enough to possess. I learned that from Meredith, who once explained that any expression of disgust in response to the natural functions of her lady parts would have me dismissed from her sleeping bag and replaced by the patchouli-scented ponytail dude who stacked fruit at the Star Market. Any guy who wore that much patchouli would be down with the blood of the yoni, she argued.

At present, though, I was doing a terrible job of being dictator of the Dictator's Club. I still showed up for work, still replaced kegs and counted the beans, but my true calling—amateur psychology while selling alcohol—had been replaced by solipsism and making out with Lena to "Words" by Low on repeat. (How I loved her when, a tear in her eye, she told me she'd been wanting to make out with someone to that song since high school, so we put it on repeat and let our mouths heal all that lost time.) Oh—I was also sending texts to Wayne, which he mostly ignored. Since Wayne's disappearance, I no longer found my bar comforting. I had learned the hard way not to make crotchety statements to Clyde and his young pals, such as, "These kids wailing on drop D like some half-assed wannabe grunge act make me want to go back to 1989 and impregnate as many women as possible so that my progeny could teach these pieces of shit what music is about."

As I age, every part of me grows soft. My ankles are chubbier and have long strands of dark hair jutting out all over them. My belly is round and my belly button is starting to turn inside out, but I can still look down and see my penis, and so can Lena, and that is all I care about. My mind—I think of nothing except rock shows that I'd like to see again, the soft feel of Lena's body, and lavender-scent-triggered remembrances of my mother.

Even my heart was growing soft. *Son!* I thought, when I saw Clyde operating the mop with military precision. Not one misplaced peanut or strand of hair remained on our floor when Clyde was on duty. He wanted this, this idea of a happy bar, and for him that included providing a stage for his friends' band to play. I would have wanted the same at his age. I became grouchy. The artistic endeavors of others became fodder for scorn and judgment. I hated those who had become what I was as a young man.

I pitied Clyde for spending the early 1990s in diapers, putting Fisher-Price toys in his mouth while those of us with 1970s births were down at the club, receiving our youthful blessings. But I admired Clyde for his initiative, and for not being afraid to call me out. "For being the one from the inferior generation, I'm clearly the one with the work ethic around here, you lazy old fuck," Clyde yelled at me from across the bar, after I refused to get off my ass and help him with the sound equipment, and I loved the boy for it. Clyde kept my mind fresh. I should have offered him a free time travel concert. I underestimated him, thinking that at the age of twenty-two he had no call for nostalgia. His favorite bands were no better than mine.

"You want a beer?" I asked Clyde.

"Maybe later," Clyde said.

"On the house. For your hard work. I appreciate it."

"I can pour it myself."

I was about to summon something nice to say to Clyde (a vague attempt to silence the scornful old man growing inside me), when a woman spun around on her barstool and said, "Fuck you, Karl."

She had dyed black hair, wore a too-tight Ramones T-shirt.

"Excuse me?" I asked.

She stood up on the bottom rung of her barstool, which still left her shorter than me. "I said, fuck you, Karl."

I placed both hands palm down on my bar and lifted myself up to seem taller. "You got a problem, lady? Because if you do, you can take your problem and leave."

The woman laughed. "Oh my god, Karl Bender, did you just call me *lady*?"

"Do I know you?"

The woman raised an eyebrow at me. "Really, Karl? Has it been that long?"

"No." I swallowed hard.

"It's Meredith McCabe."

I looked closer and saw those bottle-green eyes behind her glasses and the lines that had worn their way into the pale flesh. My knees buckled. I grabbed the bar. I steadied myself.

Kill me.

In all those years, how many hours, how many days, had I thought about holding Meredith in my arms again; lowering my nose to her head so I could inhale her scent—chamomile shampoo blended with cigarettes, whiskey, and Nag Champa. Here I was, wish fulfilled. And my stupid ass didn't even notice.

I took Meredith into my arms, her cheek against my chest. Years had passed, and in those years my license to legally sniff her head had been revoked. She must have heard my heart accelerate, pound against my T-shirt onto her face, which I had once described in a decrepit notebook of youthful embarrassments as "porcelain." (This was back when the very thought of Meredith McCabe made me write bullshit poetry, when the world would have thanked me to have just jerked off instead.)

The sight of her, the remnants of that face, the one I still kept pictures of in my wallet, in my apartment, stashed away in books I never read. Her red hair dyed black. Her sharp nose and chin now round and soft. Her once tweezed-to-a-thin-line eyebrows thicker. The black revolver tattooed around her bicep faded to blue. I felt light-headed, standing in a graveyard before my true love. I'm pretty sure my heart stopped beating for a few strokes.

"Stop, Karl. You're crushing me like a bug."

I had forgotten how small she was. I remembered her body as a bullet, tight and lean and small enough to fit in the luggage compartment on an MBTA commuter train, where I had once lifted and stowed her, on a long-ago ride down to Quincy to purchase some kind of illegal painkiller from a Greek woman with no teeth. She'd squealed like a child on a swing until one of the conductors made me take her down.

"Way to make a girl feel like an ugly old hag, Karl. Fourteen years and a high-risk pregnancy haven't done me any favors, I know, but come on, man."

"I'm so sorry. I'm in a funk. I've given up on looking at female patrons in the face, so I don't get accused of being a perv. I really am happy to see you. You're really here. How the hell are you? Let me get you a drink." I darted behind the bar to pour Meredith a beer.

"I've been sitting here for an hour, Karl. Waiting for you to recognize me. Watching you follow that natty young man with the mop around like a puppy dog. His hair really is a sight to behold."

I was the one who poured her first beer. I was probably thinking about her as I did it. "Why didn't you tell me you were coming? I would have taken the evening off. We have a band coming to play in a few hours, so . . ."

She shook her head no. "So you own this place?"

I looked around at my baby, all dressed up for Rockabilly Night. "Still making payments. But yeah. It's my baby. A bar baby. Just going to sit out the rest of life, you know, pouring beer for strangers."

"Oh, shut up, Karl. You became a huge rock star after we broke up. Or a minor one. I had that picture of you from *Spin* magazine on my fridge for years, until it, like, decomposed."

"Wow, really? That's a terrible picture of me."

"It was in *Spin* magazine."

"That article was about Milo and his short pants."

"Milo schmilo. I saw you guys play. In Boston, maybe around 2000. I didn't say hi because I didn't know if you wanted me to say hi."

I couldn't tell if Meredith was flirting, or if I even wanted her to be flirting. "Oh, gosh. You know, I think I would have wanted you to say hi."

"Well, too late now. Here I am, ten years later. So?"

"So?"

"So."

"So." I couldn't feel my tongue. "Why are you in Chicago?"

She had a guilty look on her face, one I remembered from the times she flirted with other men or asked me for money. "You didn't respond to that e-mail. About the note I found, from the girl who said you would still be in love with me in the year 2010. Well, here it is. June 2010. I thought it was time to check in and see how things were going with you. Garrett, my husband, his family is in Milwaukee. His brother got married last Saturday and

I'm taking an extra week for myself before I go home to wife-and-mother land. Visiting old friends. Hello."

The words hung in the air. So heavy.

"Hello," I said. "So . . . you have a kid?"

Her face lit up like Christmas. "Yep. A daughter. She's almost four now. Little hellion. Saoirse. Saoirse Reyna de Luz Navarro. Like that? She reminds me of me. Red hair. Likes to use her fists. We bought her a drum set. Big mistake. Having a baby at thirty-nine makes you tired, and then not getting enough sleep for four years turns you into a damn zombie. Garrett and I were not all there when we agreed to buy her a drum set."

"We." The word didn't feel like a punch. "You got married."

"I got married. I know I used to talk about how marriage was shackles and Emma Goldman and Alexander Berkman never got married, but you know. Things change. I woke up one morning and looked at Garrett and was like, "Hell yeah, let's do this forever," and so we went to city hall. We got married after Saoirse was born, so she's a bastard. That makes me feel a little less like a sellout. Garrett's nine years younger than me, too. I was like, what do you want with me, but he was into older women, I guess. It started out as just a sex thing, you know? Then it turned into a big relationship and we got pregnant, and married, in that order. We're happy. I finished college at thirty-five. I teach first grade at this little private school. My hair smells like finger paint and there's crushed Cheerios all over my car. I actually own a car. Can you believe it? Me, a teacher? I love it. We have a dog. And a house in Oakland. Owning a house is not as much fun as people will have you believe. Karl, remember when I didn't believe in possessions? I never should have changed that. I was happier when I lived beneath the pool table at Berkman. Owning stuff is stupid, but I have a kid, and if you don't own stuff people will jump up your ass telling you you're a bad parent, and maybe that does make you a bad parent. I don't know. Now I have a new hot water heater and I have to scoop dog shit from my backyard. All my money goes to Target and the electric bill. I let Saoirse have a Barbie. Am I boring you?"

"What? No." She wasn't. I needed to hear about how domestic, average, and dull her life of work and marriage and kid was, even if she was leaving out the part about hot, marital animal sex with Garrett or how adorable her dog was. I kind of wanted a dog.

"Good. Tell me about your life, Karlito."

"Uh," I noticed how badly my hands were shaking. "Well. Bar, obviously. The Axis broke up, like, seven years ago. Big steaming pile of shit breakup. I think *Spin* ran an article about that too. Milo moved to Portland and got married and had a couple of kids. I moved here. I just, run this bar. Hang out with friends. I don't play music anymore. I don't know. I'm thinking about buying a bear rug for my apartment. With the head still attached. I know possessions are stupid, but—"

"Milo has kids? How wonderful."

Meredith had developed the specific smile a mom smiles when someone is talking about kids. In that moment I felt sick, because she probably liked Milo more than me because he was a dad. Too bad I couldn't tell her about Glory.

"How's Lena?" she asked.

I blinked. "How do you know Lena?"

"The time travel girl. You read my e-mail, right? I found this piece of paper this girl gave me back in ninety-seven. Lena. Who said that in 2010, you would still be in love with me."

"And that's why you're here?" I asked. My heart was ready to leap from my chest and run down the street. I didn't want an answer to this question. I wanted to remain loyal to Lena. It was safer and easier not to get what you'd been praying for for fourteen long, stupid years.

"She said she was visiting from the future. I thought she was on drugs, and that she was someone you knew, but I thought I'd check. I think about her often. That happening. How strange it was. And how it was probably true, and how I didn't need some girl who claimed to be time traveling to tell me."

"I don't know what to say."

"She was wrong, obviously. You didn't even recognize me after I sat here for a whole hour."

I dried my palms on my jeans. "We're so busy right now. We've got a band coming in to play and I'm giving Clyde more managerial duties."

"You didn't recognize me, Karl. It's because I'm old, right?"

"Why do you say that?"

"You keep looking away from me. You don't want to see my face. You're not the only man to do that. I mean, not Garrett. But other men. I'm forty-three. You think I don't notice? I know I've aged. You become invisible to men at a certain point. Even to men my own age. It fucking sucks."

"I'm looking at you," I said, though maybe I had been paying more attention to the wood grain of my bar than to the woman I'd been thinking about for over a decade.

"Maybe it's because I have a kid. Women who have children are automatically sexless and useless. I know how it is."

"You know, Meredith. We haven't seen each other in forever. I'm happy to see you, and you want to pick a fight?"

"I love being a mom."

"Great. I'm happy for you. Want to go out and throw a few punches? For old times' sake?"

Meredith slid off her stool. She made a pair of fists, pressed them to my chest, and winked at me. "Suit yourself."

I followed her out to the yellow light of the street, where I noticed the definition in Meredith's biceps. She clearly lifted weights. She could probably take me, and I preferred it that way. Cars whizzed past, and the nauseating blue-green glow of my Dictator's Club neon sign made me dizzy.

Meredith watched the Blue Line train rumble by overhead. "I kind of like Chicago. It's chaotic," she said. "But in a good way."

I didn't want to talk about Chicago. I wanted her to hit me. "Okay, McCabe. Throw your punch. Do your worst."

"Is that Persian restaurant on the corner any good?" she asked.

"Yeah, they do a good shash—" She slammed me on the side of the head, morc of a slap than a punch. It felt like my head had been filled with tiny metal balls. "—lik."

"Want to get Persian food after I beat the crap out of you? Your treat. I hear the shashlik is decent."

She put down her dukes. Hands on hips. Still stowable in a commuter train overhead luggage bin. Still capable of doing. She was still a goddess. She could still undo me.

"Where's Lena? Does she know I'm going to break her boyfriend's jaw?"

"She's at Northwestern, grading papers. She's a physicist."

Meredith cackled. "What are you doing with a physicist, Bender?"

"What? You think a really smart girl can't—"

The punch came, and my nose felt purple. My nasal cartilage popped like popcorn. I exhaled quickly through my mouth, spraying blood onto the sidewalk. I wiped my face with the back of my hand.

"Ow!" Cold threads of pain radiated across my cheeks, toward my ears.

"Want another?"

"You think I only date stupid girls? You think I'm some kind of loser?"

"Physicist? That's too much."

I looked behind Meredith and saw Lena, in her purple Doc Martens boots, walking up the street from the el station.

"Meredith, stop, please. Don't punch me again. Incoming. . . ."

Meredith smirked and slapped me across the face, hard. "You don't get to tell me—"

The sight of violence against me registered across Lena's face. Lena ran toward us yelling, "What the fuck!"

Before I could catch her around the waist, she'd body-slammed Meredith into the sidewalk. Lena wound up her left fist and was preparing to sink it into Meredith's face, but I grabbed her and wrestled her away. We both fell backward onto the sidewalk, Lena's elbow landing right in my crotch. I yowled right into her ear.

"What the fuck was that?" Lena yelled. "Call the cops!"

Meredith moaned.

"Shit," I said, grabbing Lena by the hand and pulling her up to her feet. "Wow. Did you just—"

Lena pulled me back into the bar and flipped the lock on the door. She screamed over the bar's sound system, "What the hell? You were getting beat up by a woman on the street?"

A sharp pain shot down my thigh. I was prepared to lose a testicle over all of this. "That was Meredith. She's in town and she came to see me."

Lena didn't say anything. She stood before me, looking afraid and guilty. I grabbed her and held her to me, but she wriggled out of my embrace and said, "Don't." She raised her hands up in that leave-me-alone fashion and walked a few steps away from me. "I'm not jealous. I just don't want to get arrested for assault. I've got enough shit in my life right now," she said, and then she flipped the lock back open and ran out the door, back toward the train.

I staggered out into the diminishing Chicago sun just as Meredith, clutching her head with one hand and her messenger bag with the other, was getting into a taxi. "Karl?" she called.

I said nothing. I didn't even stop walking.

"Karl?" she yelled.

Fourteen years of pining for this woman. Fourteen wasted years.

I stopped and locked eyes with the woman I'd once loved. "Sorry," I said, and ran after Lena.

9

COMPARED TO THE wormhole, the el train was poky and old-fashioned, shaking and shuddering its way toward the Loop. I did not miss public transportation. I did not miss screaming babies, screaming adults, loud body odor, or the one-sided cell phone wailings of the angry and sexually dissatisfied.

I followed Lena to her building, one of those old-style Chicago apartment buildings made of yellow brick and real artisan stonemasonry. Lena shared a place just a few steps away from the South Boulevard train stop with another Northwestern graduate student, who she'd described as a ghost. ("She goes to law school and sleeps in her library carrel. She works at a firm downtown and probably sleeps on the floor of her office there, too.")

Lena reached into her bag to pull out her keys. "I guess you're coming in?"

"Can I?" I asked.

She jiggled the lock and gave the door a kick with her boot. "I guess."

Lena's small apartment was strewn with papers and books. They were stacked on the floor, piled on the windowsill, and set on a short wooden bookshelf, along with a menorah full of melted candles and a hot pink picture frame containing a school-type photo of a bucktoothed little girl.

"Is that your sister?" I asked, pointing to the photo.

Lena paused before saying, "That's Rachel Geduldig."

The apartment smelled like Nag Champa, cat, and girl. I sneezed.

"You're allergic?" she asked, pointing to the indignant black feline that jumped at her ankles. "Oh shit, I'm sorry. I didn't know. Look, there's just the one. My old lady kitty, Zelda Abramowitz, went to live in Jewish cat heaven last April, so only Zed remains." Zed rubbed his small kitty face on Lena's calf. She picked him up and hugged him to her chest and rubbed his ears. Zed, I sensed, wanted to run me off the property.

"I can put him in my room and vacuum."

"I think I'm okay, thanks. Why did you dye your hair back to brown?" I asked, noticing that her bright-colored streaks were gone.

"I'm a natural woman."

Lena opened an overstuffed hall closet and pulled out her vacuum cleaner. "I baked cookies this morning. Oatmeal chocolate chip. Raisins are for losers, but oatmeal is healthy, and I care about you. I had a few in my bag that I was going to surprise you with, but you're here now, so here's the whole batch."

"I love you," I blurted out, like I was drunk, which I kind of was, on sleep deprivation and fear. Unsure of what to do with my hands, or my body, I knocked into Lena's body like a toddler and pressed my lips to hers. I presented her with a love so irresponsible and weak I shuddered, because Lena deserved much better.

"Whoa there. Power down, please. I mean, love . . . That's a big deal, Karl. Even supposing I love you back, well, you're weirding me out right now. Did you have sex with Meredith? Was her punching you sexual?" She pulled her face away and insisted I unhook my leg from her backside. "Unhand me. You're squishing my boobs."

"No, I didn't sleep with Meredith. But yeah, getting hit by her is, um . . . thrilling in that department."

Lena arched her eyebrow. "You're acting guilty. Stupid guilty."

"I'm sorry. I just. I'm exhausted. Can I lie down on the couch or something?"

"You'll have to fight Zed for the couch. Zed will probably win."

Zed issued an aggro meow in my direction and hissed at me as I nudged him from the couch with my elbow. I lay on Lena's flowered IKEA couch. He stared me down with his shiny gold coin eyes. I stared him down, back. "I'm on your side, cat."

Lena shooed Zed away, and he made a jumpy retreat into her bedroom. She knelt down on the floor and put her head to my chest. "You finally saw your Meredith and felt her furious fists on your face. And you have a girls-hitting-you fetish. Why didn't you tell me?"

"It's not something I lead with."

"Well, you're here, and you abandoned Meredith on the street in favor of chasing my fat ass all the way to Evanston."

I pulled Lena to my chest and sniffed her shampoo-scented head. I shivered at the joy of pressing her ear against my sternum. I kissed the top of her head. She stayed perfectly still for a long moment, and then she stood, took a step backwards, and issued a hearty slap across my face.

"Thank you."

"You're welcome. Tell me about Ghost Woman."

"Oh, you know. The sobering result of seeing the woman you've pined after for a stupid long number of years is that when you see her it feels like . . . like nothing."

"Feels like a punch in the face, is more like it."

"That too."

With some caution in her voice, Lena asked, "Did you tell her about the wormhole?"

"No. I thought about it, but traveling with Meredith . . . I consider that cheating. Sort of an emotional betrayal. I don't want to see the past with her. How I remember it isn't really how it went down. I couldn't go there."

Lena fiddled with my zipper tab a bit and then stopped. "I'm glad we practice monogamy where time travel is concerned. It's the only safe way, really." She disappeared to her kitchen.

"Time travel isn't safe," I shouted after her. "There aren't, like, emotional condoms that prevent sorrow ninety-eight point five percent of the time."

"I actually kind of like this about you, Bender," she shouted from across the apartment. "That you and I don't use emotional condoms. We just let the messy goo of who we are fly free, threatening to impregnate us with insecurity or infect us with the pain of true intimacy. Hey, I'm sorry I attacked her, but she was hurting you, or at least that's what it looked like. I didn't know that was her. I'm generally cool with people's exes, although if you ever run into Linnea Long, you have my permission to be mean to her."

"I know you didn't know."

"You've been carrying a big thing for her for years. Hopefully, her coming to see you helped you get past a little bit of that. Sometimes you've got to break a heart so it will heal." She returned with a tower of cookies stacked on a black plastic plate.

"Since when are you a poet?"

"Since never. I'm a robot."

I winced at that statement, but kept going. "It actually hurts not to feel that way about her anymore. It's like she was just ripped out of my brain. She's all gone now. Is this okay, that we're talking about this?"

"I don't expect you to be perfect, Karl. Yes, we can talk about anything. Eat a cookie while you're doing it."

Lena was a good baker—her cookie was soft and buttery and the chocolate chips were still kind of warm and melty. "Are you sure? I feel like a dick talking about my ex to you."

"It's fine. Getting stuff out in the open is good, I think."

"Do you have anyone in your past like this?"

"I have no past."

"Lena. You have a past."

Lena dropped the cookie plate onto her coffee table, causing the tower to collapse. "Eviscerate your memory. The past sucks. The past is watching my mother die, having my stepmother manipulate my dad into not being a dad to me, getting raped at a Mazzy Star show, dating a controlling psycho for two years, getting rejected from the top astrophysics programs only to come here and have my research stolen by Justin Fucking Cobb, that sack of crap. . . ."

"Lena?" I looked up into her big, fuming eyes, welling with tears she was too tough to cry. "If it bothers you to talk about Meredith, I'll stop."

"No, it's not about Meredith." Tears ran down her red cheeks. "Fuck the past. Fuck bands. Why the hell would I want to be a tourist of my own past? My life has sucked, Karl. It only got better when I stopped feeling things. When I decided to take pills and be a robot and focus on my work and just say fuck it to everything."

"Lena." I tried to put my arm around her, but she shoved me away.

"I don't have some great big romantic love in my past. Smart girls with big noses and belly rolls get overlooked in the game of love. I've never had a boyfriend, okay? I had a girlfriend, but that relationship ended when Linnea suddenly decided that she loved God, and pussy was evil. Maybe I should have taken a cue from my stepmom and married a recently widowed third cousin."

"I didn't mean to upset you."

"Well, thanks for the apology. I appreciate it. I don't know. Obviously I like you. I have a monster crush on you. We made out to 'Words,' and that's, like, practically agreeing to marry me. I don't make cookies for just anyone. I haven't made cookies for anyone since Linnea, back in Missoula."

Lena may have thought she was a robot, but she was acting like a girl.

"You were raped?" I asked.

She nodded and looked away. "I don't want to talk about it. But that's why I react to certain things sometimes. I have a lot of triggers. That's probably why I knocked down your ex-girlfriend."

I filed this information away, knowing that we should talk a lot more about it at some point, should Lena want to. I wanted to kill the fucker who did this to her, with my bare hands.

I took her hand and ran my finger over her cat scratches and black nail polish. "She asked about you. Meredith. She remembered you. From her porch in 1997."

"Well, who wouldn't want some android telling you your ex-boyfriend still loves you in the future? I would love that."

"I didn't like seeing her," I admitted. "It's sort of like driving by your old house. It's not yours anymore and you just feel crummy when you see what the new people did to the front yard."

"Well, you did see her." Lena crammed a cookie into her mouth. "Eat another one. I put two packages of chocolate chips in the batter, because I care."

I did as I was told and took a cookie, which had a greater chip-to-cookie ratio than the previous one. Lena stared at the far wall of her living room, the one that had a poster of a Picasso dove, which, lacking punk/scientific cred, I assumed belonged to the absent roommate. I gave my girl a kiss and told her I had to go to the bathroom.

Zed hopped into Lena's lap and she squish-petted him in a way that made his head appear to shrink by the force of her hand. "Don't be mad at me, okay?"

On the way to the bathroom, I peeked in her room. Double bed with a twist of black-and-white checkered sheets. Posters of Richard Feynman and Ian MacKaye stuck to the wall with tacks; black T-shirts and white bras turned gray from the wash, wadded up on the floor; bookshelves of books with titles like *Principles of Quantum Mechanics* and *Experimental Techniques in Nuclear and Particle Physics.* No fewer than three Sleater-Kinney CD covers on the floor, jewel boxes smashed like accident windshields by Lena's careless steps.

I didn't think much about the laptop perched on the bathroom sink next to the liquid soap dispenser and Lena's Hello Kitty toothbrush holder. I barely noticed the collection of wires connected to the toilet's tank. I was accustomed to such setups at home, and I was too preoccupied with the fact that I was about to take a dump in Lena's bathroom, and that she only had one weak vanilla-scented candle on hand to mask the smell, and that I wasn't sure if we were in that part of the relationship where we could laugh off bad bathroom odors. The laptop screen was dark. I undid my pants, and no sooner did my ass touch the seat than I discovered what Not-a-Doctor Lena had been cooking up in her spare time. I passed through the floor and backward across time and fought hard against the force of travel to pull up my goddamn pants.

I landed in a hospital waiting room—orange and teal Naugahyde chairs and a muted television showing CNN, a darkish-haired Bill Clinton speaking from the White House podium. The air was dry and smelled of antiseptic and the faintest whiff of cigarette smoke. I looked out the window. Surprise, surprise, I was in Butte, Montana, staring at the big, brown mountain crowned with the slightest touch of green. The waiting room was empty except for a girl, teenage Lena, clad in overall shorts and yellow and black bumblebee kneesocks, flipping through a copy of *Sassy* magazine. She had, beside her on a table stacked with finger-worn magazines, a Super Big Gulp cup with a red straw, from which she took long sips, and a jumbo box of tissues, which I assumed was for crying.

I sat down in a chair across from her. "How's your mom?" I asked.

"Do I know you?" she asked.

"You will. Someday. In the future."

She shot me a look. "I'm fourteen, dude. Gross."

Lena turned her head away and pressed her eyes shut. She covered her face with her magazine, the cover bearing a photograph of young Courtney Love with her fat lips pressed to the cheek of Kurt, who stared at the camera with a youthful mischief, like he'd just gotten away with something.

"He dies in 1994. Kurt," I said, pointing to the magazine.

Lena shook her head. "Everyone talks about Kurt killing himself all the time. Anytime someone's depressed, they're, like, gonna kill themselves. I don't care about Nirvana. This copy of *Sassy* is a year old. My dad just grabbed a stack of stuff for me to read."

"I don't mean to creep you out—"

"Then don't," Lena said, covering her chest with her magazine. "My mother is in there dying. I'm waiting for that bitch nurse to come out and tell me my mom is dead so I can go home and cry about it for the rest of my life."

"Where's your dad?"

She shook her head. "Work."

"I'm sorry," I said. "You're the one who sent me here."

She blinked.

"What's today? The date?" I asked.

Lena shot me a look like I was stupid. "April 22, 1993."

"My own mother died last month. March fifteenth."

"That sucks."

"Thank you. I'm about to become a minor-league rock star."

"You're weird," she said. She stared at me and stared back at her magazine and back at me again.

"What bands are you listening to these days?" I asked.

Lena's face blanched. She took a handful of tissues from an adjacent box and buried her face in them. "My mom is dying," she said. She blew her nose. "Yo La Tengo, I guess."

"Yo La Tengo is nice," I said. "They have a long shelf life."

"I don't want to talk about bands!" Lena emitted a series of short breaths. Sobs she was trying to stifle. This not wanting to talk about bands thing had been a thing for Lena for a while, it seemed.

"I don't mean to mess with you. I'm telling you the truth. Your thirty-one-year-old self is a physicist who made a time travel portal out of a toilet and sent me here."

Lena unburied her face from her tissues and turned her attentions back to *Sassy* magazine, like she hadn't heard me.

"Can I give you a few bits of advice?" I asked, feeling a sickness in my gut about breaking my own rule about not changing the past. "This is important."

She looked up from her magazine. "What?"

"After your mom dies, women are going to come for your father. Terrible women who won't want to be a good mom to you. Be there to protect," I said. "Be as horrible as you need to be."

Lena gulped and sobbed and nodded and shook. She reached for her tissue box, took a big handful, and pressed the white paper cloud to her face.

"The world is big and cruel, but it's yours, Lena. Don't let anyone take anything from you that you're not willing to give."

"Uh, thanks?"

"And another thing?" I said, cautiously. "Always know that you're beautiful. Inside and out."

Lena, her babyish face as red as a rose, tossed her handful of tissues on the magazine table and walked up to me. She leaned over and gave me a hug around the neck, pressing her not-quite-at-their-final-size breasts up in my face. She lowered herself onto my lap and I put a careful, friendly arm around her back, trying to be caring but brotherly.

"I'm so sorry about your mom," I said, and then Lena, age fourteen, began to weep in the style of a girl in an old Dutch painting: all porcelain skin and heavy eyelids and the kind of light that can only be rendered by the natural world or a long-dead portrait painter who worked beside an open window. Her cheeks were smudged with black mascara trails. It hurt me to look at her, this child, already Goth, devastated and scared. This was the beginning of Lena the Wounded.

Lena shut her eyes and pressed her lips to mine. I let her linger for a second—a second too long—before I grabbed her head and pulled it away.

"Sorry, Lena. You have to wait for that," I said.

She shuddered. "I just wanted to try it. My mother is dying." Lena let her hand wander down my chest. I pulled it away.

"I'm not doing this." I pushed her off and took a long, cleansing breath, some yoga breathing thing I remember Meredith going on about long ago, and hoped to return to some sense of equilibrium, or at least control. Lena returned to her seat across from me, glaring at me from behind her magazine.

"I wish you loved me now," she said, yanking a handful of tissues from her box.

"I have to go," I said, stabbing at the buttons on my phone as if my life depended on it.

"You're just going to leave me here alone, waiting for my mom to die?" she asked, as I waited for the pull. "That's rude. You should know what this feels like."

"I'm sorry, but we have to do things in the right order," I said, as I was slurped back to the safety of now.

LENA SAT CALMLY on the couch, nibbling a cookie, Zed on her lap.

"Were you going to tell me about your portal?" I said. "I just met you at age fourteen."

Her shoulders fell. "I'm sorry. I didn't want it to be in the toilet. That's just stupid and embarrassing. I didn't . . . I didn't do it on purpose. That's just where I could make it work. It turns out it's fairly simple to create your own home wormhole if you have seven years of physics grad school under your belt. I quit school."

"You quit school?"

"The department had a hearing. Me versus the guy who stole my research. Guess who won?"

"Lena."

Lena's face grew cold. "Yes, Karl? Is there something you want to say to me?"

"You built a wormhole? And you quit school? You just quit? You let them win?"

Lena leaned back on her couch. "I was going to tell them about it. About the wormholes and the time travel. But as I was about to tell my PI about it—Liz, a woman—she advised me to leave the program, that she couldn't help me, that it was Justin Cobb against me and that he was going to win. And then I was like, Why should I tell them anything? Why would I say or do anything that would make the work of the Northwestern Department of Physics relevant, after they'd taken such a big shit on me? So I told Liz to go fuck herself and left."

"You could fight it."

Lena's bottom lip began to quiver. "You know what? Fuck this 'fight' shit. Why do I have to fight all the time when other girls don't? You take someone like me, who has been treated like garbage by just about everyone, and people think they're being supportive when they say, 'Fight. Be tough.' But what they're really saying is that I have to be the one to change, not the other person, not the way society works. Well, I'm not tough, and I am so goddamn jealous of the girls who get to be weak, who get everything they want by just sitting there, looking pretty and dumb. Fuck you for telling me to fight."

Zed jumped off her lap as she dove at me, arms open. I held her while she cried, big walrus tears, chest heaving against mine. I wanted to talk to her about the portal in her toilet, why it sent me back to her past, not my past, not 980. And how, all of a sudden, we'd met each other before, in 1993, on the worst day of Lena's life.

"I used my portal to pay my rent this month," she said, standing up to brush cookie crumbs off her lap.

"What?"

"Also, my roommate's in 2007 right now, fiddling with the Harvard Law School admissions department's computers. She thinks if she'd gotten into Harvard, her life would be better."

"Uncool, Lena. Extremely uncool."

"I don't need a PhD as long as I have the wormhole. The wormhole will provide enough money to live on, as long as I have it."

"Lena. Where's Sahlil? I called his office today and was informed that he's dead."

Lena looked away.

"Lena, where is he?"

Lena hurled her cookie at me. It nicked my nose and went *splat* onto the wall behind my head. "Where do you think he is? He paid me twenty thousand bucks. Cash. He was a big, fat, sobbing mess of a man who wanted one thing and I was able to give it to him. And now he won't sell the building and you can continue to be the source of DIY time travel in Chicago. Why should he be miserable? Besides, unlike some time travel peddlers, I don't have lofty, discriminatory practices. I'll send whomever, wherever they want to go."

"Lena, damn it."

"I need the money. I've got grad school loans to pay, even though I'm not getting my degree. He promised me he'd be back. He just needed to see Freddie one more time."

"His wife thinks he's dead. His office has been shut down."

"Well, maybe he lied. He told me he just needed a week. We have an appointment for his return on Friday. Do you think he's a flight risk? You know what? If he is, I don't care."

"We have a moral responsibility—

"People shirk their moral responsibilities all the time, Karl! Northwestern's physics department had a moral responsibility, didn't they? People see a weak target and then it's like you're a urinal cake, and they piss on you just because they can. Don't lecture me on moral responsibilities."

"Karuna thinks her husband is dead."

"Karuna's better off with a pile of money than a husband who cheats on her with a dead rock star."

"Maybe, but that's not up to you to decide. I hired you to get Wayne back, and have you? No, you haven't."

Lena looked around for something larger than a cookie to throw at me. "Wayne doesn't want to come back, you idiot! And as far as moral responsibilities go, the world doesn't need another physics professor. The time travel biz will generate far more money than a teaching job ever would, and that's a good thing, so don't be riding my ass about your stupid morals, okay?"

I raised my voice. "Lena, I just met you at age fourteen. That just happened, on your toilet."

"That was you? In the hospital in Butte?"

"Yes."

Her face softened. "That was you. That was amazing. Did you just do that? Right now?"

"That's where I was when I was in the bathroom. With fourteen-year-old you." I held out my hand.

"That was you. That was you, right now." She came to me and placed her ear against my chest. "Strange, since I have absolutely no memory of that ever not happening."

I slumped down next to her on the couch.

Lena, bigger now and age appropriate, sat on my lap and put her arms around my neck. "Karl, you meant the world to me that day. You told me I was beautiful and that was the first and pretty much only time I ever heard anyone say that. How can you say that changing the past is a bad thing? You saved my life."

We held each other on the couch. Body to body. Soul to soul. Lena removed her shirt and bra and pushed me back on the couch, unhooking my belt with an excitement and desire that I hadn't yet seen in her. "Is this okay?" she asked, as she brushed the cookie crumbs off her hand and wrapped her fingers around my cock.

"Yes," I told her, and reached up for her lips for a kiss.

After we finished, our naked, slippery bodies pressed together on the couch, I felt a sense of dread that I don't usually experience after orgasm. I asked, "Lena? What's your stepmother's name?"

"You just put your face in my crotch and now you want to talk about Judy?"

"Her name is Judy?"

"Yes. Judy."

I swallowed hard. "And your sister's?"

"What sister? I've only met Judy's son, Eric, like twice, so I don't really think of him as a brother. Dad and Judy only got married five years ago."

"Wasn't your dad married to someone named Hana?"

"What? No."

"You had a half sister named Rachel. And a stepmother named Hana." I glanced around Lena's apartment. "Where's that photo of Rachel? It was right there," I said, pointing to the bookshelf where I'd just seen it.

"Who's Rachel? I'm an only child. I have a thirty-three-year-old stepbrother who I've met twice, once at the wedding and the other time a few months ago."

"A few months ago? You haven't seen your father in years!"

"I saw him last April. Right after Zelda Abramowitz the Cat died, I went home for Passover. Judy's great. Montana Jew, born and bred. She and my dad are totally awesome together. We should go to Butte to visit sometime. They just got a horse."

"A horse?" I shouted as I reached for my pants. I'd essentially murdered Lena's thirteen-year-old sister. Removed a young person from the universe. How did this work, exactly? Was Hana bitching her way through a day of wife- and motherhood in Butte, only to be wrested from her reality into one where she'd never had a child? Was Rachel Geduldig sitting at her desk at school one minute, only to disappear?

"Are you talking about Hana Lieberwald, my dad's freaky cousin who tried to marry him right after my mom died? Did I tell you about her? Yeah, he saw the light on that one. Guess that would have turned out horribly."

My face went red. "Your dad married Hana. Before I went to the bathroom."

"Really? I listened to you. To what you said in the hospital. I was there to protect. I convinced my dad that Hana was bad news and she got a clue and took a hike."

I walked toward the window and looked down at the courtyard below, trying to understand how I could change so many lives in the space of what was supposed to be a trip to the can. I could disappear any of the people I saw from Lena's apartment, walking and minding their own business. Living the lives they were given through time and circumstance. I could kill, murder, erase, redact, alter, all with the power of time travel.

"I just accidentally killed off a thirteen-year-old girl I never met, when I was supposed to be taking a dump."

Lena pulled back on her shirt. "Karl, I don't have a sister."

"You did. You had her picture right here." I said, pointing to the spot where the frame had been, not ten minutes before. Lena had never said much about her sister, other than that Hana had never let her hold the baby Rachel, always accusing Lena of having dirty hands or being too "angry."

Lena got up and put her arms around me, pressing her cheek into my back. "I don't know why you make such a big deal about the wormhole being just for rock concerts. Changing the past helps people. Wayne could have unmurdered John Lennon if you'd have just sent him to 1980. Where's the bad in that?"

"It's bad, Lena. It is because it is. I just hurt a lot of people. People I don't even know. I want to be good. I want time travel to be a force for good."

"But it is a force for good. It's how we know each other. I wouldn't know you without time travel, and you're the best thing in my life right now."

Zed and I made eye contact as I looked at him from over Lena's shoulder. I'd come to Lena's to find refuge, and instead I became a child murderer. I was a horrible piece of shit to everyone but

Lena. Maybe that's the way it was supposed to be. But I couldn't just chalk this up to being a good boyfriend. I couldn't make what I did good.

Don't lose Lena? She was right here, hugging me, but something was different. She felt lighter in my arms. The grief and stress that I felt from her when I'd arrived at her place had faded. She was giggly. I had never seen her giggle before.

10

WAYNE WAS STILL in his pre-Columbian Utopia and I was still in Chicago, barkeeping. Freed from her obligations to the physics department at Northwestern, Lena spent almost every waking hour trying to get Wayne back, barking at me to bring her chocolate, pad thai, and tampons. (Yes, I walked down to the Jewel and bought 'em. Tampons. No problemo, because I'm a man in love.) She smiled at me warmly when we sat opposite each other, eating pad thai on my couch. Eating tofu pad thai with Lena in my living room, straight from the Styrofoam takeout box, Lena reaching over and stealing my lime wedge without asking, Lena demanding that I spoon my small hill of pad thai crushed peanuts onto her pad thai because she likes them more than I do, smearing a tamarind-orange kiss across my mouth when she is done with her pad thai, me agreeing with her that we should have pad thai takeout again the following night because it's so yummy, and barely talking is the closest I have ever come to family dinner.

Lena was my family, and I drank up the familiarity of her simply existing in close quarters. I loved watching her shoveling noodles into her mouth, plucking fallen bits of bean sprout off the shelf of her breasts. She was living and breathing next to me, and to me, that was magical.

Lena labored. I wondered if I could convince her to destroy the portal she had made in her toilet if she succeeded in bringing Wayne back. Once Wayne was back, I was destroying mine, even though that meant never seeing another rock show in the past, ever again.

Lena didn't want to. She worried that she wouldn't have money to eat ("Pad thai is eight ninety-five plus tip, Karl!"), and I'd remind her that the wormhole had already brought in mad bank, and that I would buy us an Airstream trailer to live in. ("I may love you, Karl, but I've smelled your farts, and I doubt an Airstream trailer has sufficient ventilation to allow our relationship to blossom in such tight quarters.") We could be like an old-timey medicine show and take time travel on the road, she said, with dollar signs in her eyes. Just add our scientific magic to the nearest rest stop toilet, hit Send, and watch the money flow in. "His and hers Airstreams," she said. Then she added, "I want a Mini Cooper."

What roads we would follow if we became time travel snake oil salespersons, we did not know. She'd be Clyde Barrow and I'd be Bonnie Parker. We'd shoot our way across the West. I would serve my Clyde B. with foot rubs and pad thai and holding in my farts, and she would spin mad science like the wizard she is, tossing high-dollar patrons backwards in time, leaving piles of gold doubloons at our feet, which we would then take to our Airstream trailers to toss on the bed and make love upon. Perhaps we'd stow away on a steamer ship bound for the New World. Perhaps we'd build ourselves a New World. I'd leave the bar in the care of the real, Bonnieless Clyde, and when Lena and I fell upon hard times, failing to find work as carnies or circus freaks, we could crawl back to the Dictator's Club on our bellies and resume simple lives of keg tapping and toilet scrubbing. I'd let her do the books. She was the smart one, after all.

I thought Lena should reapply to grad school, but she said it didn't work that way. In her small, incestuous academic science universe, her name was mud. Astrophysics was through with her and she was through with astrophysics. Lena said her new career goal was to be the mermaid girl in a carnival somewhere, but really she was going to make bank selling time travel trips and fuck me if I tried to stop her. She'd disappear me to a never-ending Barry Manilow concert in 1982. One where he sang Christmas songs.

I knew the future, because I'd seen it. In my older years, I'd be busted and rickety, like old furniture, with some ill-defined avocation or perhaps a government allowance that permitted me to purchase ointment for my hemorrhoids. I suspected that Lena supported me, down the road, that she returned to school, got her PhD, and that her career as a physics professor paid our rent and our undoubtedly high water-pumping bill. And in spite of not knowing what bumps lay ahead in the road of our relationship, I believed that she and I were happy and in love. This woman who, in the future, would be an endowed chair of the physics department at the University of Washington, even though university operations are suspended in the post-A world, would be in love with me. I knew that because I had peeked inside our tiny, watertight home and had seen the covers of the books she would write, and the shiny gold awards that she would win. For reasons I could hardly fathom, she would choose to stay with me, even as I would inevitably disappoint her.

On days when I should have tended my bar, or just cuddled with Lena, enjoying the effervescent parts of her new personality, thanks to the removal of the evil stepmom, I set the portal in reverse and hurled forward, to the strange air and odd water dwelling of my future. I peered in the windows, just so I knew that everything was okay. I felt dirty. I tried to hide it, to pretend it wasn't necessary. But my name is Karl John Bender and I am an addict. Addicted to the calm of knowing what my future holds. I found peace in seeing my dotage. My ugly mug. The strange texture of my future waterproof carpet. I was comforted by Glory, the teenager who insisted that, in 2010, Lena was married to someone else.

I learned some other things, too. Friends, you will have to wait twenty years for this sandwich: algae paste (a green umami filling spread on puffy bread), topped with pickled sprouts and radishes. It sounds odd, with echoes of hippie notions of health and nutrition, but it's delicious, salty and strange. I tried it when I traveled forward to 2031 to see Lena. I had to talk to her, to fifty-two-year-old her, and I was hungry, so I popped into the Post-A Cascade Zone 1 Sandwich Store, a red plastic Quonset hut of a building that sold one sandwich and one sandwich only. I committed a future faux pas. When I was asked to wave my wrist over a white box on the counter to tender my payment of $26.75 for the sandwich, I had to explain to the dark-haired girl behind the counter that I didn't have a wrist box thingy. I told her I had cash and she said that nobody had cash. I put a twenty and a ten on the counter. She said she couldn't make change and I said that was fine.

"Excuse me," a woman shouted. "Karl?"

I spun around. Lena at age fifty-two, wearing a short-sleeve flowered dress and rubber galoshes, stood behind me, arms akimbo, racing stripes of crimson anger across her puffy face. Her hair was the basic brown of wooden furniture, with a few strands of gray in the front. It made her staid and bankerish.

"Hello, " I said, moving toward the metal chute where my sandwich was scheduled to slide out (wrapped in edible rice paper so sweet it's called dessert wrapper). I did not take her into my arms. She looked basically the same in her fifties as she did in her thirties. Maybe a few extra lines around the eyes, but she had on thick black glasses (will those ever go out of style?), so you could only see her crow's-feet if you looked hard. She carried herself like a woman with a measure of success. That she had stuck by me all this time made my heart do somersaults.

She seemed standoffish, not moving toward me, clutching the grab bar on the counter of the sandwich store so she wouldn't fall down (post-A buildings had a tendency to sway). "Karl, you've been time-stalking me since I was fourteen. I marry you. You have nothing to worry about. You have to wait. Just like you told me in the waiting room at the hospital in ninety-three."

"I'm not stalking," I lied.

"Go back." Lena gave out two loud, over-the-top sobs. She pushed me away and barked, "If you love me, you'll get the hell out of here. Leave us alone. Go live your life. Go be patient." Lena raised her voice and said, "I know Karl—you, right now—sends you messages. Please leave us alone. Leave Glory alone."

But I'm here because I love you.

"I just want to know," I said.

"You don't get to know, okay?"

She turned to leave. I caught her by the wrist. "Lena, please. Just one thing. It doesn't have anything to do with you or me. Does

Wayne come back? From 980? You know, my friend Wayne DeMint? Remember?"

She shook her head from side to side. "Wayne got exactly what he wanted. Now get the hell out of here. We're not ready for you yet."

I looked down at Lena's bare arms and neck.

She didn't have any tattoos.

11

THE ENTIRE PAINFUL saga of Hana the Stepmonster may have been wiped from Lena's history, but she still maintained her maudlin, hard-edged attitude. Still, she had done her job: she had figured out a way to get us back to 980 and then back to 2010. Or so she said, in the strange language of physics. I only understood every fifth word, but apparently we were bringing along an electrical generator.

Lena's tattoos were right where I'd left them. Tattoo removal might be really effective in the future, but that didn't seem to explain why age-fifty-two Lena's arms were inkless. Lena dug her tattoos, talked endlessly about how much she loved her tattoo artist and what each of her tats meant to her. I told her I ran out of open tattoo real estate a long time ago, and she said she saw some free space on the backs of my thighs, and anyway, it was time to get a cover-up on the skull with the banner that said "Merry Death" on my chest.

"In terms of suicide, escaping to an undamaged hunter-gatherer society isn't the worst way to do it. You can't choose heaven; heaven chooses you. But this would be sidestepping logic and theology and just going directly, should your idea of heaven be spearfishing with Wayne DeMint all day," Lena said. She wore her puffy blue winter coat and a gray woolen hat topped with kitty ears. She stuffed her coat's pockets with Skittles, Cadbury Creme Eggs, bottles of Wayne's favorite expensive root beer, and a small, stuffed, anthropomorphized corncob that Wayne had bought for me at a gas station on his way back from a comic book convention in Des Moines. These items, we'd decided, would be the bait that would lure our Wayne home to the present.

"Why are we talking about suicide?"

"I have nothing to live for."

"What about me? I thought I was your boyfriend," I said.

"I'm really bad at relationships. I appreciate the interest, though."

"I appreciate the interest? What's that all about?"

"I think we're just fucking."

"We're doing more than just fucking. For that matter, we don't fuck all that much."

"I'm on antidepressants," she said to the wall. "Sex doesn't feel like anything to me. Not anything special, anyway." Lena turned back to me. Her cheeks were scarlet. "If we stay in 980, no more Effexor. I'll be effex-ive all on my own."

"Do you want to talk about that?" I asked. Lena seemed fairly into having sex with me the first time, post meeting her in the hospital waiting room at fourteen. She was wet and eager to please and told me what she liked. The second time we had sex, six minutes in, she pulled my hand away from her clit, explaining that the chances of her orgasming were nil. Then she turned her back to me, curling over like a pill bug. The third time, she offered me a hand job and said she was on her period. There had been no fourth time.

"I'm not into sex, okay?" she yelled. "If you want to sleep with other women, feel free."

"Lena, what the hell?"

She was doing this thing where she wouldn't look me in the eye. She kept turning her back to do something or other. "I don't want you to think that this is a romantic trip. In fact, this is a stupid trip. A dangerous trip. Wayne doesn't want to come back. Maybe I won't, either. Maybe *you* won't."

"Maybe," I said. I took her hand and led her to the bathroom. She pressed her lips to mine and sat on the toilet. Then she fell. Slipped right of my arms, made invisible by the pull. I followed her down, my pockets full of protein bars, two solar phone chargers, and my toothbrush, taking her at her word that we would be able to come back to 2010, and that we'd want to.

980 Mannahatta
a report
by L. R. Geduldig, not a PhD

On the day Karl Bender and I traveled, it had been approximately eighteen days since Wayne Alan DeMint of Chicago, Illinois, was mistakenly transported to the year 980 via wormhole. The cause of this mishap was human error. Committing that human error was the very human, very sexy Karl Bender (formerly of the Axis—#1 Feminist Indie Rock Band w/mostly male lineup!), who contacted me via the Northwestern Physics Department Web site and requested my expertise to help him to return Mr. DeMint to the present because he liked my T-shirt.

The wormhole tethering-and-release system designed by

Mr. DeMint (formerly of the computer science department at MIT) included a programming flaw by which the reversal of the string pull originated in an electrical charge. The source of the electrical charge came from holding one's cell phone in one's hand, but was aided by atmospheric electrons discharged by common electrical items such as lightbulbs, radios, or air-conditioning systems. Pre-Columbian North America, lacking incidental electrons, make a return trip difficult.

After this mishap, Mr. DeMint assimilated himself with a native tribe living on the Island of Manhattan and, finding comfort in their way of life, chose to remain. Able to use his cell phone, he sent several messages to Mr. Bender describing this people's way of life.

OBJECTIVE: In an attempt to persuade Mr. DeMint to return to the year 2010, Karl Bender and I traveled to 980 Mannahatta Island. I was excited to travel to the year 980 due to the unobstructed visual access to celestial bodies. Astronomic curiosity. Mr. Bender wanted his friend back. At the time of this writing, I'm lukewarm on Mr. DeMint as a person, but I am lukewarm on most people, so Mr. DeMint, should he ever read this document, should not take it personally.

Aside from astronomic interests, I was also interested as to why Mr. DeMint would want to leave modernity to live with an ancient tribe. What would he find nourishing about living amongst people with whom he could not communicate verbally using modern American English, people with whom he lacked biological or social ties?

GEDULDIG HYPOTHESIS #1: Green. In 980, the green of the trees is so intense that you have to stop and refocus your eyes. I grew up in kind of a brown place—Butte,

Montana—so maybe I have more of a reaction to green than others. Upon my arrival on the shores of ancient Mannahatta, I was immediately seduced by the green. It was no longer winter, definitely spring, with red and yellow flowers growing on the floor of the forest. Long, gossamer strands of light poured down from the sun through the trees. Knowing that the tribe relied on fish for a portion of its diet, I suggested to Mr. Bender that we circumnavigate the perimeter of the island. Mr. Bender, agreed and, being the beta of this expedition, followed two paces behind at all times.

It took us about an hour to find Mr. DeMint and his adopted indigenous family. I believe that the encampment is in the modern day West Side Highway/West 75th Street area. I found Mr. DeMint sitting cross-legged in a circle with other men in the tribe. In the center of the circle was a pile of tendons harvested from the carcass of a hoofed animal.

Mr. DeMint saw us moderny-moderns (Mr. Bender was looking extra butch in his leather jacket with a vintage AXIS BUTTON ON THE COLLAR!*—two cultural signifiers that would be lost on a tenth century Lenape tribesperson), and immediately jumped up to hug me. He ran toward me shouting my name, even though we'd never met. Mr. DeMint delivered long, meaty-smelling hugs and explained that he and the men were making stringed musical instruments. They also make arrows, pants, baby slings, baskets, and bone tools, but we happened to come on stringed instrument day.*

Mr. DeMint turned down my offer of Skittles and Cadbury Creme Eggs, so I stuffed them into his dirty, rough-looking hands. He handed these gifts back to me. "This stuff is so ugly. So gross. The packaging. And all that sugar and artificial flavoring. I only eat fish and nuts now and I feel great."

Mr. Bender didn't hold back. Like a true man of the early twenty-first century, he yelled "Fuck you!" before crying into a giant fern frond he had plucked from a knee-high bush.

"We don't say that here," said Mr. DeMint. My first impression of him was this: unsatisfied, entitled, horny, over-mothered, unable to dress himself. . . Okay, maybe I'm projecting here. At least Mr. DeMint was not clad in the classic Men Who Annoy Lena Uniform of pleated khakis and a tucked-in oxford shirt. He wore some cross between a leather kilt and big, floppy board shorts, and a fur vest.

While ~~my boyfriend~~ Mr. Bender started telling off Mr. DeMint, I went for a walk. Hearing "SELFISH ASS FUCK BITCH SELFISH MISSING PERSONS REPORT YOUR MOTHER IS WORRIED" against the gentle call of a long-extinct bird did not make for the optimum 980 experience. But that aside, Mannahatta was the most beautiful place I'd ever seen. Winter was over and everything was luscious. Tall trees, a mossy carpet on the ground, bushes hanging low with plump, purple berries, frolicking deer seemingly content to offer themselves to you as dinner. The silvery shimmer of unpolluted waters. Fish actually leaping out of the water, making lissome pirouettes above what was not yet called the Hudson River. I helped myself to a handful of blackberries from an adjacent bush. Sweetness! I cupped my hands and drank from the river. Cold, clear, a little fishy. Then I heard a booming voice:

"ASSCHICKENS!"

I returned to the scene of bad language, well hydrated. A storm between two men was raging, and honestly, I'm not very good at refereeing fights between men. This one had fits and starts of Mr. Bender threatening to pummel Mr. DeMint's head but ended up being mostly yelling followed by laughing about something stupid. The two men were standing practically nose to nose, shouting in each other's faces. They stepped away from each other when I reappeared and I told them it was cool with me if they wanted to make out.

"We're fighting," Mr. DeMint said.

I asked why someone said "asschickens."

"That was me," Mr. DeMint said. "I was making fun of Karl."

Mr. Bender laughed. "Inside joke, and you're on the outside."

I was happy they were being playful, if they were in fact being playful. I do not understand men.

Then, Mr. DeMint proudly told us he could play "Love Will Tear Us Apart" on his stringed instrument. It was a little ukulele made out of wood. The strings, he said, were made from rabbits. Dead rabbits. Nonvegan strings. "I bet you think that's disgusting, but it's not."

We sang "Love Will Tear Us Apart" in full voice, in our native language, which was English tinged with sorrow and longing.

I recognized my weakness in this mission: Unlike my stepmother, Judy, I am not a warm, engaging person. So asking Mr. DeMint to please rejoin his friends and family in the future had the effect I assumed it would have: very little. Mr. Bender, stressed out about Mr. DeMint not wanting to come home, went straight for the Young Man I Want You Do To What I Want style of persuasion. Did he not know that the Chicago P.D. have his name on the missing persons report? Did he not understand that he was The Heart and

Soul of the Dictator's Club. He did not know. He did not care.

Mr. DeMint had finally found it. Utopia on his terms. Don't we all want Utopia on our own terms? The only Utopia on my terms that I've ever had were the birthday parties my mom threw for me when I was a kid. It was Lena's day and Lena got to do whatever she wanted, and all of her friends were there. Perhaps 980 for Mr. DeMint is an endless birthday party where he doesn't have to do unpleasant things like compromise, show up for work, have his heart broken in myriad ways. All the little shit snacks that regular life feeds our brains had stopped for Wayne. All input was positive. By the looks of it, there was no depression in 980.

I have observed those who are in love, and their eyes are so clear. There are changes to the brain's chemistry when one is in the presence of their loved one. I have started to see Mr. Bender aim those special eyes on me (I can feel a certain warm smile creeping onto my face when we are together), and I can say with great certainty that Mr. DeMint is in love with his life in 980. He is in love with his tribe. They, to him, are better than us in 2010. Like a returned Peace Corps volunteer, he only finds fault with the world we live in. We're judgmental. We're reliant on a dehumanizing economy. We're selfish and have no idea how to live and share in a collective, even as we pay lip service to the word. We don't know what love is. He said that. That he had felt more love in his three weeks with the ancient native people than he did with his family in Wisconsin, or at The Dictator's Club.

"What does this love feel like?" I asked Mr. DeMint.

"It has a smell," he said. "Have you ever made marshmallows from scratch?"

I told him I had not. Mr. Bender said his sister had, and then asked Mr. DeMint if he would like to marry his sister. (Answer: no.)

"You know how you, like, are dating someone, and eventually the sum of their faults causes you to start looking for someone else? Someone with fewer faults?"

I told him I did.

"It's like there are no faults here. No way to be wrong. No disappointments. No possessiveness or jealousy. No hairsplitting. No analysis. No expectations other than to be kind and true." As he said this, a long-legged gray bird walked up to him, unafraid.

"I fish with this guy," he told me, pointing at the bird. "He's my fishing buddy. Also Kelho and Teranhatmo, the two guys over there with the big pitchfork things. That's what we use to fish. Pitchforks." Two short, bald men with very thick eyebrows in fur/leather skirts were walking about with pitchforks along the shore of the river.

Okay, I asked. Those are all negatives. What are the positives?

"Everything is shared. These folks don't know any enemy except weather and wild animals. Food is abundant. Women are slightly more revered than men, as they have the power to give birth. Everyone sleeps in a big puppy pile in a hut heated with burning embers. I think about how many nights I slept alone, or beside someone I was sure didn't want to be sleeping beside me, and I think, wow. What a sad life I've had."

"You've had a fine life," I said.

He disagreed vehemently, shaking his head back and forth. The bird, his fishing buddy, copied his motions. "I only want love without judgment. Love where you live is conditional. There is no such thing as unconditional love."

I looked over at Mr. Bender, who was on the verge of losing it again, his lip quivering like mad. Which, I guess, was a form of judging. Or at least privileging what he wanted over what Mr. DeMint did, which was a big no-no in 980.

"Hey Wayne, do you have any idea how much you mean to Karl?" I asked. "I mean, your friendship? Look at Karl! It's like he's at your funeral."

Mr. DeMint looked over at Mr. Bender's shaking body.

I was impressed that Mr. DeMint was crying, too.

"He is at my funeral," Mr. DeMint said. He then walked over and threw his arms around Mr. Bender and Mr. Bender pushed him off.

"You're such a hypocrite," I said. "Railing on about unconditional love but treating your own best friend like an inconvenience. Don't you love Karl? Karl is crying! Do you understand how upset this man has to be for him to openly cry?"

"Men cry here all the time. I can't cry in Chicago."

"Men cry in my bar all the time," Mr. Bender said.

I held Mr. Bender and let him cry on my chest. I hope my love felt pure and unconditional, and, above all, real. I have to work really hard, I'm afraid, to be outwardly loving. But I am trying. I hope Mr. Bender can tell.

Until meeting Mr. DeMint in 980, it had never occurred to me to hold my friends 100% responsible for my happiness and well-being, and then crap on them when they didn't deliver. Maybe this is why I have historically had so few friends: I held them to such low standards. (This is the part where I'm trying to be funny. Mr. Bender and I should just accept that we're funny-looking and inconsequential, that neither of us are worth giving up life with a sky with two moons and unlimited sushi-grade fish.)

"You guys should stay," Mr. DeMint said, fidgeting around with some sort of knifelike tool. "What do you have to go back to? Neither of you are super tight with your families. You're not in grad school anymore. Stay and skin some rabbits with us."

"No," I said.

I watched Mr. Bender clench his fists. "Lena's got science, and I've got Lena," he said

"Pffft," said Mr. DeMint.

All of a sudden it was TIME TO GO, like a bad party where a fight was about to erupt. But I also kind of wanted to stay. I was not done drinking in the extreme green and clean, and the night sky was absolutely ripe for some serious astronomical inquiry. The stars were like a thousand diamonds, a beautiful perfect view of our cosmos. I couldn't sleep because the sky was so alive with brightness. All the time I've spent squinting into a microscope to see this and there it was, right in front of my face. The night sky swirled purple with an elegant lattice of stars and planets. Venus. Jupiter. Right there. Illuminated. Close. Breathtaking. I couldn't sleep because all my life's work was dancing in front of my face, reminding me why I chose celestial bodies as my field of study. I regretted not bringing along pen and paper. So strange—my first impulse was to get up and find a CVS to buy pen and paper. In 980. I got some pictures, though.

There is an asteroid hit on Earth projected for the year 2029. It's been something of an obsession of mine for years. I think I saw my asteroid. A small, flaming rock in the sky, alarmingly close to Earth that I could see it with my eyes but not close enough that it altered the earth's surface temperatures. It looked like a second moon, just hanging there next to the real moon, calm but furious. I'm curious to know why its trajectory was stalled a thousand years ago. I took a lot of pictures of it. The sky was so clear. It was churning with light like those glow-in-the-dark star stickers we used to glue to our bedroom ceilings.

Mr. Bender had that wounded look. Like he wasn't saying what was on his mind.

Mr. DeMint and I hugged, and I didn't mind his old meat smell. He sort of blessed me, I guess, like a holy man. I don't believe in heaven or hell, but this might have been the closest I got to knowing a god. Mr. DeMint told me people think being rich is the answer but he just gestured to the egrets with fish in their beaks that had gathered around us as if to hear poetry and said that this was the answer. Pointy birds and fish. He decided to take me up on the offer of American snacks after all and gobbled his Skittles and handed me the wrapper to throw away in 2010 (no landfills, he said, and chided me for attempting to pollute his lands). He told me about his favorite video games and TV shows, and how sometimes he wants a Taco Bell bean burrito, even though they're nasty.

I've known a lot of angry men in my life. Mr. DeMint wasn't angry. Mr. Bender was angry. And I chose Mr. Bender and his anger over Mr. DeMint and his fish. I'm not sure why I failed to be seduced by Utopia the way Mr. DeMint was. Maybe I know where I stand in 2010.

Maybe I'm not ready to retire. Maybe it was the thought of never hearing Joy Division except on a homemade ukulele ever again.

"Take this back with you," Mr. DeMint said, pressing his iPhone into my palm. He pulled the solar phone charger out of the pocket of his leather pants. "Mourn me as if I am dead."

Mr. Bender presented his clenched fists to Mr. DeMint.

Mr. DeMint shrugged off his friend and asked, "Got any paper? A pen?"

I told him there needed to be a CVS in his tribal village. I managed to find a napkin, though, in one of my coat pockets, and he took a burned twig and used it as a pencil.

"Dear Cops, I have suicided," he scrawled. "Wayne Alan DeMint says no to life. Dead! Love, W. DeMint. June 4, 2010."

In the event that someone from the Chicago P.D. ends up reading this, I have in my possession a few photographs taken in 980, to prove that Mr. DeMint in fact suicided by time travel. My heart aches for his mother.

He stuffed the paper into my coat pocket. Mr. DeMint and I were finished. Or rather, he was finished with me. And with Mr. Bender, who I knew would need some serious post-travel care and hugs when we got home.

I watched Mr. Bender scream at Mr. DeMint that he regretted the wormhole, that it did more harm than good, and, that, in the wrong hands, it ended up being a tool for selfish actions rather than collective good.

But then there's the matter of Mr. Bender and Ms. Geduldig. Without the wormhole, the collective good of Karl and Lena, Time Traveling Super Couple, wouldn't exist. I hate to think Mr. Bender would want to destroy the thing that brought us together.

Mr. DeMint ran back to his tribe, who were cooking and scraping and playing weird music in a clearing in the woods. Skipping, like a little boy, bathed in sunbeams. I, like a mother, holding a handful of his candy wrappers, feeling burned.

12

I RECEIVED LENA'S report a week after we'd been back. This, after a one-week no-contact order from her. She claimed that she "needed some space" and that her trip to 980 had "scrambled her brains." I told her I could respect that, even though I was worried that such an order meant something more grim. Lena was my BFF, privates-touching or no, and not being able to smell her hair or trace my finger along the red and black loops of her shoulder tattoo brought me no shortage of sadness. But ever since we'd returned to our modern era—smack at the front door of the Dictator's Club—I couldn't seem to talk to her, either. Saying good-bye to Wayne had turned my mouth into a dead, cottony hole. And I couldn't breathe. My lungs still full of all that clean Mannahatta air, my skin still hot from the burn of rejection. Recalibrating to 2010 after traveling from so far back was hard. But I also wanted to talk about 980 with the one person in the world who understood the stars. Or why the hell I got to have this wormhole in the first place.

I was sorry to have to live the rest of forever without Wayne DeMint. I had taken the suicide note that he'd given us to the police, who quickly wrapped up the case. (I expected more investigation from Chicago's Finest, but apparently a scrawled-on napkin was evidence enough for them that there was no foul play.) I closed the Dictator's Club for a week in mourning, pasting to the front door a sign explaining why we were closed, with a copy of a photograph of Wayne's sweet little boy face and "Wayne A. DeMint, October 23, 1973–June 4, 2010" written across the bottom.

I needed to pull my shit together and go to work. I needed to stop time traveling . . . but I also needed one last trip. I programmed the wormhole to send me to 1976 West Hartford, to my home and my long-gone mommy.

I peeked in the windows of my childhood house and watched my mother smoke her extra-long cigarettes and watch *The Young and the Restless* on the heavy, wooden on-the-floor television with chunky silver knobs. I wanted to hug her, touch her long, well-sprayed mass of blondish curls and her pointy polyester collar, but I stayed outside, my knees grazing the sharp branches of those gnarled, waist-high bushes that grew little red berries that my mother would encourage me to eat when I did something bad. I stood there watching, not wanting to disturb the normalcy of Melinda Bender, age thirty-five, as she lifted her skinny cigarettes to her mouth and then over her amber glass ashtray for two taps, her few moments of pleasure when her brats weren't wrecking the place and her husband wasn't wrecking her life, not knowing when she'd die (1993) or what her children would become. I cried, sure, and wanted to stay a few more hours in hopes of moving to the kitchen window to watch my mother stir tuna fish and canned mushroom soup into noodles, her thoughts elsewhere as she shoved the casserole into her harvest gold oven. But after a while I realized that the body will just keep crying about the same thing forever. The human brain, when faced with years of sorrow, never gets a clue and shapes up, and time travel only makes it worse.

JUST AS I was feeling settled and ready to resume my relationship with Lena and Clyde and the bar, I got an e-mail from Milo Kildare, with a photo of two miserable-looking children in top hats and goggles, flanking a baby with tubes up its nose, lying in a bassinette.

> There's a new little bad-ass on the scene.
> Declan Ulysses Kildare
> Born July 10th, weighing in at 2lbs 3oz.
> Much love from PDX,
> The Kildare Familie
> Milo, Jodie, Edgar, and Viola
>
> P.S. Don't call him Elvis, please. Or Napoleon Dynamite.

And then:

> Brother Karl:
>
> Three words: Axis Reunion Tour.
>
> I know you're gonna say no, so three more words: Daddy Needs Money.
>
> Don't do it for me. Do it for Declan. Do it for Jodie. Please. This is the hardest shit I've ever had to deal with. This little old man Jodie and I made, this sad old rocking-chair wrinkly cranky little can't-breathe man Declan. I can't look at him

without wanting to rip my own lungs out of my chest and shove them down his throat so the little man can get some air. Declan's got some chest wall deformity going on and his little lungs are all messed up. He's in the hospital with tubes stuffed up his nose and he doesn't even cry. He can't breathe on his own. We have to wait a few years for surgery, and of course we don't have insurance. He was supposed to be born in October. I've attached a picture. Please say yes to the tour. We can't afford this. My baby is full of tubes, and the other two are monsters. Edgar smashed one of my guitars and Vi won't stop crying for, like, a second. I haven't slept in a month.

Vi drew you a picture. I'll mail it to you if you give me your address. SAY YES, BENDER. YES BENDER YES.

You were always the smart one.

Love,
Milo

P.S. I've gone ahead and hired my friend Jill's booking company. We kick off in Chicago on August 28. How convenient for you. Then Boston and NYC, then West Coast with TRINA. Berkeley/Portland/Seattle. Trying for some Philly/Prov dates as well. SAY YES!

The Axis was successful, for a late-nineties East Coast indie band. The fact that the band had any fans and made any money was because of the charisma of Milo, the front man described by *Puncture* magazine as "a human rubber-band with a vibrato and swagger that charms the pants off those Morrissey fans with a sense of humor." Milo was, at worst, an attention slut who made up for his lack of talent with a fearlessness and larger-than-life stage presence that naturally dwarfed the other three people on stage. Sam Hecker, the drummer, and I took it in stride, but when Sam had the chance to join another band and tour Australia, Milo called him a "diaper wanker" in the middle of a show, in front of a capacity crowd in a DC club. Sam cried. When I pointed this out to Milo, he said, "Yeah. I guess I shouldn't have told everyone about his diaper thing."

Trina Aquino, a fellow Tufts student who answered an ad I placed for a bass player, left the band to go to law school back home in San Diego, right before Frederica Records released the band's last album, *Big, Bigger Love.* Trina later wrote an article for *Pitchfork* about women of color in the late-nineties indie rock scene and called Milo a "a maniac; the most selfish human being I've ever encountered." Milo's daddy's lawyers drew up a slander suit, but Milo refused to sue Trina, citing free speech as a beacon of American values. Trina and I hooked up once, behind the 40 Watt Club in Athens, against a parked Ford Fairlane.

Toward the end of my time with Milo, he unilaterally decided that the Axis needed to make a concept album about his love for amply proportioned ladies, and Milo blames my departure from the band at the end of the Big, Bigger Love Tour on my discomfort with his chosen subject matter. Milo, a string bean with hips so narrow he often searched the children's section at the Goodwill for high-water pants that fit tightly around his frame, made public his sexual preference for large ladies at a show in Atlanta. The crowd went wild. Buck wild. Young girls wrote "I LOVE YOU MILO!" in lipstick across their quadruple-D chests. Between songs, he gestured at what was poking from the crotch of his maroon polyester pants and said, "See. Atlanta girls give me a boner." I begged him not to do shit like show off boners on stage, told him that it was creepy, and probably illegal, but he never listened to me for a minute, ever, even before he first took the stage to sing the Axis's most widely played song, "Pin Cushion."

His predilection for heavy ladies was something I'd noticed over the years but had never thought to say out loud. His girlfriends were always plump, rosy-cheeked hipsters who stuffed their Rubenesque bodies into plus-size thrift store frocks. But one day he just unloaded it all in song, and because of the reaction he got in Atlanta, he expected me to play lead guitar on such tracks as "Pin Cushion" and "Jodie's Song (The Softest Love)."

My last exchange with Milo as a member of the Axis went something like this: He had rented us a rehearsal space in Roxbury and had put up a photo of himself on the mirror in the men's room with a speech bubble saying "WATCH YOUR ASS, I OWN IT NOW." He'd also helped himself to forty dollars in cash out of my wallet, to pay for his herpes medication, because he thought his dad might find out that one of his fleshy fuck buddies had contaminated his rich-boy dick if he used his credit card, which his family was still paying, even though Milo was past the age of thirty and, for a while anyway, was making enough money to pay the bills.

Before we went to the studio to record *Big, Bigger Love,* I tried to get Milo to reconsider. "I don't care that you're into large women. I'm just saying that this is a bad idea for the band. People are going to make fun of this. Also, I feel like you're trying to use my hand to jerk yourself off, and I'm not into that."

Milo was always a fidgety motherfucker, and he was practically doing a Saint Vitus' Dance in the studio's parking lot when he said to me, "Does anyone give Rivers Cuomo shit for making concept albums about his love for Japanese women? Every single song is about him ramming it in some Japanese chick." I told him I didn't know what he was talking about, and he kept going about Rivers Cuomo, and I stopped talking because there was no point.

Miles Oglethorpe Johnston V, a descendent of plantation-ruling slave owners in Georgia, christened himself Milo Kildare the way James Osterberg named himself Iggy Pop. (He rejected other monikers he'd made up for himself, such as Dick Suicide and Johnny Velvetone, for sounding too sexual or too Las Vegas.) Young Milo collected porcelain dishes and lace handkerchiefs and enjoyed horrifying his dates by telling them that he grew up in a house with African American servants and that he often came home to find his father having his way with Anita, the nanny, either next to or in the family swimming pool. He'd hit on women by saying that he learned to play guitar because he liked having his hand near his crotch. He wrote overly personal fan letters to Michael Stipe and claimed to be bisexual from 1991 through 1993. He briefly had an affair with a male anthropology professor well into his sixties, and once, back when we shared a terrible apartment in Somerville, busted into my room at three a.m., high as a kite to tell me and Meredith all about giving his first blow job. We dropped out of Tufts because we were going to be successful at this music thing, and also because we were pulling 2.0 GPAs and were about to be kicked out. Milo bought me a guitar, a Danelectro, red and white. We were starting a band because he had to do something to make Michael Stipe love him. Milo never smoked but he did have a similar oral fixation relationship with Dum Dums pops, usually root beer flavored.

"Perhaps you'd like the album better if it were called *I Love Anarchist Bitches with Crabs Who Steal My Money*?" Milo had asked.

I raised my fist with the intent of following through with a punch to Milo's mouth, Dum Dums pop and all, but I knew he was a limp-wristed rich kid used to his big cretin of a daddy fighting his battles. A punch, I knew, would end with Milo's face wrapped in bandages and Miles IV sticking twenty lawyers up my ass, taking every last guitar string I had to my name.

"Oh God, Bender. Put your fist down. You're from West Hartford, for Pete's sake."

"I'm sick of you running your mouth, Milo. You're going to ruin our band's reputation if you keep talking like that, and I for one am disgusted by you."

He ignored me. "Think of all the big, beautiful women who will come to our shows and buy this album. We're just doing musically what my luscious pen pal Jodie Simms is doing with her size acceptance zine and her Web site, at Reed College, out yonder in Oregon. God, she's hot. I'm a pin and she's my cushion. Anyway, it's an untapped niche market, plus—*plus*—Bender-face, I mean it all. I'm being sincere here. You're being a naysaying little prick. The Axis is my band, and you do as you're told."

"Oh really?"

"Yes. I made it up, I paid for all the equipment, I book the shows, I got you out of that filthy apartment and over that dumb homeless dyke you were shagging. I saved your freaking life. I even gave your sister something to remember Boston by, and you—you are just sitting there like King Dumbfuck."

Needless to say, I told him exactly how I felt about him, put my amp in the backseat of my Honda Civic, and sped away. Contractually, though, I was obligated to play the tour, and I needed the money, so I gritted my teeth and came back. Girthy lasses from Dallas to Duluth threw their XXL panties at him on the *Big, Bigger Love* tour, and afterwards, the Axis officially over, he moved to Portland and married his longtime long-distance crush, Jodie Simms, the proprietress of *Fanny,* an indie-famous riot grrrl fat acceptance zine that contained size twenty-plus dress patterns and black-and-white photographs of nude, ripply flesh.

LENA CALLED AND said she was ready to come over to my place and hang out. She allowed me a dry, closed-mouth kiss and announced she was on her period. I asked her if she wanted to get food and she said no, she wasn't hungry. So we were on the bed, fully clothed, me fighting tears and reading one of those old *Puncture* magazines I'd been holding on to for years (the one with Neutral Milk Hotel on the cover), she knitting a winter hat. Her only words to me in the first hour of all this were, "I don't know why I'm making this hat. I hate winter."

My phone rang. A 503 number. I handed it to Lena.

"It's Milo Kildare. Answer it for me."

"Really? I get to talk to him?" The fact that, even after I told her what a ding-dong narcissist he is, she was still excited to speak to him slightly broke my heart.

"Hello? This is Lena. Karl's girlfriend. Yeah, I know who you are. You're a pin and I'm your cushion." My girl was all electric and happy now, with Milo's voice streaming into her ear. Fucking Milo. Even though he was a stranger, he turned Lena's cheeks all scarlet over the phone. I never took Lena for a starfucker, but here she was, being a starfucker of the most traitorous sort. "Yeah, I saw you play in Chicago a few years ago. The toy piano thing. And I saw you in Portland in oh-one. I've lost some weight, but only because I was poor grad student up until about two months ago. Now I'm an entrepreneur. Jodie was always such a hero to me. Please give her my best. . . . I don't know, you'll have to talk to Karl about that. He's around somewhere. Hold on."

She flashed a furious grin and sang in full voice, "This is the start of a revolution! I'm the pin and you're my cushion!," before sliding off the bed and into the bathroom.

"What do you want, Milo?" I said.

"You get my e-mail?" His voice sounded old-man weak.

"Yeah. Sorry about your kid."

"The worst part about all of this is how hard it is on Jodie. She's a flipping mess, bro. Her hair's all gray now. Viola asked her if she's turned into a witch. I'm not kidding. My house is like a mausoleum full of crazy people. I'm getting the snip on Friday. No more Kildare offspring. Hey, I like your girlfriend. What's her name? Tina? Gina? Nina?"

"Lena. I assume you're calling about the tour."

"Dude. Sam turned me down."

"You treated him like crap. Remember? 'Diaper wanker'?"

"Sam had a soul. I don't blame him, really. I've got us another drummer. Eve Showalter. From the Dixie Lizards and Holy Anna. Portland bands. You'll like her. Lesbian. Really good at Scrabble. Mean beats, plus she has a plum tree in her yard."

"How much money are we talking?" I tried to sound at least a little rude.

"Eve Showalter babysits my two older kids a lot. She's really neat. She babysits them for free, even, because other than a little bit of Axis money that still trickles in, and my Web design work, which has dried up because I can't concentrate because my son Declan is in the hospital, I have zero income. Jodie's been carrying us. Shit, dude, even Trina's on board for this. And she's, like, a lawyer. She's taking time off work to play our Portland, Seattle, and San Fran dates. Trina is a goddess."

"It'll be good to see Trina again."

Milo began to talk even faster. "We're selling our house. We're moving to Macon to live with my parents. Karl, remember my dad? Big Daddy Johnston? He's still banging Anita, after all these years. True love. Seriously, amigo, I don't want to raise my kids in front of that man. That's just . . . I mean, I love my parents, but one of the conditions they've placed on us living with them in their gimondo palace is that we change the kids' last names to Johnston, and my little brother is, like, this nutjob conspiracy theorist who's living in the back house with fifty guns and some girl he met at AA, and my mom is, well, no point in saying anything about her except praise Jesus for Xanax. But Declan, you know, he needs lungs, so . . ."

"If I'm going to take time off of my business, that's going to cost me money, so I need to know what I'm getting out of all of this."

"This is Declan's tour, man. This is all about Declan."

"I have a business to run. . . ." I said. Lena, who had returned to the foot of my bed, made a disapproving noise with her tongue.

"If my son dies," Milo said, in that tone of voice, high and child-like, the tone that jettisoned my internal locked box of anger toward him. "If my son dies, then what? You going to be okay with that?"

I heard Jodie in the background say, "Milo, give me that."

"Karl? It's Jodie. Hi."

"Hi, Jodie. Very sorry to hear about your baby."

"Yes, Karl. Look, don't go on the tour. Milo is just looking for a reason to get away from me and the kids. Understandable. Did he tell you we're moving to Macon to live with his parents?"

"Yes."

"Can't wait to raise my daughter in that house. Edgar will be treated like a little king, but Vi will have to learn early to develop an eating disorder if she wants a date to the Daughters of the Confederacy cotillion, of which Milo's mom is the head. Declan . . ." her voice trailed off. "Declan will be treated like crap for not being athletic or something."

"I'm sorry, Jodie."

"Everyone is. Everyone's sorry, and Declan weighs three pounds, and I haven't slept in months. Don't do the tour. Reunion tours are embarrassing. Here's Milo again. 'Bye."

"I'm sorry," I said.

"Bendo, look. I'm going to level with you. I have a lot to apologize for. I was a jerk, I was selfish, I should not have said some things that were said. But dude, you owe me an apology, too."

Milo wasn't exactly wrong on this point, but in light of his situation, and in light of the Milo superfan in the room, whose hands were wrapped in gray woolen yarn, I wasn't up for rehashing the past.

"You quit the band because you didn't want to do *Big, Bigger Love,*" he said.

I covered the ear part of my phone with my hand so Lena wouldn't hear. "That's not why. You were being a control freak—"

Milo's voice rose. "The album embarrassed you. Fine. But you know what? That album saved lives. Women wrote letters to me and Jodie, saying that they *were* going to kill themselves, that they felt ugly because they were big, that it meant something to them that a guy in a cool band was madly in love with a woman who looked like them, and that if it wasn't for that album, if it wasn't for a famous guy like Milo Kildare saying that chubby chicks are beautiful and worthy of love and sex and beautiful lives . . ."

I clicked the phone on to speaker so Lena could hear. I wanted her to curl up beside me, to put her head on my shoulder, to let me put my head on the softness of her bosom. She sat on her quadrant of the bed, marinating in disappointment. She silenced her knitting needles.

Milo's tinny voice railed on. "There are at least five girls out there whose lives we saved. Who I saved. That we know about. So you know what? I don't need an apology. My kid is sick. Do the tour and help me save my baby's life."

I looked at Lena. Her eyes welled with tears.

"My best friend killed himself recently," I said. "So things around here are very emotional."

Milo paused. "I'm sorry to hear that, bro."

I covered the phone's receiver. "Did you write a letter to Milo about *Big, Bigger Love*?"

Lena's eyes got big. A tear fell from her eye. "Yes, but I never sent it."

Lena, in her bed quadrant, didn't have to say it. If I didn't do the tour with Milo, she'd stab me with a knitting needle. Or worse. I'd lost Wayne. I didn't want to lose Lena.

"Lena wants me to do the tour. You saved her life." I looked at her. Lena's face betrayed no acknowledgment of this statement. "I need to think about it."

"If my son dies, I'll kill myself, I don't think you really know how all this feels, Karl. Karl? Hello?"

Lena threw down her knitting. "I can't believe you. I can't believe you have to be convinced. Christ, what do you need? A blow job and ten grand and a five-hundred-volt ego stroke?"

I hung up with Milo and threw my phone aside. "What?"

"What *what*?"

"The bar doesn't run itself, Lena. If I want to pay my rent and eat, the bar has to stay open. Besides, is a tour really going to make enough money to pay Milo's bills? You factor in gas and the cut the venue takes . . ."

Her bottom lip quivered.

Lena dove for the roll of TP that I kept on the table next to the bed, pulling at it for several loops, which she used to dab her eyes. "Why is it so damn important to you that the wormhole only be used to see rock shows? We can fix everything bad in the world and we don't, because you're hung up on music, and control. I used the wormhole to travel to Butte yesterday, just to surprise

Dad and Judy. I took the wormhole instead of flying on a plane. You'd rather be poor and misunderstood than go against your senseless set of so-called morals. I told Dad and Judy—"

Judy. Just Lena saying the other, better stepmother's name made me want to jump in front of a bus. "Judy! Great for you that I accidentally got you a stepmom who didn't treat you like Cinderella. You still dropped out of Stanford and made a mess of things. What else do you want, Lena? What else didn't quite work out for you in this life?"

She blotted her tears some more. "You have no call to be mean to me."

"What did you tell your parents?" I demanded. "About the wormhole?"

"Nothing," she spat, and I didn't believe her. "People in this world are hurting and we can help them. Your friend's baby is dying. You don't want to help people, and you don't even want to make gobs of money off the wormhole. You have cash from the wormhole, so whether or not you shut the bar down for a few weeks, it isn't going to take food off your plate. You could have more money than you know what to do with. Enough to just hand Milo a check and say, 'Here you go! Medical bills solved!'"

Her disappointment with me was unbearable.

"I don't get it. Who are you?" Lena crawled over me to get off the bed, took two heavy, barefoot stomps across the bedroom floor, picked up her bag, and headed toward the door.

"Who am I?" I asked. I watched her slide her feet into her ratty old Converse sneakers. I had wanted to buy her a new pair. "I don't want that kind of power. Do you think I want the responsibility that comes with, say, destroying the airline industry? With fighting the government for the power to time travel?"

"You can't stand to lose. So you don't play. And you don't give a shit about your friends."

"Milo and I aren't friends. Sorry to mess up the Axis's mythology for you, but I haven't spoken to him in over five years."

"His kid is dying." I followed her down the hall, where she was sitting cross-legged on the floor, tying the laces of her sneakers.

"Where are you going?" The sick, sour fear of her leaving me crept up from my stomach into my mouth.

"I don't know, Karl. I have my own wormhole. I could go anywhere. Do anything. But don't worry. I don't know what to do with power, either."

"Why are we fighting?" I asked. I loved Lena and wanted to be a good boyfriend to her, but she was being difficult at every turn.

"Do the tour. You wouldn't know me if there had never been *Big, Bigger Love*. Go serenade some fat chicks. Make 'em feel sexy for five minutes," she said, slamming the door behind her so hard a section of my cinderblock and plywood vinyl album shelving area collapsed, splaying mottled, frayed jackets across my living room floor.

I decided to leave those records lying in a mess. Symbolic value or something. Maybe if I left them there, fanned out across my floor, Lena would come back.

E-mails I sent after deciding I'd do the tour for Declan and Jodie and Milo and Lena:

FROM: dickbartender@hmail.com
TO: merrydeathmccabe@hmail.com

Dear Meredith,

Thanks again for paying us a visit at Ye Olde Dictator's Club. Sorry about that random street assault. Guess what? I woke up a few mornings ago sneezing blood. I went to the urgent care place and damn! Hairline fracture to the nose. I wonder how that happened? Well, $100 copay and a bottle of Vicodin later, and here I am, walking around with a splint on my sniffer. Booya. I have definitely lost my bartenderly authority and mojo with this thing. Thought you'd like to know.

I hope you're okay. Chicago is a dangerous city.

Best to Garrett and your daughter (how the hell do you spell her name? Soiearshe? Swordfish? Soysauce?)

Karlito

P.S. If there is a song that ever saved your life, could you tell me what it is?

FROM: dickbartender@hmail.com
TO: brookemariebender@hmail.com

Dear Brookie,

Sorry I haven't called in a while. I know you probably aren't happy that dad is incarcerated, but when I got your message, I high-fived my fridge. The cops are just doing their job, and dad brought on all of this himself. A bomb threat? What the F?

Anyway, question: If there is a song that ever saved your life, could you tell me what it is? I'm taking an informal survey.

I love you, Brookie Cookie. You're my favorite sister.

Love,

Karl

FROM: dickbartender@hmail.com
TO: Jodie Simms fannymadness@hmail.com

Jodie:

I know you're really busy right now, but let me ask you a quick question: if there is a song that ever saved your life, will you share with me what it is?

Xo,

Karl

FROM: dickbartender@hmail.com
TO: Future Karl benderkarljohn03201970@postacascadezone1.vpx

You're sixty-one. What is the song that saved your life?

FROM: merrydeathmccabe@hmail.com
TO: dickbartender@hmail.com

Karl—

I'm sorry about the fracture. Other than a few scratches and a bruise on my butt, I'm fine. Not interested in pursuing my assailant, since I think I know who she is.

S-A-O-I-R-S-E.

"Don't Dream It's Over" by Crowded House.

—MM

FROM: brookemariebender@hmail.com
TO: dickbartender@hmail.com

Hey little brother!

So nice to hear from you. Not much going on around here, just work and the new puppy. His name is Rex and he's cute as hell (photo attached). Our dad didn't have a bomb. I have no idea why he phoned in a bomb threat to the Walmart but he did and he's in jail. His lawyers are bleeding me dry. I know you won't send a penny to help, but if you could find it in your heart to help ME, not him, and send some money, I'd appreciate it. He has a court date in November. There was no bomb, of course. He's all talk. He's always mad at something or someone. You know they garnish his Social Security so he has basically no income, right?

I don't know that I have a song that saved my life, per se, but I do think it's nice that Milo wrote that song about big women. The "this is the start of a revolution" song? Did he write that about me? I don't know if you know this or not, but I slept with Milo years ago, that time I came up to Tufts to visit you. He was very, um, forward. (insert Brooke blushing) The Axis was never really my thing, but I'm just really happy this song exists, and not just because the lead singer and I have done the deed! I think my favorite song is "The Greatest Love of All" by Whitney Houston. Go ahead and make fun of me all you want. I know you're sitting there doing the gagging motion finger thing.

My boyfriend Sean and I are going to Disney World next week and taking the puppy with us. I hope dad stays out of trouble from now on.

Wish me luck!

Love,

Brookie

FROM: Jodie Simms fannymadness@hmail.com
TO: dickbartender@hmail.com

Karl—

For me, it's Rebel Girl by Bikini Kill but something tells me this question is about Pin Cushion. I'm right, aren't I?

Milo leaves for Chicago tomorrow. Good luck with the tour.

—Jodie

P.S. Declan says thank you!

FROM: Future Karl benderkarljohn03201970@postacascadezone1.vpx
TO: dickbartender@hmail.com

Karl:

No song saved my life. You don't believe in that shit and neither do I. The song that ruined my life, however, is "Fade Into You" by Mazzy Fucking Star.

These days, I'm partial to the Post-A Federation Jug Band. When you spend your days in hip waders shoveling mud with Team Golden (the sixty- to seventy-two-year-old division of muck-diggers and manual labor artistes) you want to sing a particular kind of work song, and I think the Post-A Federation Jug Band really hits it where it needs to be hit. Yes, they play jugs. Economic realities of the post-A world require you make music like a 980 Lenape tribesman on an instrument made of rabbit carcasses. The national guitar string supply is long dried up. Two years ago, I traded my last pack of Ernie Balls for a box of soymilk so Lena and Glory could eat some cereal, because that's love.

You 2010 hipster fucks could have taken the work song to a new hipster-fuck level, but there wasn't a need, I guess. You don't know what you've got until it's gone.

Enjoy flushing your toilet and watching your poop disappear! Ah, the good old days.

—Karl

13

AT THREE FIFTEEN, the front door of the Dictator's Club opened and, as the darkness of my bar gulped the sunbeams that crept in, Milo Kildare's silhouette appeared. Twenty pounds heavier? Check. Brown curls now streaked with gray? You bet. Ancient cardigan with holes in the elbows, just like back in the day? Of course. And, in tow, refusing to hold his hand, his six-year-old son, a whimpering young boy with a mass of brown curls, his eyes downcast, toting in his hand a tiny plaid suitcase.

"Old friend," he said, reaching out and taking my hands into his. I registered the slight southern twang in Milo's speech with a hint of nostalgic joy. With a look of gratitude that I'd never seen on his younger face, he kissed the ball that he'd made of my hands. "Karl John Bender, the keeper of my secrets, the keeper of my riffs. Meet my eldest son, Edgar Ian Simms Kildare. Edgar, hold out your hand to Uncle Karl so he can shake it. There you go. That's the stuff. Shaking hands." I shook Edgar's cold little hand and he shook mine, only he wiped his hand off on his shirt when we finished.

Milo propped Edgar up on a barstool and had me pour the kid a ginger ale. Edgar looked like a mini Milo, or rather, a mini twenty-year-old Milo, with his blue eyes and dark curls tumbling past his eyebrows. Milo had him dressed in a white T-shirt and jeans. Hell, even Milo was wearing a white T-shirt and jeans, and that old burnt-orange cardigan I remembered from days of old, only he had removed the fabric sunflower that one of his female admirers had given him, which once hid the Izod alligator logo. I took one look at Milo and saw that all of his buzz and theater and energy—what made Milo insufferable but successful, miserable but admirable—had evaporated.

"Well, do I look old and defeated or what, old friend? You look absolutely the same. Must be the wine, women, and song that have kept you in amber all these years. Actually, no, it's that you don't have kids. Kids age you. Kids are little Amish cameras, stealing your soul. Am I right, little man, or what?"

"Yes, Daddy," the child said by rote. Edgar had opened his little plaid suitcase and removed a laptop, which he placed on the bar. He sat up on his knees and turned on a cartoon.

For Milo, who looked to have aged about thirty years since the last time I'd seen him, I poured a Makers. Milo propped his head in his hands and slumped over my bar. Milo explained that Edgar was going to stay with some friends of Jodie's who lived on a farm outside of Madison while we did the Midwestern portion of the tour.

Milo placed his hand on the boy's head. "There's going to be horses at Matt and Kimmy's, right, Edgar?"

Edgar nodded his head and sucked hard on his ginger ale straw.

"Horses, and what else?"

Edgar pulled the straw out of his mouth. A shiny strand of saliva stretched from his lip to the straw. "Sheep."

"And what else?"

"Iris."

Milo looked up from his son and met my eyes. "Iris is Matt and Kimmy's daughter. Kimmy was Jodie's roommate at Reed. Great people. Helping me and Jodie out by taking care of Edgar for a week."

"Got it."

"Viola, my girl child, was supposed to go to Matt and Kimmy's too, but when we told her, she flipped out and didn't want to leave Declan, so she's in Portland. Helping. Vi likes to help. She's four and she owns a hundred aprons."

"Sorry about all of this, Milo."

"This is Edgar's first bar visit. What an honor and a privilege to have that experience at the Dictator's Club. So manly! Too bad Uncle Karl isn't wearing shirtsleeves and a handlebar mustache. Right, Edgar?"

Edgar clicked his little laptop and ignored his dad.

"Hey Edgar! Karl was my best friend in college. He was in the Axis. What's your favorite Axis song?"

Edgar looked up from his laptop. "The one about mommy."

"They're all kind of about mommy," Milo told his son.

Not exactly true, but I didn't want to ruin this father-son moment. For a second, I was jealous that Milo had a son with whom to share the legends of his life. I'd never taken an interest in parenting, mostly because my own parental duo had been such a shit show, but there it was: a soft pang of desire to be called Daddy by someone small.

"Karl, do you have coffee? I probably shouldn't drink. I'm so tired."

"No, but I can send Clyde to get you one."

"I haven't slept in months." Milo stared into space for a bit.

"Daddy's tired," Edgar told me, pointing his small finger at his dad's head.

"I can tell."

"He's tired because Declan's going to die."

Milo's body stiffened. "Edgar, no, buddy. Don't say that. We've been over this."

"That's why my sister cries all the time," Edgar told me. He pushed his empty glass toward me. "Can I have more?"

"You know," Milo said to me, dabbing his eyes under his glasses. "I don't know what to do with that. I'm so tired I'm not thinking straight, and I know I should say something to prevent the situation here from accelerating, but what do I do? Could you . . . could you correct him?"

Milo looked like the one who was about to die. I turned to Edgar. "Declan's not going to die," I said. "Sometimes babies are, like, fixer-uppers. He's just in the hospital being repaired, like an old car." Edgar trained his eyes on his drawing and reminded me he needed seconds on ginger ale.

I looked to Milo for some evidence that my brief parental assist was at least semisuccessful, but his eyes were closed, his head slipped from his hand onto the bar. "Do we really have our first show in two days?"

"Yeah, buddy," I said. "Go take a nap on the couch in my office."

"I have to take the train up to—what is it? I have it written down—somewhere north of here, and hand my kid off to Matt and Kimmy tonight. And then we can get to rehearsing. Is that kid you were telling me about going to play with us?"

"Clyde? He's crapping his pants over meeting you."

Milo looked pleased by that news. "That's sweet. Nobody wants to meet me anymore." Milo's eyelids fluttered and I was reminded that the ancient rumor about him was true: he really did get tattooed-on eyeliner. "Goodnight, buddy. I love you, Edgar. Uncle Karl will keep an eye on you."

Milo Kildare, he of fire and ire, spit and spirit, was now a chewed-up mess, not unlike my bar towel. I had no idea how he would pull off an Axis show. I caught myself from saying, "I went back in time and saw us play the Big, Bigger Love show in Portland, back in oh one, with my girlfriend, who cried when you proposed to Jodie at the end. Twice. The first time it happened, and then again, a few days ago, when we went back in time and watched."

The main reason Lena and I had gone back to that show in 2001 was so I could see her, age twenty-two, twenty pounds heavier in a red plaid dress, holding hands with her heavier, also plaid-clad college girlfriend, screaming and crying in the front row as Milo rattled on about starting a revolution. Lena and I wandered through the crowd, me averting my eyes from the stage, not wanting to look at the stooped figure, to the left of Milo, shamefully plucking guitar strings in a corner while all the chubby chicks in the room had a collective indie rock orgasm.

"You have to understand," Lena had screamed in my ear over the music, standing three feet away from her jumpy, screaming younger self. "Guys in my high school threw food at me in the cafeteria and called me a pig and a slut. A guy held me down and told me I was too ugly to rape. Then he did it anyway. The only person I could be sexual with was a woman who looked like she could be my sister, and even that was hard. Then I heard this song, and that mind-set that I'd been in, that I was hideous and undeserving of love, began to change. It's been a slow process, but this really was the start of a revolution for me."

I hugged her and yelled above the sound, "You are beautiful!

You really are!" I told Lena she was beautiful again, as if I were grinding those words into her face, making her take them like medicine. I loved her so much, in the thick of her pain and her redemption, and I didn't know if she could hear me, so I told her again that I loved her, and again that she was beautiful. Lena's face went pale.

"You can say that all you want, but I'll never really believe it," she said, and turned away from me.

I should have told Milo this story. He really did save Lena's life. Our band did. That's why I agreed to do the tour. So I could tell him, eventually. But right now the poor guy was asleep with his face on my bar.

I helped Milo to the couch in the office and set up Edgar with another round of ginger ale so I could call Lena.

"Hello," she said, ice cold.

"Hey."

"What?"

"What? What do you mean, *what*? How are you?"

She waited a few seconds to answer. "Horrible. How are you?"

"What happened?"

"Nothing. Forget I said that. How are you?"

"Tell me what's wrong," I said. "I'm concerned."

"Usual stuff regarding my life. Nothing you don't already know about."

The flatness in her voice startled me. "Fine. Milo's here. We kick off the reunion tour on Saturday. Want to come down and meet Milo and his kid?"

"Can't."

There was a pause, one that made me worry. Lena on a good day would be on the train in five seconds to get here to meet Milo. "I have to miss the show," she said.

"What? Why?"

"Karl, I'm sorry. I tried. I thought I could do this, but I can't."

"You can't do what?"

"I have a job interview on Monday. In San Diego."

"What?"

"I have to get out of Chicago. For my own sanity."

"Lena . . . are you kidding me? I thought—"

"I have an interview for a teaching position at a community college there. You only need a master's for that, and I need a job. I can't operate an illegal wormhole forever."

"Lena. Please don't leave."

"Karl." Her voice cut out a bit on the phone. "We can't be together. I'm undateable. I can't do a relationship."

"Can we at least try? I mean, I thought we were trying. I thought . . . Look, I'm going on the tour to save Declan. Do you want to come on the tour? I really want to try. I really want you to come on the tour."

"No," she said without missing a beat. "I can't come on the tour and I can't stay in Chicago. I can't be your girlfriend. I'm a robot, remember?"

"Stop that. You're a woman. A smart, amazing human being. What is this about anyway? I got rid of your bitch-face stepmother and got you a better one."

I could tell that she was fighting tears. She didn't have to fight them. She could let them win with me. "Well, thanks. I guess I owe you one."

"You don't owe me, but I need you to stay."

"It's just better this way. Justin Cobb is filing a civil suit against me. He just got his PhD and a postdoc at fucking Princeton and he can't keep his goddamn claws off of me. I need to get out of Chicago."

"So come on tour with us," I said. "You can be a roadie."

"I'm going on this interview, Karl. It's really the last way to salvage my career. And praise Einstein and Rosen, because I just had to write a big, disgusting check to a lawyer because of Justin Cobb. All of the money I got from Sahlil is paying for lawyers."

"Lena, you can change all that. Fix it."

"What?"

I buried my pride, my rules. My voice cracked, but I said, "The wormhole. You can change or do anything."

"What are you saying, Karl? Go back in time and kill Justin Cobb? Oh, hey, Sahlil's back. I think he and Freddie Mercury broke up. He won't tell me what happened, but he's back. He calls me sometimes and wants to chat, like friends. His wife still thinks he's dead. He's on the lam. Turns out he didn't realize that faking his death came with all manner of legal difficulties, like insurance fraud."

I took a deep breath. "Use the wormhole. Get rid of Justin, even if you have to kill him."

Lena's sharp cackle of a laugh blasted into my ear. "Wow, murder? Really? Who do you think I am, Karl? Besides, I thought you had moral objections to changing the past. You didn't even want to unmurder John Lennon."

"Look, just . . . whatever it takes," I said, feeling the sweat of desperation crawl on my forehead. "Just go back and get rid of this Justin guy so you can finish school. Get him off your back. You should come down here and meet Milo."

"A PhD isn't going to make me happy. Nothing is. That's always been the problem."

"I love you, Lena," I said, the words feeling like the burn of a hundred tattoo needles. "I love you and I need to be with you."

Things got quiet on her end. "You sure you want to put that out there, cowboy?"

"Yes."

"I don't think you know what you're saying," she said.

"You don't love me back?" I asked. "I've heard you say you love me before. You look at me with love eyes. Do you want me to beg?"

Silence.

"Please don't leave Chicago."

She was quiet for a while. "I'm still going to go to my interview in San Diego. I can't just not show up for that. They probably won't hire me, but I have to go."

"Fine," I said. "Good luck."

"When do I get to meet Milo?" she asked.

"Right now. Come to the bar. He's asleep on my office couch. I'm babysitting his son."

I wanted Lena to come. I wanted to be with her, even if it was just for her to ogle my old bandmate for ten minutes and then leave.

"I'm in the middle of packing. My flight's at six a.m. Oh well. I can live without meeting Milo Kildare."

She was quiet for a bit. Then she said, "You don't even want me anyway. You want fifteen years ago and I want to be left alone."

I heard the click. She'd hung up.

A few minutes passed. I fought the urge to travel forward to see Lena in post-A land. If I hadn't had the Axis show that night, I would have done it, traveled forward to make the sting go away. But I didn't. I sat and forced myself to sit. The nice thing about working in a bar is that there's always something to wipe: tables, the bar, the brassy accents on the bar, tinkle sprinkle in the bathrooms, the jizzy puddles of liquid soap that collect beneath the dispensers. I began to wipe down my bar, methodically lifting glasses and paper coasters, wiping around Edgar Kildare as he noodled on his child-size laptop. I enjoyed deepening the cracks in the wood through the power combo of moisture and the force exerted by my goddamn hand. I'd been dumped by the one known person who knows how to operate a wormhole. *My future wife.*

"All the adults are sad," Edgar said, looking up from his computer screen at me.

"Yes," I said, honoring the little man's observation. I forced myself to smile and look busy. A six-year-old boy who was much worse off than me was watching, after all, his watery eyes following me from beneath his little houndstooth driver's cap.

I recognized the music coming out of Edgar's little laptop. "What are you watching, Edgar?"

He spun his laptop around to show me. He was on the Frederica Records Web site, watching a video entitled "The Axis at T.T.'s Cambridge 09-30-99."

His little finger jabbed at the screen, leaving a mark. "That's you and Daddy and Auntie Trina," he said.

"Yeah. You like that? You like our music?" In the video, the crowd was screaming and howling as Milo wiped his forehead dry with a white towel after a particularly strenuous performance of the song "Trina's Tarantella."

Edgar shook his head and shut the laptop. "No. I just like seeing Daddy when he's happy."

14

THIRTY-SEVEN PRESOLD TICKETS for the Axis with Small Factory, eight p.m. at Schuba's, as of three o'clock.

Clyde did some Googling and sneaking about on indie rock blogs and Web sites—an intel mission on my behalf. Apparently, some hard-core Axis fans planned to fly in to Chicago from Phoenix for the first reunion show. Some expressed joy over our regrouping, and some expressed scorn at the very notion of old farts like us thinking we had a right to go near drums and guitars and microphones ever again. References were made to plus-size panties and bras with cups as big as parachutes sailing through the air and landing with a leaden thud at Milo's feet. *Pitchfork* did a small write-up about Milo's son's medical troubles and linked to a Web site where fans could donate money for Declan's hospital bills.

Forty-one sold by four o'clock.

"Are you sure they're not coming out for Small Factory?" I asked. "Small Factory hasn't played in forever."

"No, no, they're out for the Axis," Clyde assured me.

I'd left six messages for Lena, sent three e-mails, and made a big deal out of putting her name on the guest list, even though she'd given me her regrets. No response. I nervously looked at my phone for signs of Lena every five minutes.

She could be anywhere, at any time, doing who knows what.

Fifty tickets sold by five o'clock. I didn't know we had fifty people willing to pay twenty-five dollars to see us play.

"Shut the false modesty off, dude," Clyde advised. He'd been studying the bass parts of every Axis song since he was fourteen, and would be playing with us at our Chicago and East Coast shows.

I was anxious, but not about the shows. I'd made peace with the fact that I was a mediocre guitarist. I questioned whether the Axis had the right to call this a reunion tour when only two of the four people playing these shows were in the original lineup, and when the hired-gun bass player was born in 1989. And I had no call to judge Milo, but the dude was not in the best shape.

Milo was lounging on my office sofa with a laptop balanced on his middle-aged paunch.

"How's it going?" I asked.

He looked dazed. "Fine. Took the train up north to deliver Edgar to Kimmy and Matt. Only a small amount of separation anxiety there. Just talked to Jodie. No changes with Declan today. You know. Kind of feeling like a horrible parent for not being with Declan right now, but Daddy's gotta make the money so we don't starve, right?"

"I don't know, man."

Milo's old angularity had rounded. He looked baggy and beaten. "Don't have kids. They just break your heart."

"I don't think I have to worry about that," I said, knowing that wasn't true. *Milo's kids are friends with your kid.* Even if Glory wasn't my bio kid, she was still going to be mine in some way. It broke my heart that, in two-ish years, Lena was going to get pregnant by some other guy, some physicist named Park.

"Tell me about your friend who died," Milo said. "You said that you had a friend who killed himself not too long ago. Is it okay to ask about that?"

"Yeah," I said. "It's fine."

"I don't want to kill myself. But I think about it a lot. That wouldn't solve anything. That's the thing. That guy didn't have kids, right?"

"No."

"Kids make you permanent. I hate permanence. It's weird. I had no trouble at all committing to Jodie. I have no lust in my heart for other women. But permanence still bothers me. I remember when a Sharpie exploded in my laundry in college. In my whites. You remember? I had a fit. My precious underpants turned gray. I had such problems then."

I laughed. "You had your charms."

Milo rubbed his eyes. He looked exhausted. "Not to be dark, but how did your friend do it?"

"Um," I thought of what Lena had said about helping Milo. "Time travel."

"What?"

"He time traveled away from us. He decided to stay in the past. The year 980, to be exact."

"What does that mean? That he's not actually dead but in a mental hospital? Or you just don't want to talk about it?" Milo yawned and closed his eyes.

"No. It means that he time traveled. We had a . . . a thing called a wormhole. It really worked. He traveled in time back to the year

980 and decided to stay. He lives with a native tribe on Manhattan Island and catches fish all day. My girlfriend . . . Okay, probably my ex-girlfriend . . . She and I went back to 980 to try to get him to come back to the present, but he refused. I can show you the report she wrote about the experience, and the pictures she took of the sky. There were two moons."

Milo bolted upright and rose to his feet. Milo was maybe five foot seven without shoes on, but he took up more space than I did, especially when he was pissed off. "Fuck you, Karl. Fuck you fuck you a million times fuck you!" He threw his laptop on the cushions at the end of the couch and stood up in order to get up in my face.

"I'm not lying."

Milo's eyes were bugging out of their sockets. A giant blue vein appeared on his forehead. "Oh my god. Bender, you're a lying, manipulative turd dangling from the asshole of decency. Your friend died and you have the gall to make up some story, to dick with me? News flash: I am in no mood to be dicked with right now."

"Milo, I'm not lying. I swear. He time traveled. I can time travel."

Milo's sagging face turned the color of plums. I kind of hoped he'd hit me. I could take a hit from him if it would give the man some peace. "I've got a half-dead fetus in a plastic box for a son, I'm three hundred grand in the hole for medical bills, and you're sitting here telling me your dead friend died by time traveling?"

I let Milo make me feel small. "I don't know what to apologize for here, but I'm sorry if I offended you. I'm telling you the truth. That's how I lost Wayne."

Milo kicked my couch. Six kicks in rapid-fire succession, with the toe of his cowboy boot. "I know you make fun of me. I know we're not friends anymore. I know my fat acceptance album makes you want to barf. But for fuck's sake, Bender, could you maybe just humor me? Could you for once be the bigger man here? Did it ever occur to you, mister never got married because he refused to get over his bug-infested, anarchist girlfriend from fifteen years ago, that my best friend, my wife, is the one person in the world I can't talk to about what I'm feeling right now?"

"Milo, my girlfriend could be anywhere in the space-time continuum. Let me put it this way: you could go back in time and watch a Miaow/Durutti Column show at the Haçienda."

Milo turned his back to me. "I have to go to the bathroom."

I followed behind him as he flung open the men's room door. He went into one of the red-partitioned stalls and slammed the door.

"We don't need a time machine to travel," I said. "That's what we're doing tonight, right? Playing our old songs. We haven't played together in nine freaking years. We have no new material. We're going to pretend like time hasn't passed, even though we're old and irrelevant."

Milo yelled through the stall door, "You may be old and irrelevant, but don't pin that on me."

"Oh, sorry, Milo. You're twenty-seven and at the height of your abilities."

He kicked the stall door. "Can a man shit in peace, please? Go away."

"Okay. I'll be out here when you're done." I turned, but before I could step back into the bar, the stall door swung open, revealing Milo, still pulling up his pants. He leaped in front of me and slammed the door to the restroom shut.

"Prove it. Show me you can time travel. I want to do it."

I didn't respond.

Milo grabbed me by the back of my neck. "If you're holding out on me for any reason, Karl, I will kill you. I will kill you with these two hands." His unbuttoned pants slid to his ankles. "My will to live these days is pretty minimal, so don't think I'm bluffing."

I held up my own to hands to show innocence. "I'm not holding out. Swear."

Milo buttoned up his pants. "We're going," he said.

"We're going," I said, and so we went.

MILO LOOKED AT the closet, my piss-poor DIY technology, the smudgy black accelerator exhaust on the walls.

"That's it? It's a closet."

"It's a wormhole. The Einstein–Rosen Bridge. Not a machine but a portal. A slip in space-time."

He nodded, running his finger across a thick black wall smudge. "Low tech. What is this black crap on my finger?"

"Accelerator residue. Carbon, basically."

"Why does it do that?"

"I don't know. The force of the hole kicks back this black soot and it gets all over my walls." Lena never exactly explained this phenomenon to me, but she was better about wiping down the walls than I ever was.

"Okay, where do you want to go?" I asked.

"The future," he said. "I want to see my three kids as adults."

"Milo, no. No forward. Just backward."

"Fuck backward. What is past stays in the past. I want to see my kids. I want to know that Declan will be okay."

"It only goes backwards," I lied.

"Okay, maybe I'd like to go back and meet Jodie for the first time again. That was my favoritest day ever. Meeting Jodie. We'd been writing to each other for over a year after she interviewed me for *Fanny*. Amazing, beautiful letters. She took me to that Ethiopian restaurant on Hawthorne that we don't go to anymore, since the kids won't eat spice. She was so beautiful, in this yellow sundress and little Mary Jane shoes, her hair full of rain. Gosh. . . . You know, honestly bro, I'd rather just relive it in my head. I don't need to see dorky me shoving handfuls of spicy goo in my mouth, trying not to look like an ass in front of twenty-two-year-old Jodie, who was so confident and gorgeous."

"Well, let's see a band play. REM, Athens 1980, in the church."

"Why? I mean, really, why? I was nine when they played that show. And that show sucked."

"Bill Berry played that show."

"Stipe couldn't sing back then. I bet he made everyone uncomfortable."

"You had a boner for Stipe!"

"I had a boner for everything. I was twenty."

Milo ran his finger through the accelerator smudge again. "Because rock music is all about legend. It's all artifice. I mean, really, we're doing this reunion tour, right, and all these people are going to show up, and we're going to play some shit from *Big, Bigger Love* and *Dreams of Complicated Sorrow,* and maybe we'll do a cover of "Bela Lugosi's Dead," just to get the crowd riled up, and everyone's going to clap politely and then go home to their lives and their families and stare in their refrigerators and try to decide whether or not their milk is rancid, or if they need to go to the dentist, or if they're about to run out of toilet paper. The departure from reality that a rock show provides is as temporary as whatever time travel shit you're peddling. Even if it's real."

"Okay, fine. You want to go back to the bar and practice?"

Milo pressed his knuckle to the wall, as if testing it for softness in the event that he chose to punch it. "I want my son to be okay. That's all I want. This tour is for him. I really, really don't want anything else. And it's a feeling that scares the shit out of me."

"I want to help you. Don't think for a minute that I don't. I just don't know how to do that without simply erasing him. Making it so he was never conceived, never born."

Milo rubbed his sleeve across his eyes. "I don't want to erase him. I want him to be whole."

I told him that I would send him back to 1998, to the first time he met Jodie Simms, on that summer day in Portland. I remember Milo taking that trip—seeing him off to the airport after a show we'd played in Salt Lake City, of all places, and then going to Portland a week later to play an Axis show and seeing Milo and Jodie together for the first time. When Milo wasn't onstage, they were smooching and holding hands. How in love they were, and how silly and cute they looked, Milo of the twenty-six-inch-waist pants and Jodie Simms, the original pincushion, his big, bigger love. I wish I'd taken a picture. Mismatched socks on the outside but a perfect pair on the inside. I looked at them, sitting beside each other on the little wooden stage at the club, Milo standing on his tiptoes to kiss Jodie while we were supposed to be doing a sound check, so sure that in my life I would never find my sock, my big love. Is it a blessing or a curse that my wormhole can return a person to their life's most perfect moment? For me, it was both. As much as I loved going back and seeing my younger self wrapped around Meredith McCabe at T.T.'s as Galaxie 500 played "Blue Thunder," it was also painful to see how much I've changed, how much I'd lost. I hoped that Milo would think his trip back to 1998 was a blessing. It was all I could give him.

Milo perked up. "Okay, send me to Portland. June 3, 1998. Best day of my life."

And so I sent my old friend back to see his best moment one more time. To lurk around an Ethiopian restaurant and look at his twenty-eight-year-old self.

I called Lena. No answer.

As I sat waiting for Milo to come back, the lights dimmed and there was a popping sound and Lena appeared at my feet, prone on the floor, an iPhone in her hand. She coughed and struggled to stand. I saw that she was crying, that her face was red and puffed up.

"Lena." I leaned down to pick her up, but our hands didn't meet. I tried again to grab her but couldn't. She was on a different level. A different level in the present.

"Karl. I'm trying to. I need—" And then there was another popping noise and I grabbed for her but she disappeared.

A minute or two passed, and then the pop sound returned, as did Lena, or at least the image of Lena, still untouchable, still crying.

"Karl. I'm on the wrong level. I'm in a loop. I'm trying to . . ." Her voice sounded muffled and distant, like she was across a noisy room. "I can't—"

I tried to grab her hand as she reached it out to me, but I couldn't. Her hand was ungrabbable. And then she disappeared again.

I looked at the laptop screen. It had gone dead after I'd sent Milo away. Did sending Milo disrupt whatever Lena was up to? I made sure all the wires were where they were supposed to be. The laptop issued a hoarse beep before twinkling out, and no amount of banging on the keys made it work again. And then Lena reappeared, only for a few seconds, iPhone in her hand, screaming my name before disappearing like a switched-off television.

"Lena?" I took out my phone and texted her: *WHERE ARE YOU?*

1996. THE NIGHT I WAS

I pressed the laptop's On button again and the screen turned white and issued a rather sick-sounding beep.

I managed to get the program up long enough to see her coordinates.

"Shit."

Another sickening beep, and then the answer flashed on the screen. The last transmission: December 15, 1996. San Francisco, California.

It was then that knew where Lena went. She was back in the night she never wanted to talk about, and something I'd once said to Wayne popped into my head: *"You want to be a superhero? Put on your cape and fly."*

Only I didn't know where my cape was or how to put it on. The wormhole's computer system went dark.

15

I SAW THAT Lena had sent me an e-mail four hours earlier:

FROM: Lena G. l.diggy@hmail.com
TO: Karl dickbartender@hmail.com
SUBJECT: Break-up e-mail
DATE: August 28, 2010 07:04AM CDT

Karl,
I know it's tacky to break up via email, but I don't have time for a phone call, or the stomach for an argument. So here it is: break up. Goodbye. Over. Out. See you later.

Can we do a brief exit interview before I go? What the hell did you see in me? Will you at least indulge me by hitting reply and telling me why you wanted to date me? You didn't even really flirt with me or pursue me. You just kind of came on all strong, like nabbing me as your girlfriend was a foregone conclusion, (Elliott tattoo and all, I guess) and I figured that decent, mostly-bullshit-free people are interested in me once every five hundred years so I might as well go with it. I'm accustomed to men not liking me like that. They have to be okay with the fat, and a lot of men are, but once they hit the smart, game over. Being both chunky and intelligent while also being a woman is discouraged in our culture, even in our nation's mid-ranked university physics departments, where dudes outnumber ladies ten to one. One would think that having a pussy and being able to discuss the latest Higgs Boson discoveries would be a plus but it's not. Add trauma and loss, and you can see why I prefer the life of a robot.

You told me to go back and change the thing that would allow me to stay in grad school. You even suggested that I murder Justin Cobb, which is probably the nicest thing anyone's ever said to me. Did you know in addition to getting raped at the age of eighteen to the song "Fade Into You" performed live, the really excellent man who attacked me also slammed my head against the pavement and gave me a concussion? And as hard as I tried to stay at Stanford, the residual memory loss and occasional seizures pretty much prevented me from doing schoolwork in any meaningful way. So I went home to Butte and was given a part-time job at the MT Tech financial aid office processing paperwork. I also enrolled in a dance class to help me regain my sense of balance. The State of Montana took away my driver's license after I drove my dad's Volvo into the call box at a Wendy's drive-thru during a black out. Thirteen years ago—I've never tried to get my license back.

So no, I can't murder anyone, having almost been murdered myself (like a light bulb breaking). I'll continue to go about my business, being the human equivalent of a toilet for overconfident, talentless vermin like Justin Cobb. That's my life. I'm done fighting.

Keep this in mind, Karl: I could have saved my ass in grad school by telling the department about the wormhole. In fact, somehow they already kind of knew about the existence of a functioning Einstein-Rosen Bridge somewhere. If I had told them, not only would the department have gotten flooded with dollars by a number of private and government entities, but the Geduldig vs. Cobb issue would have been decided in my favor. I still would have broken up with you but not because of feelings or because I'm constitutionally undateable, but because I'd have been up to my ass with work and wouldn't have had any time.

I was their charity case. My dad's a Northwestern alum and he and a friend of his who's on the Board of Trustees pulled some strings to make up for my post-attack shoddy academic record.

What I really wanted to do was keep my mother from dying. But all the time travel in the world cannot prevent cancer cells from growing and spreading. Cancer is far stronger than a time-space slip. And I'm not a doctor. Not any kind of Doctor.

But there is something in my past that I can undo, and that is not to be a fucking idiot at the age of eighteen. To not be the girl with the 170 IQ who answered a personal ad in SF Weekly written by a guy looking for "a cute young girl to take to see Beck and Mazzy Star at the Cow Palace." I wasn't cute and I knew lots of things about calculus and quantum mechanics, but I didn't know that I shouldn't accept free concert tickets from a stranger.

During Mazzy Star, the guy stuck his dirty face into my

neck and started kissing me. Rather than tell him to stop, I said I had to go to the bathroom. My plan was to hide from him until the show was over and then sneak away in a taxi. He followed me into the bathroom, dragged me out, and accused me of trying to run away from him.

I screamed, but Mazzy Star was onstage playing, and "Fade Into You" sucked all the sound out of the space. I can't listen to that song. The nineties have been over for how long and you still hear it in every coffee shop in Chicago. This is why I stay home a lot.

All I remember was him slamming my head against a wall and telling me I was too ugly to rape, but that he was going to do it anyway, and I should be thankful that any man would want to fuck something as fat and hideous as me.

A very nice couple who had gone outside to smoke weed found me with my head all bloody and my skirt torn away and called the cops.

There is this part of me, a rather large chunk, actually, that doesn't want to be a robot, that wants to do miraculous things like have a healthy relationship and a satisfying career. But every time I suffer a setback I look at my options and they're either kill myself, or go back to Butte and live with Dad and Judy and their new horse. Then I met you. Then the wormhole happened. And now I have a third, better option.

Delete, delete, delete.

I'm going to use the wormhole one last time. Then I will kill it, much to poor Sahlil's horror (I've grown to really feel for the guy—he's not bad, just needs to come out and get some therapy). I can't stop cancer from colonizing my mother, but I can undo the night I was raped. I can delete the one night that turned me into the Lena you claim to love.

Thanks for everything. I promise I will not rat out your wormhole to the physics feds.

—L.G.

I jerry-rigged the controls on that busted-ass computer and landed on the ground level at the Cow Palace in December 1996, a mob of moving bodies in black T-shirts. I saw this "guy" and I saw Lena—fifteen feet and too many bodies in front of me—standing with her, and he's got his hand too low on her back, and Hope Sandoval is onstage in a cloud of purple light and she's about the size of a pencil eraser, and then I saw this guy leading Lena by the hand. I pushed through the crowd, the thick throng of bodies. I didn't keep my eye on anyone but Lena. Lena, age eighteen, and Lena, age thirty-one. She was just a kid who wanted to see Mazzy Star and maybe Beck, and then suddenly and without warning, while Hope's eerie voice spilled out of the speakers, this asshole broke Lena's glasses, her spotless academic record, the essential Lena-ness that was already halfway to being the steely, sad-eyed woman I knew and loved so much. I was there, too, and I watched the woman I love, Lena, age thirty-one, know her strength and use the wormhole for good as Hope Sandoval finished up the final strains of "Blue Light."

Lena told me once that she wished that she could be weak. She's not weak, and that's the thing about her that makes me happy. She's strong, even if it hurts. I watched as she, with a half-life-worth of anger and resolve, flickered into this dark night and tried with all her might to get back what was taken from her. When Lena, thirty-one, saw me elbowing my way through the crowd, she screamed, "No! No! Go back! I don't want your help!" She pushed me hard on the chest, so hard that I fell backwards. "Karl, no!" she yelled, all scars and tears, "I have to do this myself!"

She flickered in and out and I reversed my pull and went back to the apartment in 2010 to see if she was there, but she wasn't. I shot myself back to 1996, setting the controls to land at the Cow Palace two hours earlier, around the time I guessed she and the guy would have arrived. I walked up and down the aisles of the parking lot, hoping to see her, hoping to find some way to help her, or at least let her know that I was there for her, but I couldn't find her.

I wandered around the crowd, looking for Lena, knowing exactly where and when on the floor I would find her. She made eye contact with me and yelled, "Karl, go away!," and then I saw what she did. She wasn't weak at all. Older Lena rushed up behind the guy, snapped his neck backwards until he slumped down to the ground like a sack of flour. She kicked him in the head, even though there wasn't room enough for her foot to go back far enough to make the kick count. Then she made eye contact with her eighteen-year-old self and screamed at her, not from the violence she had inflicted to save herself, but because, in that moment, looking into the scared eyes of the girl who had the rot and the hurt this night burned into her, the two Lenas separate instead of one, Lena—the one I love, the older, the wounded, the beautiful—evaporated.

"Get away! You're so stupid! Run! You're so stupid!" she screamed into her eighteen-year-old face, even though she wasn't so stupid. She never was. But I talk trash to myself like that, and she does, and we all do, and that is why we look back in time and suffer.

I watched Lena disappear. Lena, age thirty-one. She transformed into bubbles, like the top of a freshly poured seltzer.

Eighteen-year-old Lena pushed her way through the crowd as some guys tried to grab her and security pushed their way toward her, and I stood there as Mazzy Star filled that huge stadium with that song you hate. The song played and she moved away, toward the exits, followed by security, fading into herself, fading away. She wouldn't have to leave Stanford, and her life would be easier, and I watched, knowing that when I came home there wouldn't be the Lena Geduldig I knew, but maybe a healthier one. I could live with the changes. I wanted to.

I wanted to be the one to save her. To rush that asshole and kick him and kill him and be her superhero. But I understood that, here, she needed to be her own superhero. This undoing belonged to Lena and Lena alone. I tried to understand what "Don't lose Lena" meant, if losing Lena was the best thing in the world for Lena. I was the loser here, the biggest loser, because I lost her, and I was told so many times not to.

LENA IS GONE now. Her phone number belongs to a liquor store in Skokie. The photo that helped me find her is no longer on the Northwestern physics department Web site. She doesn't live in Chicago. She never did. She's Dr. Lena Geduldig, PhD.

16

FROM THE *NEW* *York Times* Weddings and Celebrations page, May 3, 2009

Lena Geduldig and Derrick Park

Dr. Lena Rose Geduldig and Dr. Derrick Yoon Park are to be married this evening at Cassiopeia, an event space in Gloucester, Mass. Rabbi Tamar Sandel, director of the Jewish Women's Resource Center in Boston and a friend of the bride's, will officiate.

The couple met at Massachusetts Institute of Technology in 2004, where they both earned doctorates in physics.

The bride, 30, will be a postdoctoral fellow in astrophysics at the University of Washington in Seattle in the fall. She is a graduate of Stanford University.

The groom, 32, will also be a postdoctoral fellow in

astrophysics at the University of Washington. He is a graduate of Columbia University.

She is the daughter of Dr. David Geduldig of Butte, Mont., and the late Gloria Schiller. The bride's father is a professor of geological sciences at Montana Tech.

He is a son of Dr. Sang Hoon Park and Dr. Emily Kim Park of Verona, N.J. Both of the groom's parents are oral surgeons in private practice.

apartmentsinlove.com: The Moon and the Stars

Lena Geduldig and Derrick Park, astrophysicists both (they're the smartest couple we've profiled, ever) share this stylish abode in the heart of Seattle's Ballard neighborhood.

THE SURFACE OF LAST SCATTERING:

The adventure blog of L. R. Geduldig, Girl Physicist

March 20, 2010

Well, gosh golly! UW student Hannah Ashford-Clark wrote an article about me on the Women in STEM Committee's website, calling me "Bad-Ass Female Scientist of the Month." This is quite an honor. I've worked with the Women in STEM Committee since I arrived at UW last fall, and I've enjoyed getting to know the many women here who are dedicated to advancing the role of women in the sciences and in mathematics. I did not know that Hannah admired me so, seeing as she is majoring in chemistry and has not taken a class with me, but apparently my storytelling at the W-STEM lunch meeting last month about dealing with two of my creepiest male colleagues at MIT really struck a chord. I'm getting a lot more offers for lunch dates. I've never been popular before, so this is strange, but I love W-STEM, so I'll take it.

I really am chuffed that Ms. Ashford-Clark chose to write about me, but because I think we as a community of women scientist all benefit when we point out our own institutional oppression (yep, I said it), I'm going to say something, and I hope it doesn't hurt your feelings, Hannah (and if it does, please come by my office hours and talk to me—). If you click on the link, you'll see that in her article, Hannah dedicated one paragraph to my work on quark entanglement and acceleration as it relates to the Einstein-Rosen Bridge and three paragraphs to my marriage to UW Physics Department hottie Derrick Park.

In a perfect world, noting my work would come before noting who married me, but the world isn't perfect. Women are taught to see their value raised by the men who choose them as partners. Who are we without love? (Answer: the same somebody.) If you go through everything that's ever been written about Dr. Park and his work, my name appears exactly zero times.

I guess it's cool to be part of a physicist couple, and my husband and I occasionally collaborate on our research. If you look at our career trajectories, Derrick has had it a lot easier, and he will readily admit to this. We're super lucky to have gotten postdocs at the same institution and are grateful to not have to live apart to further our careers with parity. But when I mentor young women in the sciences, I want to talk about science, I want to talk about our advancement, I want to talk about the challenges that come with being a physicist while also being a woman, because there are many. I'm successful because I work hard, because I pushed myself even when the voices telling me I wasn't good enough were screaming in my ear, because I spent a lot of nights crying on the floor of my office because I felt stupid and hopeless and wanted to quit. But fortunately I found my way out of that through a lot of love, luck, and straight-up faking it until I made it.

If this is a matter of being inspired because a chubby, nerdy science girl from Montana found true love, I get it, but I prefer to focus on the work. Many of us have a long road ahead as we begin our careers. We're here to do the work. We're here to support each other, to make sure other women succeed, and to not give up when giving up seems like the choice everyone around us wants us to make. Let's keep sight of that. And though I'm really honored, and maybe a little confused, by the attention I've been getting lately, I definitely do NOT want anyone to look up to me for any reason other than my research and what I contribute to our community of female science students, not because I'm married to the guy who teaches Intro to Quantum in a sick leather jacket.

A partner who will support you in your career is probably the most valuable thing you can have as you move forward, and, sadly, the most rare. Don't settle, is what I'm saying.

Here's a link to my latest published paper, "Gravitational Wave Disturbance in Space and Time and Inflationary Models of Cosmology."

Here's a video of my lecture at the International Congress of Cosmologists conference in Antwerp last summer.

And here's a picture of the moose antlers winter hat I knitted for my dad.

AFTER HOURS OF furious Googling, after hours of hoping to find what I had lost, I closed the lid of my laptop and prepared my body to cry. I removed my T-shirt, lay on my office couch, bellowed, gasped for air, pressed my T-shirt to my face, and contemplated calling Brooke and telling her everything, because she was now literally the last person on the face of the planet who gave half a crap about me.

When I was done with my cry, I paused to look at my empty bar, the reddish light of my neons keeping everything looking like a sad, murky dream. I sat down at the bar, in Wayne's favorite seat.

"Wayne," I said to no one, catching a glimpse of my stupid mug in the mirror behind the bar. "Nothing in my life right now can be fixed by going back in time to see a rock show. Now what?"

I needed my own bartender.

WHY I REMEMBER LENA BUT LENA DOES NOT REMEMBER ME:

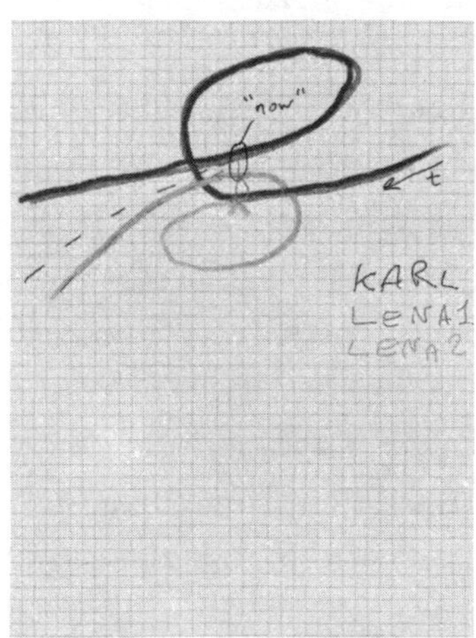

I sat down at my desk with some colored pencils and the pad of graph paper that Lena herself had left behind at my apartment

(I've never bought graph paper in my life, and *yet there was graph paper in my apartment, hello!*) and drew out the linear time paths of our lives. My drawing may be a failure. I don't trust my ability to use applied physics, problem solve, or draw lines with colored pencils, but it seemed plausible when I drew it, though my science-minded pals Wayne and Lena were unreachable because of the very concept of time travel, so what the hell do I know about anything?

Lena and I were on the same linear time trajectory (along with the rest of the world), but then, when she managed to avert her assault at the Cow Palace, Lena off-ramped into a different reality, thus disappearing Lena 1 and leaving Lena 2 to exist as the sole physical manifestation of Lena Rose Geduldig—the one who had never met me. Having averted the experience that led her away from Stanford and toward me, she went down a different path, like she pushed herself out of the way of an oncoming truck. Lena changed her own life.

Why am I the only idiot in the world who remembers Lena the way she was?

The heart has a long memory. Or at least mine does. (Exhibit A: Meredith.) Maybe love is science and science is love. Maybe I was meant to be that guy, the guy who loves women who don't love him back, or simply don't remember him at all. Or maybe Lena was right, even though this was so unscience-y that she didn't want it to be true: that love is what kept Wayne in 980, what propelled Sahlil back to 2010 without using the wormhole controls. Love, in its infinite power, had something to do with the function of the wormhole. Lena hated that, but it was the only explanation that made sense to me.

Science and love. One is bigger than the other. I regret not having that conversation with Lena when I had the chance.

17

I LOST LENA, and took a day off of work to engage in some masochistic Internet searching, but dagnabbit, the Axis rocked our first reunion show right on schedule.

The dicks at *Pitchfork* deemed our Chicago show "lackluster, owing to the obviously preoccupied Kildare and his equally dazed-looking guitarist, Karl Bender." Milo was exhausted by the situation with his baby as well as his trip to Portland, 1998, where he saw how unburdened by life he and Jodie looked: well rested, dressed in darling outfits, full of the hope of youth and the battery power of new love. "Now we just look and feel like shit," Milo said. "I try not to be sad about it."

My excuse? I had lost a loved one. Wouldn't *Pitchfork* love to have access to my wormhole? I was so indie cool about it that even *Pitchfork* never heard about me or my portal. Typical Karl behavior:

me being bitchy about a bad review instead of focusing on repairing the great chasm of loss and sorrow in my life. I didn't like being Sad, Alone Man. I had my health. I'd lost two friends, but I wasn't in danger of losing a child. Still, there was this small part of me that really wanted Lena to see me play "Pin Cushion." To see how far I'd come in embracing Milo's masterwork. In Chicago, I stood at his side and played that song with great duty and reverence. I'd even written "Lena" on my left wrist, below my crocodile tattoo, so she'd be there on stage with me in some symbolic way.

Her life was better without me. She had a husband and a daughter and a better job. Who doesn't wish good things on the people they love? The world was rid of one heinous rape and one horrible stepmother. Collateral damage: Rachel Geduldig, the Northwestern physics department, and me.

Another drink, bartender.

Milo's son Declan passed away in his incubator two days after we played the first reunion show in Chicago. The four of us—Clyde, Eve Showalter, Milo, and I—were on our way to New York in our rented tour van when Jodie called, and after we'd pulled over to a gas station so that Milo could kick the wheels of the van and scream so loud that the manager of the gas station came out and asked us to leave, we gunned it to the nearest airport, which happened to be Pittsburgh. We chipped in three ways to pay for his expensive last-minute ticket and sat with him until his flight was called, at which point we canceled all of the East Coast shows and turned the van back toward Chicago.

Milo had something to live for, I realized. He had Jodie and their family. I said this out loud, somewhere during hour three of our silent-save-for-the-stereo ride through miles of nondescript Ohio farmland. Eve, who was somewhere in her fifties, decided to ignore my proclamation. Eve spent the time in the van talking about her partner and their teenage son, who was rebuilding his own VW bus, and her chicken coop and living roof house. She had things to live for. Rather than address me and my insecurities from the van's driver's seat, she asked for the attention of young Clyde and offered him general life wisdom.

"Don't be afraid to do what you love, and don't be afraid to keep doing what you love, even if it doesn't turn out the way you wanted it to. Don't be afraid to love someone because you think society will laugh at you. Don't be afraid to cry or let other people define for you what being a man is. Always love and protect your friends. A lot of people think Milo Kildare is an egomaniac or a pain in the ass, but he's the best example of how to live I know."

Clyde nodded. He did not look my direction, though I kept glancing over at his face, hoping to just be acknowledged as an older person with something of value to offer.

I resumed bartending and time-travel-induced depression. Urges to call Lena were quelled by pounding my head on my bar. This is bad form for a bartender. A good barkeep must always display a modicum of self-containment. I resented the clock and its glacial, forward movements.

I shut down the wormhole. A few people contacted me about it—Clyde's good-looking indie rock pals, mostly, and Sahlil, who was bumming around 2010 with a Freddie-shaped hole in his heart, trying to get back to the seventies. I had no one to talk to about the wormhole, except for Sahlil. For this reason I was unusually happy to hear from him when he rang me one afternoon while I was in my bar serving beer to frat dudes who had the stones to ask me why there were no TVs showing sports.

"What happened to Lena?" he asked. I heard street noise and sirens in the background. The number that he called from came up on my phone as unknown. "I tried calling and e-mailing, and nothing. Is she mad at me?"

Sahlil. I shivered. "You remember Lena?"

"Of course. Where is she? I need to use her wormhole. I have money."

"She went back in time and changed something in her past," I said. "Something really bad. Now that that's gone from her past, everything's different for her. She's in Seattle, married to some other guy, and a very fancy professor and . . . and I'm happy for her."

"I would like to go back in time, but not very far. Just back to the day I asked you to send me to Freddie Mercury. I want to have never known him. Going back to see him was a mistake. Can you hook me up, friend?"

"Dude, I just told you that Lena completely altered the course of her life and all you can talk about is yourself?" I felt my fists clench. "Lena was raped, you selfish ass!"

Sahlil cleared his throat. "Thank you, Karl, for pointing that out to me. Freddie told me that I should be a more compassionate person. I'm sorry about Lena."

"What else did Freddie tell you?" I asked. "Why did Freddie even like you? I don't get that one bit."

"Nothing I want to share. But I will say that time traveling to meet the man I've idolized since I was a kid ruined everything I've got. Money, my gorgeous wife, my family. Just sitting next to him and listening to him talk. His ideas were like falling rubies. True gifts. I've never felt love like that before, and it isn't real, and fuck you, Karl, for ruining my life. My life is shit now." Sahlil sounded oddly calm while telling me I had ruined his life, and though I didn't actually believe his life was ruined, I was painfully aware that Sahlil was the only one that I knew of who was in the same spot as me: suffering from time-travel-related heartbreak and loss.

"I didn't mean to ruin your life. You were the one threatening to sell the building, remember?"

"Well, you did. Or I did. Or time did. Being born in the wrong time and the wrong place keeps you from getting what you want. I should have sold the building, but Freddie meant more to me than money. Will you help me undo it?"

"You were friends with Lena?" I asked, wanting Sahlil to answer in the affirmative, wanting some sign that Lena affected someone else's life. "Tell me about her?"

"Lena spoke to me of nothing but business. But from what I know of love, if she loved you, she wouldn't have disappeared."

"Lena and I have technically never met. That's the rub. That's why I'm sitting here in my underwear with a broken heart. But you remember her? That's great news. Hey, Sahlil? I know I sound like a teenage girl when I ask this, but did she ever say anything to you about me?"

He was quiet for a bit. "Can you send me back in time to undo it? Please? I'm in a lot of pain here. I have about a thousand in cash. I can get more after it's undone. Things are very bad, Karl."

I thought about helping Sahlil. But enough damage had been done. "No, man. The wormhole is gone. No more time travel. I don't want your money."

The line went dead, and when I tried to call back he didn't answer. I tried again, hoping that he'd contact me or show up at the Dictator's Club so I could talk to him, even though I knew talking wouldn't help.

That made three people lost to the wormhole.

Two months later I heard from Milo. With the support of Jodie, his friends, and his therapist, he had decided to reschedule the Portland and Seattle shows. He wanted to get the band back together so he could feel something other than pain. I was to fly to Seattle to meet up with him, Eve, and Trina the week before Thanksgiving, and was invited to spend Turkey Day in Portland with Milo, Jodie, their kids, and their friends.

"Demand seems to be high for the shows," he said. "I want to do it around Thanksgiving because I'm thankful for what I have, which is an amazing wife and people who still give a damn about what I do." His voice sounded about a million miles away from his usual power-mad self.

Besides: Seattle. *Seattle.* Where New and Improved Lena happened to live. Derrick Park, too. And in came this text from Glory:

> YES, DAD LOVES THE AXIS. HE'S A BIG MUSIC GUY. HE HAS A DEPECHE MODE TATTOO. EMBARRASING. ACTUALLY, YOU TWO ARE KIND OF FRIENDS NOWADAYS. YOU SENT HIM SOME OLD AXIS DEMOS RECENTLY AND HE WAS WATTS INTO THEM.
>
> AS FOR YOUR QUESTION. THEY DIVORCED IN 2022. 2022 IS PROBABLY NOT THE BEST TIME TO FLAG DOWN MOM. SHE WAS MAJORLY DEPRESSED AND ALSO WORKING ON SOME HIGH-LEVEL TRAVEL TECH STUFF THAT ULTIMATELY ENDED UP FORMING THE GLOWORM COMPANY. I THINK IF YOU SHOWED UP THEN, YOU WOULD EITHER GET DISSED BY HER OR MAYBE EVEN KEEP HER FROM WORKING ON THE SPEECH DILATION MODULE, WHICH IS THE TECHNOLOGY THAT ALLOWS ME TO TEXT YOU ACROSS TIME. WE DO NOT WANT TO MESS WITH SPEECH DILATION IT IS WATTS THE TITS RIGHT?
>
> I STALK YOU, TOO. AT YOUR BAR. I SAW EDDIE KILDARE AS A LITTLE BOY THERE ONCE. I WATTS HAVE A CRUSH ON HIM BUT HE HAS TWO GIRLFRIENDS AT ONCE AND IS FAMOUS. DON'T BE MAD AT ME TURNABOUTS FAIR PLAY.
>
> I'M NOT MAD, GLORY. BUT SERIOUSLY, I LOVE YOUR MOM.

YOU DON'T REALLY KNOW HER, TURDFACE. YOU'RE MAKING SHIT UP ABOUT HER RIGHT NOW. SHE'S NOT WHO YOU THINK SHE IS.

I'M WILLING TO TAKE MY CHANCES. SHE'S HAD HER HEART BROKEN, THAT'S ALL I NEED TO KNOW TO WANT TO BE WITH HER.

OK, BUT SHE'S KIND OF NOT VERY FUN. SHE'S A TOTAL SLUT FOR HER WORK, EVEN BEFORE THE A. WON'T LET ME DO ANYTHING EXCEPT SCHOOL AND TEEN CORPS, WHICH ARE LEGALLY MANDATED BY THE GOVERNMENT DUH LENA. SHE ALSO PUT ME ON RESTRICTION NO TRAVELING LIKE SHE CAN STOP ME THOUGH. ANYONE CAN HACK HER PROGRAMS WHATEVERS MOM.

I'M SURE AT SIXTY, I'M NO PARTY.

YOU KIND OF SMELL BAD, BUT EVERYTHING SMELLS BAD HERE, SO WHATEV. ALSO, YOUR FEET ARE VERY DISGUSTING. PROMISE ME WHEN YOU GET HERE YOU WILL WEAR SHOES AT ALL TIMES. I'M TELLING YOU THIS NOW SO WHEN I COME HOME TONIGHT YOUR FEET WILL BE COVERED. SERIOUS. YOUR TOENAILS ARE YELLOW.

GIRL, YOUR TEETH ARE BROWN!

SAD FACE. BEFORE THE ASTEROID THEY WEREN'T. EVERYONE'S TEETH ARE BAD NOW. DON'T BE MEAN.

SORRY.

WHO'S THE TEENAGER HERE?

I SAID SORRY.

I'LL TELL LENA THAT YOU'RE FLUSHING THE TOILET ON NONFLUSH DAYS.

ICE COLD, G.

I loved that kid so much.

I put Glory up to asking her mom if she'd gone to see the Axis play the Showbox the Friday before Thanksgiving in 2010.

MOM SAYS YEP SHE AND MY DAD WENT TO THAT SHOW.

I asked if she remembered meeting me there.

MOM SEZ NO. I HATE THAT PIN CUSHION SONG SO DORKO. MOM PLAYS IT A LOT. HOLD ON.

SHE SEZ STOP USING ME FOR PERSONAL INFORMATION. I LIKE TALKING TO YOU. WHAT'S THE POINT OF TIME DILATION IF YOU CANT TALK TO PEOPLE IN THE PAST? LIKE WHOEVER HAS THE BEST STORIES? GOT2 GO. TEEN CORPS HAS A PARTY TONIGHT. L8S!

I FLEW TO Seattle to play the rescheduled Axis reunion show. My head and heart were not anywhere. I did what I always did, pined away after a girl I couldn't have, which led me to scheming in my head around seeing Lena 2.0, solely with the idea that we would meet and I would feel nothing and she would feel nothing, and that I could go home to Chicago and feel nothing until the next heartbreaker waltzed into my life. My hope was this: that her new life trajectory had left her content but complacent—given to socially accepted life goals, Crate and Barrel furniture, mall shopping, and talking about her car—or so science-y that the two of us would have zip to talk about, as stentorian, formulaic gewgaw fell from her mouth, a result of having spent her Stanford years not deejaying college radio and not feeling like an outcast, rendering her far too lame to date someone as cool as Karl Bender.

What if her heart was no longer bruised? What would it mean to love someone who was whole?

I INDULGED IN just a little more Internet stalking. Dr. Lena Geduldig, assistant professor of physics at the University of Washington, was still a member of a riot grrrl-ish knitting organization. There were glossy photos of her and Derrick's stylish astronomy-themed apartment, complete with mural of the constellations on the ceiling, on a couple of interior-design-porn Web sites. She served as adviser to the University of Washington chapter of Women in STEM, a student organization for female undergrads in the sciences. I even found a few of her wedding photos—my girl in a white dress, cleavage bursting over the top of an antique white lace gown, holding hands with Derrick Park in his gray pinstripe suit and top hat, or standing between her father and stepmom Judy, smiling, looking truly at peace. I quickly clicked away from those. And then I hit the jackpot: Lena was scheduled to give a presentation entitled "Plucky: The Physics of Guitar Strings" at a smart-people-get-drunk event called Spirited Discussions, held in the basement of an expensive Capitol Hill bar the night before the geezers of the Axis were set to rock the Showbox just like old times.

From the Spirited Discussions Web site: "Lena Geduldig holds a PhD in physics from MIT and is currently an assistant professor at UW. She is also a huge music geek and can talk your face off about nineties indie rock, from Sebadoh to Sleater-Kinney to the Axis. Lena explains—with science!—how the size, shape, tuning, and length of certain guitar strings produce specific tones and how these tones inform the various subgenres she identifies throughout the indie pantheon."

I was the guitarist for one of the listed bands. Could Lena Geduldig be talking about me and my guitar strings? Conducting science-y science on recordings of my ancient ax-playing? Thinking about me in a vague way? With science? Was I arrogant enough to think that?

I had to remind myself that this Lena didn't give a rip about me, that I was nursing a dumb, piney crush on a stranger who was married to someone else—but who would love me and marry me, but not today, not next year, not for a while. *Reunited* wasn't the right word to use to describe going to see Lena in Seattle. As far as she was concerned, we 'd be meeting for the first time.

SPIRITED DISCUSSIONS TURNED out to be a more popular event than I'd thought it would be. I thought I'd stroll in the bar in my slim jeans, order a brew, and take a seat, but the place was packed asshole to belly button with bodies clothed in corduroy and tweed, and the bar's air was hot and stuffy and smelled lightly of pickles. Everyone kept their jacket on while engaged in conversations that required large gesticulations with the hands not wrapped around cocktail glasses. I jammed myself in between two burly guys in riding caps, leaning against the side wall, who spent the preshow moments furiously dicking around on their phones.

I wanted to lecture them about living in the present, but when the pot calls the kettle black, the kettle kicks the pot in the face.

I slugged my beer and waited for Lena to take the little stage, which was a plywood riser illuminated by an IKEA floor lamp. I waited, and then Lena, dressed in cuffed jeans, a tight black T-shirt that made her breasts look enormous, appeared behind the microphone. This Lena possessed the grace and effervescence of those content with their lives: a confident approach to the microphone, hair cut into a sensible, frizzy bob, natural brown with a few flossy strands of gray poking out around her hairline, illuminated by the IKEA lamp. This was a different Lena, a woman without ghosts, with a stepmom who didn't ruin her, a career that had worked out, and a physicist husband with stupid skunk hair who quite possibly loved her for all the right reasons.

"Hello, Seattle," she said, smiling. I wondered if the Lena I knew would have ever willingly, smilingly, lectured for fun in a bar basement, happy to be there, giddy even. I didn't think so, but this Lena was eating up the attention. "Thanks for coming tonight, especially my students, who think they're getting extra credit for coming to a bar. I'm Lena. I'm a physicist who never really stopped being a college radio deejay. An example of how I blend these twin passions is that I geek out on figuring out the string gauge and tunings used by my favorite bands. This is one of my favorite songs."

The familiar licks of "Pin Cushion" came on over the speakers, and I just about melted into a puddle of love. It was the first time I felt nostalgic about "Pin Cushion," seeing it not as a requiem for Milo's penis but as a song favored by a beloved lost friend.

Lena's everlasting smartitude had taken on a gigglier quality. She mouthed the words to "Pin Cushion," imitating a joyful scream on "This is the start of a revolution." That she still loved the Axis rocked my face off.

"Remember this song?" Lena said, pointing upward at the music. "If you were an overweight college girl in glasses circa 1999, "Pin Cushion" was probably your battle cry. It was definitely mine. But all politics aside, those first few string strikes—*duh nuh nuh nuh*—provide a good example for an extended discussion on wave velocity in a steel string. A few factors relating to aural tone include length and tension, which leads into my long lecture about the significance of tuning and how each of these notes makes a physics nerd such as myself immediately want to calculate the tension, mass, and length of each string. Now, 'Pin Cushion' utilizes a nonstandard guitar tuning scheme—"

"It's an open D," I yelled. I felt a little ashamed of yelling at her in a bar that had temporarily converted itself into a sacred holy temple of the celebration of arcane knowledge. I didn't want to be mistaken for a heckler. I was excited that she was talking about me, and that I existed in her new world.

"Yes, it's an open D. How do you know that, Mister Guy Who Heckles Physicists in Bars?" She squinted and visored her eyes with the side of her hand so she could get a good look at the schmuck who yelled "open D" like a rude clown. She moved the neck of her IKEA floor lamp to shine in my face, and as I squinted and received the blinding that I so deserved, Lena's face suddenly fell. Gone was the bubbly performer. She looked for all the world like she was going to puke.

She gasped and clasped her hand to her mouth, a look of horror darkening her face. I began to feel bad for interrupting her. "Oh my god," she said. "It's you."

The crowd turned and looked my way, and I assumed that everyone in the room expected to see Milo Kildare and not the Axis's thug guitarist.

"Sorry," I shouted at the stage, feeling like a class A schmuck. "I didn't mean to interrupt. I'm not Milo, by the way. Just the guitarist."

"I know you're not Milo. I know who you are." I didn't expect New Lena to be a fan girl for me. She had been so damp in the pants for Milo when I knew her, it didn't occur to me she would have any opinion on ugly old me. But here she was, breathing heavily, wiping sweat from her hairline, looking for all the world like she was about to lose her shit in front of an audience.

"You're the guy from the hospital, when my mom died. . . ." She clutched the lamp to prop herself up. Lena wobbled. "I'm sorry. Sorry everyone. Give me a minute." The two women who were running the show rushed to her side. One handed her a water bottle and the other asked her if she wanted to continue. She pointed in my direction. I was the guy from the hospital and she was onstage, crying, looking my way through her tear-smeared glasses, until the taller of the two hosts put her arm around Lena's shoulders and led her offstage.

The lights went up and the crowd was told that we were taking a twenty-minute intermission. I barely had time to peel my raggedy, ashamed self off the wall of the bar before the shorter of the two host women approached me. "Dr. Geduldig wants to talk to you," she said, and I followed her up the stairs to the main part of the bar, which was darker and quieter. Lena was sitting in a wooden booth, her cheeks a scarlet mess, sipping on a ginger-colored cocktail.

"Hi," I said, sliding into the seat across from her.

She looked at me as if I were a scary ghost. "You're the guy from the hospital in Butte in 1993, when my mom died," she said, her voice crackling.

"Yes. That was me. I'm really sorry for scaring you. I can explain."

She shook her head back and forth and then, more to the table below us than to me, she mumbled, "I've been waiting for you. All these years. To find me."

I had to play my cards correctly. I reached across the table and took Lena's hand. It was still a chubby hand, but had red-painted fingernails done nicely instead of chewed-up black ones. There was no red and black squiggle tattoo on her shoulder or notes written to herself on her palm. Just a gold wedding band topped with a tiny round diamond on her finger, so ridiculously plain and so not the ornate or old-looking ring I imagined Lena would have picked for herself that I wanted to rip it off her finger and throw it in the street.

She let me hold her hand, squeezing her fingers on mine in response. "You changed my life." She covered my hand with hers. "After you disappeared from the waiting room, I went into my mom's room to have what ended up being our last conversation. I told her about you. And what you said to me."

"You did? Why?"

"Because you were there. Because I was fourteen and my mom was dying and you were the first person who was nice to me and talked to me like a regular person in a long time. Mom looked me in the eye and said, 'Lena, you're going to marry that man someday.'"

News of Lena's mother's prophecy made me shudder. My own mother, who died a month before Lena's did, made no such proclamations on her way out of the mortal coil. She just said she was sorry. Then she was gone, and the nurses came in and Brooke and I were swept out of the room into our sad, separate lives. I wished I'd had a mom who wanted to talk about my life after, what she saw, what she hoped for me.

"You married someone else," I said.

"I know. For all good, logical reasons. But my mother didn't say, 'You will marry the Depeche Mode fan boy from New Jersey in your lab at MIT.' Even if she was having a chemotherapy-induced psychic vision at that moment, that was the last thing she said to me. Of course I wanted it to be true. Very badly I wanted it to be true."

"You never told me that. Before you disappeared. When I knew you."

Lena let go of my hand and hunched over the table and sobbed, her back shaking with every gasp for breath. I wasn't sure what to tell her. That there were two versions of her life, which both led her to me?

I put my hand on the back of her head and stroked her brown curls. "Lena, you're beautiful. You're brilliant. We could talk about time travel sometime, and how you have what it takes to develop wormhole technology for the masses. Maybe we will get married someday."

"Who are you?" she asked.

"Karl Bender from the Axis."

She let out a low laugh. "Right. If only I'd bothered to look at the guitarist's face. All those years."

"You saw me at age forty in the hospital. My age now. So you wouldn't have recognized me in the nineties. I started looking like a gray, haggard fat-ass after the band broke up."

Lena dabbed her face with her napkin bouquet, wiping away some semblance of worry. "So when are we going to get married?" she asked.

"Right now," I wanted to say. Or, *"Far in the future, according to your unborn daughter."*

"Lena."

"I'm joking. Okay, I'm kind of serious, actually," she said.

"Something wrong with Derrick?"

Lena shook her head, manic and frazzled as if waking up from a nightmare. "How do you know his name?"

"Glory told me," I said.

"Who's Glory?" she demanded, and I instantly regretted saying Glory's name. I sensed deep in my gut the error I had made.

"Are you going to tell me who Glory is?"

"Nobody."

My phone buzzed with a text from Glory: WHAT THE HELL ARE YOU DOING? DON'T SAY MY NAME TO HER!

My body went cold. Glory could spy on me? "Nobody," I said again.

Glory texted again: *I HATE YOU. HOW DARE YOU DO THIS.*

Lena grabbed my hand and asked the question again, gripping hard to squeeze the answer out of me. My phone buzzed again. "Could you give me a minute? I have to answer this." I stood up and walked down to the front of the bar, near the door. Lena kept her eyes trained on me as I stood and typed away at her yet-to-be-born daughter.

YOU'RE TRYING TO KILL ME.

ARE YOU SPYING ON ME, GLOR?

No response.

GLORY, WHERE DID YOU GO?

Glory's texts always arrived immediately. The bending of time meant that transmission had no time lag.

GLORY, PLEASE LET ME KNOW YOU'RE OKAY.

GLORY?

I went back into the bar and sat down across from Lena.

"Who's Glory?"

"Like I told you: nobody."

Lena suddenly seemed pissed. "Don't hide things from me, either. Don't come here all wanting to see me and then lie to me when I ask you something important."

"Why would I hide anything from you? I barely know you."

"Glory. Not born yet, technically? Is she half Jewish, half Korean? Asian-looking girl with my giant Jew schnoz? Derrick and I joke about that all the time."

"Lena."

"What I've been working on at work. Time-dilation telephony. She can talk to you, can't she? It works? Someone not born yet can communicate with you. Twenty years from now?"

I cleared my throat. "To everything there is a season. Let's respect the season."

She snorted, that same snotty snort I remembered from the first time I met Lena at the Dictator's Club. "Let me tell you something: I hate the season."

Oh, Lena. How could I not love you?

I knew I had to shut up about Glory, and I wasn't doing a very good job of it. It seemed strange that I knew more than an MIT PhD about time travel, but there it was.

Lena pushed her glass out of the way. It scooted across the wooden table, leaving a wet trail of condensation. With a sideways glance, which caused me for the first time to notice the silvery wisps of eye shadow brushed across her lids, she leaned forward and said, "Here's a proposition: I'll quit asking you questions about all this if you come home with me."

I shuddered and said, "The Lena I knew never would have asked that."

Lena pulled back. I wanted to wipe off that dumb eye shadow. "Derrick's out of town. I have a hall pass."

"Really?"

Lena nodded in a seductive way that was also kind of nerdy and a tiny bit a turnoff.

I was happy that she was now the kind of woman who put her desires on the table, and that she had sexual desires in the first place. I was even happy that she had what was maybe a very communicative open marriage that allowed her to bed the occasional ex–rock star/time traveler when it was convenient to do so. My Lena never would have worn a saucy look on her face, knowing with intuition and clarity how to push a man's buttons, leaning forward to touch my hand. My Lena pushed me off of her, rushed back into her clothes before I was done, told me she was sorry, went back to her science always promising to try harder to like it next time. A pang of guilt for wanting back someone broken, who took so many pills she couldn't really feel sex, ran through my body.

"I think it's excellent that you can ask for things like that." My voice cracked. I sounded like a teacher proud of a student he didn't think would succeed but did. "And I'm flattered."

Her face fell. "Okay, take it as a compliment. I like you. I've liked you for years. And I want to talk to you about time dilation."

I took her hands. "I can't go home with you. I mean, I'm happy for you. But you were more, I guess, *mine* when you were punk and angry. You're married, and confident and successful." That was a cruel thing to say. She didn't owe me anything, much less a life that made her frustrated.

"Well, I think I'm pretty punk. Open marriages are punk. And as for what I'm wearing: I came straight from work and generally don't rock my Melvins T-shirt when I teach cosmology to undergrads. And why the hell would you want someone who wasn't confident and successful?"

"I'm sorry. It's just . . . startling to see you this way. You don't need me. Did you need me before?"

"Need you? In the hospital when I was fourteen? You bailed. That hurt my feelings, but I'm sure you didn't want to be seen as being inappropriate with a teenage girl. I didn't get that at the time."

I debated in my head how much information to lay at her feet. Lena was agitated, in a way that made me feel relieved; the offer of a one-night stand was off the table. "No. Before you went back in time and changed your whole life. You lived in Chicago. We ran a time travel business together. I know you don't remember."

Her demeanor brightened. "So it's possible. Time travel."

"Yes."

"So the work I'm doing that's getting known around the physics department as a joke and a waste of money isn't for nothing?"

Not a joke or a waste of money, but a dangerous toy that even I, a low-key, mostly responsible guy, couldn't stop from breaking his heart. "No. Well, yes. Maybe."

"You were time traveling the day we met, in 1993?"

"Yes."

She took a long breath. "Good news, as far as my project goes."

"Not really. I hope you know what you're getting into."

"I think I do," she said, so confident and radiant.

"There was this other version of you, Lena. Where you had a different stepmother, where you were a rape survivor, where you went to Northwestern and had your research stolen. My best friend, Wayne, traveled away to the year 980. I wondered why I haven't gone back in time and changed something in my past to make my present better. And then I realized that what made my life better wasn't time travel."

"Don't say it," she said.

"It was the day you walked into my bar and became my friend. And then my girlfriend. I miss you."

"I don't want to hear about some 'other me.' I'm happy with my life."

"The thing is, in either version of your life, you found time travel and you found me. This comforts me. It means that the tattoo on my knuckles actually isn't total bullshit." I held up my hands. *AMOR FATI.*

"That's sweet of you to say," Lena said. She let me hold her hand.

"I wasted a decade and a half of my life looking backwards, waiting for the past to come back to me. And it did. And it made me happy for a while, but then I lost the two people who I cared about most because of it. And those two people are at peace and I'm not. I'm not okay. The wormhole took away my best friend and my girlfriend."

Lena pulled her hand back. I searched her face for the road map back to where I wanted to be. She reached into her purse and pulled out her phone. "Do you want to come home with me or not? If the answer is yes, I have to text Derrick."

There it was. Reductive. Unromantic. I wanted a moment of connection and she was turning it into a booty call/wormhole information mining session. She didn't know me or care about me. She just wanted to ride my pogo stick and then tell Derrick Park all about banging the guitarist from the Axis—and by the way, time travel is possible; let's go get some grant money. Maybe she wasn't using me, but I wanted all of Lena, even in her new, more cheerful state. If I did go home with Lena, did her, and told her everything the previous version of Lena told me about the science of time travel, she and Derrick would celebrate with champagne, multiple high-dollar scientific grant checks, and copulation that would eventually lead to the birth of Glory Rhiannon Park. This Lena had all she needed, and almost all that she wanted, and I wasn't on either list.

"I'm in love with you, so I can't."

Lena looked at me like I was a weirdo. "If you think I'm worth loving, why am I not worth screwing?"

"You're worth a lot, Lena Geduldig. More than you realize. Even though we're strangers, and probably will be for quite a few more years, I came all this way just to see you. And I see that I am not needed. As a younger man, this would have hurt me, but now, seeing what you've become, it makes me happy. You can stand proudly on your own. Or with Derrick, who I'm sure is a better man than me."

She looked toward the wall, at a framed photo of Kurt Cobain that the bar's management thought was a good idea to hang up. "It's not really about being a better man," she said, not looking at me.

"Your mother would be so proud of you."

Lena's hands begin to shake. She dropped her phone into her bag reached into pulled out a green tube of lip balm, which she swiped across her lips.

"Would you get me another drink please? A whiskey ginger." She rattled her glass so that what was left of the ice cubes made a swishy clang against the glass.

I stood up to do as I was asked. A final courtesy before I walked out, let her go, and went home to mourn. At the bar, with my back turned to her, I heard Lena yell, "I'm sorry. I've gotten a very disturbing text message and I have to go."

She ran out the door of the bar.

I gave chase. It was dark and wet out, and a few yards down the street. All of Seattle's street water was aglow with the color of neon lights. Lena's shoes gave out and she slipped on a puddle lit Pepto pink from a neon gay pride sign at a bar across the street. She called out in pain and I saw her look around for me. She'd dropped her phone and it slid across the sidewalk to my feet. I picked it up and read the message: MOM? IT'S GLORY. YOUR DAUGHTER. YOU HAVE A DAUGHTER ON AUGUST 6, 2013. TIME DILATION TELEPHONY WORKS. WHAT ELSE DO YOU WANT TO KNOW ABOUT YOUR LIFE? GET AWAY FROM KARL AND I'LL TELL YOU.

But before I was able to get to her to help her up, my phone beeped. I reached into my pocket. No sooner did I glance down and see that, somehow, Wayne's travel app had been activated than I was in the tunnel. An unexpected, unwanted pull had sucked me away. I was slurped down across time with enormous force, just as I was about to reach out my hand to help the woman I once loved make that connection I still wanted, and to tell her about the girl who sent her that text.

WHEN I LANDED with a thud, the first thing I saw against the starriest, brightest sky I'd ever seen in my life was that pair of not-forgotten blue eyes fighting with the sky for the right to be called the twinkliest.

"Friend."

Wayne reached down and helped me to my feet, upon the sodden, soaking earth of Mannahatta Island, circa 980 AD. He forced me into a big bear hug, slapping my back and telling me how happy he was to see me. I got a big whiff of his pre-Columbian body odor, like roasted lamb kebab, and the campfire burning sweet, pine-smelling wood behind him, and the smell of my own anxiety. A giant tear rolled down my cheek. Wayne wiped it away with his dirty, calloused hand. He was dressed in furs and leather but still wearing his ancient, filthy white Adidas, which he'd worn the day he disappeared. With kneesocks full of holes.

"You're dead," I said, shaking myself free of his loving embrace. My right fist balled up and I was about to punch the guy in the gut, because he broke my damn heart, brought me my girl but made me lose her. But then I saw Wayne's face, which looked older and wizard wise, all wrinkles and innocence. "Do you know how horrible it is to see someone alive again who you'd accepted had died? Who you mourned and cried over? Oh my god. You told me to mourn you and I did." I wanted to punch him and hug him some more. Selfish weirdo. Wise wizard. Wayne.

My chest was tight, like my heart was going to burst. I wanted to peel my skin off. But there was this giant sky, an overwhelming cosmic Lite-Brite set, a hundred billion stars like tiny firefly butts weaving a starry blanket overhead. I couldn't hate anyone. Not with these smells, the psychedelic green in the trees. No cars, no pollution, just cheerful Wayne, happy to see me again.

"We're all dead, if you think about it long enough," said Wayne. "The only person in the year 980 who misses you is me, right? And that's just the bullshit of human ingenuity. Want some fish? We're chowing down on some big, meaty trout. Me and my traveler pals, that is. Follow me to the fire." Wayne skipped off into a thicket of tall trees. Just beyond, I could hear the sound of surf waves slapping the land and smell the pure salt of what would one day be called the Hudson River.

Seated around the roaring fire in a clearing of trees was a cluster of white-jacketed young people, girls in ponytails and boys in white paper caps. I recognized them immediately as 2030s-era Post-A Teen Corps workers. Future teen time travelers. Glory's peers. They seemed tough and over it all, and I guessed that traveling to 980 to hang out with Wayne was their equivalent of loitering in front of a convenience store.

"Look, everyone," Wayne said. "My best friend Karl Bender from Chicago has come to visit. Ms. Park, if I'm not mistaken, you were the one who bent the hole to bring him here?"

Glory sneered at me—not in that scorned teenager way but with true, burning contempt that tore through my heart. It was the first time I felt that special step-hatred that the children of the remarried possess toward their parents' new loves. I'd never had to see it, but Lena did, and even if she didn't hate Judy the Good Stepmother, she'd probably had her moments of you're-not-my-mom anger.

"Yep, that was me," said Glory. "I just got into your janky 2010 phone and hacked it. You're working with such ancient technology, it's surprising that no one else has bent you against your will. Anyone with half a mind for travel can do it. GloWorm's technology would never allow for a hole bending quite like the one I just pulled off. Your stuff's all pre–travel security. You wouldn't get in a car with no seatbelts, would you? Plus, Seattle streets are, like, pffft. Easy sleazy."

I wanted to correct her and say "peasy," but in 2031, maybe the expression had changed to "easy sleazy." I'd grown accustomed to the 2031 intensifier *watts,* which made absolutely no sense to me.

I walked up to Glory and crouched down to look her in the eye. The grass below was mossy and warm against my palms as I pressed my hands down into the soft, ancient earth. Glory was pulling fish meat off the bone, her dirt-smeared fingers digging underneath the fish's skin, and popping oily bits of it into her mouth.

"Glory, you time-kidnapped me? I thought we were friends."

She swallowed her fish. "I thought we were friends, too, Karl. So I don't know why you were in Seattle right now messing with Lena, trying to kill me."

"You're the one who freaked her out by texting her. You're why she ran away from me," I said, sounding scoldier than I intended. "Look, I didn't mean to make her cry."

Ignoring my question, she said, "You didn't mean to mess with my life, either, I'm sure."

"Wait, what?"

"Mom never told me about whole hospital waiting room thing. And what a big deal it is to her. Until now. You were going to get me unborn. Disappeared. It happens all the time. Where I come from, people's parents go back in time and abort their kids after the fact. She's going to leave my dad for you, before I'm born, because of some dumb thing Grandma Gloria told her before she died. But you didn't know that. You were just being dumb and trying to get in my mother's pants. Lena and Derrick's marriage started going downhill when she started to be more successful than him because of the whole time dilation telephony thing. And I know when that started. Before I was born."

Glory was watts pissed, even beneath the celestial twinkle blanket. How anyone could be pissy underneath *that sky,* which was silver and pink and brilliant and unreal, was beyond me.

"Hey look," I said, pointing up at the sparkles. "Two moons." The twin orbs were suspended scarily close to Earth, as if they were hung with string from a bedroom ceiling.

Glory said, "That's not two moons, idiot. That's one moon and the 2029 asteroid."

"We're trying figure out how to avert the asteroid hitting Earth," a green-eyed girl in a Teen Corps jacket said. "We just happened to run into Wayne, traveling backwards. He's a cool guy."

Wayne beamed. "I'm just a guy with a simple life. I don't know if that's cool or not. It just is."

"Are you going to send me back to 2010?" I asked Glory. "I'm not going to disappear you."

"I could disappear you, you know. I know more about bending than you, Bender. Bender's gonna get bended." I hadn't heard a Bender pun since high school and had been hoping to keep it that way.

"Glory, I thought we were friends."

"Look, she'll go looking for you. She'll go after what she wants. That's how it is with Doctor Lena. She does whatever she wants. My dad, too. It's easy for them. For all the suffering their time travel modules have brought the world, they use all the technology to avoid unpleasant things in their own lives, like dead parents and broken hearts."

Glory must have known that something about her parents' marriage was doomed from the start. I wanted to know more about what she meant by this, how Lena and Derrick avoided broken hearts with time travel. Time travel did nothing but break my heart.

"I'll put her off until after you're born. I promise."

I tried to put my hand on Glory's back, but she shook it away. "No. You ruined it. She saw you. That wasn't part of the plan, man. She had never seen you between 1993 and the White Night until you started messing around with traveling forward. And now she knows and she can't unknow. She wants to make good on her mother's prophecy. That prophecy is a big deal to her. Now I have to call Grandma Gloria and ask her not to say that. Undo, undo, undo. My whole life is undo. Ever call a dead grandparent? It's creepy."

"Does she remember me from 2010 in Chicago? You seem to know about that. Nosing around my bar. Spying on little Eddie Kildare and me and your mom. Did you see her big swirly red and black tattoo on her shoulder? The Lena you know either never got that tattoo or had it removed. I bet it was the former."

"She has a tattoo. On her back, above her ass. A line from a song. 'The Moon is a Light Bulb Breaking.'"

"Really?" I said, and pressed my mossy palms to my eyes, because crying in front of a teenager, no matter what year it was, was courting disaster.

I felt the old familiar blanket of longing for a woman I couldn't have. What the hell was wrong with me? That Lena number 2 had still gotten the Elliott Smith tattoo had to mean something.

I said to Glory, "I can't keep changing the past."

"My survival is dependent on revisions, Karl, and it's all your fault," she said. And then, swiping her fingers across her wristlet, she was gone.

Her post-A friends gave Wayne friendly slaps on the back of his leather vest, said good-bye, and disappeared too.

I began to cry. I'd helped to make an entire generation of young people's lives harder. By accident.

Wayne stood there and watched me sob. I tried to enjoy the leafy, sweet-aired goodness of 980, but I longed for the comfort of car exhaust, the easy pain of existence as I knew in it my bar life. If I knew I had caused someone pain, at least I knew that I'd get that pain returned to me if I were home, in the city, in 2010, at age forty, with my good years behind me. I'd get mugged. I'd disappoint my twenty-one-year-old bar-back/bass player. I'd get my heart broken by a physicist. Nothing on Wayne's utopian island could touch me, and I couldn't stand that. What did it say about Wayne that he needed a life with no bumps and bruises? You can't write music in such a life. You don't need music. I needed to be where my heart could get broken.

Wayne, smiling like his old car salesman self, patted my head. "Buddy, tell you what. Let's go to sleep under these magnificent stars. In the morning, we'll get you sent back to 2010."

I let myself cry. If there was anyone that wouldn't judge me for it, it was Wayne. "I really do love Glory. In a weird, parental way. I never wanted kids, but a kid who can time travel like a badass? I didn't mean to make anyone's lives harder," I said. "I just wanted to see some rock shows in the past. Damn, I really miss my mom. Glory has technology where I could call my mom and talk to her. But I don't know that I want to."

Wayne nodded. "I miss my mom, too."

"Are we all just looking for an easier life?"

Wayne nodded, breathing deeply and taking stock of the pine-sugar air, the canopy of stars, the campfire. "How much of our true selves we have to give up just to get through the day. The thing is, we do rely on other people for happiness, and you 2010 people need to quit pretending like you're okay being alone, eating salad out of a bag in front of your computer, when what you want is a family and lovers and people who can see into your heart."

"You're right. But you could have had that in Chicago."

A deer-type animal approached Wayne, nuzzling its compact face against Wayne's thigh. He reached down to pet it. "Have you ever talked to Glory about Post-A Teen Corps?"

I hadn't even thought to ask what she did all day in her white coat. All I knew is that it had something to do with drywall. "No."

"Those 2030s kids complain a lot about the asteroid. They don't have a choice of what to do with their lives. Glory gets to go to college because of who her parents are, but most of her peers are going to be working for government rebuild projects their whole lives, for basically no pay. They don't get to have dreams or freedom like we had. We had 'Go figure out what you want, and make sure it pays a lot of money.' Glory and her friends don't have that. But they do have each other. They're a tight little bunch. I asked Glory who the popular kids at her high school were and she asked me what that meant."

"What 'popular' meant?"

Wayne nodded. "Karlito, it took an asteroid to get rid of high school popularity." Wayne, even well into adulthood, even in popularity-free 980 AD, still wore the bruises of high school unpopularity. Marijuana and not giving a shit somehow erased all that for me, but not for Wayne.

"Wayne, I want to go home."

He nodded, and then picked a stick up off the ground and started chewing on it. "Home is a slippery thing. What we yearn for is often not what we really need. I have what I need here. Love of the unconditional sort. I don't have burritos or written language or gummy bears or you, but I do appreciate my life of fishing, woodcraft, and sleeping in the big pile next to the fire. And all those stars up there. Nothing here hurts except physical pain."

Wayne put his arm around me and pulled me to him to kiss my forehead. "I hate to be the one to remind you this, but you do have access to a wormhole that goes forward as well as backward."

"There's no electricity," I said. I wanted him to fix it. Do something for me, one last time.

Wayne yawned without covering his mouth, aspirating a hot, fishy stream of breath in my face. His teeth, much like Glory's, looked cracked and rusty. "Well. Let's go to sleep, buddy. You really should try the fish while you're here. Tomorrow we will take my wooden canoe out and fish. And talk some more about your problems. It's dark now, and I'm needed in the pile. Good night, friend."

Wayne turned and walked away, abandoning me on the shores of Mannahatta Island, with no coat or knife or anything.

"Wait, you're leaving me here? Alone? Wayne!" I screamed after my friend.

But Wayne had already disappeared into a dark thicket of woods, and even though the shine of so many stars illuminated his face with the gentlest of white light when he stood right in front of me, the stars of 980 were not enough to allow me to see or to follow him into his woods, where he lived with his family.

I sat and listened to the whistle of the wind, the gentle crash of waves off in the darkness. The calmness should have reached me—everything around me on this untouched island, pure, blameless, and ready to nurture me as it had my asshole buddy who had just abandoned me.

Wayne left me alone in a forest. Like I'm a child in a Grimm's fairy tale.

Major parental abandonment trigger.

The stars and wind would not calm me. I felt all the ugly things inside me bubble up to my surface, especially my longing for Lena.

I could smell the earth and the smoke from the dying embers of the Lenapes' fire. The entire island was asleep, even the four-legged, hooved animals and the twig-legged birds and the bugs and the people. And I could not be still. How Wayne could leave the chaos of Chicago, the dull hope of my bar, the conundrum of his existence, for this strange green void was beyond me. I missed home, and I finally knew where it was.

I thought of Sahlil's ability to circumvent Wayne's wormhole program and come home without us telling him how, and how he said it was love that brought him home. At the time, I dismissed it as cheesy, and Lena dismissed it as unscientific. But, abandoned as I was, and finding no succor in my aloneness, left to sleep on cold, soft ground with no blankets (he didn't even offer me an animal skin or to help me make a fire), I began to reconsider.

I took out my phone and stared at the glow, feeling like a schmuck because I was beneath so much ancient sky sparkle. I snapped a picture of the 980 diamond star blanket overhead, knowing I'd never see a sky so beautifully unreal again in my life. I snapped that picture because I knew that Lena had taken a picture of this sky when we came to 980 together. I wanted to show Lena a picture of this perfect sky.

Lena.

If time is one long line, then somewhere on that line, Lena loves me. On my time line, I love her longer, but we do overlap somewhere, which meant that Lena number 2, the more fortunate one, loved me, somewhere. Her daughter had told me so. Before bending me to 980 to screw me over.

Smart kid.

I yanked the red laces on one of my boots, pulled it off my foot, and threw it into a berry bush.

I could will myself home to my mom and West Hartford, or I could will myself home to the home of my choosing, to the person who would choose to live with a bulldog-faced, washed-up indie rock dude and call that guy home.

Home. Wanting it bad enough. Wayne knew that I just had to want it bad enough. I wanted it bad.

I waited and wished and scared myself and finally the hole came for me, sucked me in, and I fell back. I landed in Seattle 2010, on that wet street in front of the Capitol Hill bar, right after Lena fell down.

"Who was that text from?"

"What text?"

"The text that freaked you out and made you run out of the bar?"

"I didn't get a text," she said. "I thought you were walking me to my car."

"No. Are you okay?" I asked.

"No," she said. "I fell on my butt and it hurts and I just got it tattooed yesterday and the area's sore."

"You got a tattoo yesterday?"

"Yup. On my butt."

"May I ask what you got?"

"If you help me up, I'll do you one better."

The crowd from Spirited Discussions was starting to file out of the bar. "Uh, okay. If you want to flash me your ass on a city street with a bunch of people, I won't stop you."

Lena took me by the hand and led me behind a Honda Accord parked alongside a building. She pulled down her drawers, exposing her plump butt at me, the tattoo on her right cheek still haloed in red.

"It's a pincushion, in honor of the song."

A red, tomato-style pincushion, full of pins, was permanently etched into her bum. Whoever did it did a nice job. This Lena still had good taste in music.

"Come home with me?" she asked, pulling her skirt back up. I saw a little glimpse of "The Moon is a Light Bulb Breaking" across her back, written in a cursive instead of the block lettering that Lena 1.0 had. Maybe this Lena wasn't that different from the one I knew. The same, but changed just enough for her to pick a different typeface for her Elliott Smith tattoo.

Lena looked at me, expecting a yes.

My heart hurt. I couldn't hurt the future, though. "Oh, Lena. I want to be the guy you come home to, not the guy you screw and then kick out."

"You do realize that most men don't say things like that. Most men want it the other way."

One of her sandals had flown into the street. I waited for some cars to pass before I ran out into the street to grab it for her.

"I'm not like most guys. I'm clingy and needy and weird."

"Derrick's banging some poet in Ann Arbor as we speak. He's coming back tomorrow morning. He doesn't want to miss the Axis show."

"I've grown mushy in my old age. I'm a big, gooey romantic. Sorry."

She seemed disappointed. "Okay. Well, thanks for being honest."

"Maybe I'll see you at the Axis show tomorrow night," I said. "Milo Kildare would love it if you showed him your pincushion."

I hoped that, if she came to the show, then that meant something. That she'd be with me someday later, when we could be a family. After her divorce, when she was a little more worn down, she and I could cling to each other like pool floaties in order to get through our older years with a little comfort.

"I'm not showing my butt to Milo Kildare. That guy? Are you kidding me?"

THE AXIS TOOK the stage at the Showbox in Seattle, a club we used to play with some frequency, and one large enough to lend some cachet to our reunion appearance, but I could feel that the audience was only about half full. I tried not to be bothered by it. The Axis was kicking out some pretty good shows, despite the thin, white ghost that was Milo, and the reason we were playing again in the first place. There was Trina, behind her old navy blue bass, Eve at the drums, and Milo, possessed by his indie rock duende, standing up on the monitors, opening his frilly pink button-up shirt, yelling "I Believe!" into his microphone. I played the shit out of the Seattle show, with special care taken during "Pin Cushion." The second it was over, I dropped my ax onto a cluster of cords and combed the crowd for Lena, calling her name, looking for her, hoping that I could see her standing next to Derrick, happy in some way that didn't involve me, except it did.

I wiped my dumb guy tears on my sleeve, and then I saw Lena and Derrick. They stood in the middle of the crowd and were hard to miss. Lena was practically twice his size (he was maybe five foot four, and skinny like a toothpick—they looked like a Goth version of Milo and Jodie)—and Dr. Derrick had that dumb white stripe in his hair and his dumb leather jacket with a bunch of spikes on it like it was 1985. A dumb white stripe, a trying-too-hard jacket, and my girl. I had to be happy for them so they'd stay together for the next twelve years, make Glory, who would then tell me exactly when I should show up and be Lena's second husband. The fifty-year-old Lena was the girl for me.

From the van on our way back to Portland after the show, I texted Glory to apologize for almost messing up her birth. I prayed for the best—that she was still a teenage drywall expert without popularity problems in the 2030s. Just to be safe, I left a voice mail message on Dr. Lena's work number, telling her to make sure to have a kid in 2013, that the future of humanity depended on it.

With great humility, or so I thought, I released the expectation that Dr. Lena would respond to this in any way, and when she didn't, I merely kept my mind on my bar, my hand on my bar towel, my focus on my life, however small I'd made it. So very tiny it felt, without my two best friends, like a sweater I'd put in the dryer on accident, like a dumb-ass.

Text from Glory: THE WORST THING ABOUT YOUR GENERATION IS HOW PATIENT YOU ARE. IT'S LIKE YOU FORGET YOU CAN BEND TIME. EVEN MOM WHO LIKE INVENTED IT. NO ONE MY AGE WAITS FOR A SINGLE DAMN THING.

CLYDE BOUGHT THE bar. I sent Brookie the money. My precious vinyl and the stack of *Puncture* magazines went to my bar patrons. Sahlil's office let me out of my lease a little too easily. Finally, I had nothing left to hold on to.

18

THE AEG-13 ASTEROID, that long-anticipated fiery rock that ruined Europe and the dreams of an entire generation of American young people, hit the town of Kansk, Siberia, at 11:07 p.m. Pacific Time on the twenty-seventh of April 2029. It was a cataclysmic event that knocked the axis of Earth off kilter, set Siberia on fire, and drowned most of the Pacific Islands, to the tune of no more Japan and very little Hawaii. On that night, fifteen-year-old Glory spent the evening at an end-of-the-world block party on her street in Seattle, where she, Lena, and her friends and neighbors would not miss the fiery ball of matter as it collided with Russia and burned, drowned, or turned to dust millions of people. Seattle spilled. The Alaskan Way tunnel filled with water, then collapsed. The Space Needle remained affixed to the ground with a series of anchors and chains, but tipped at a charming five degree angle, like the Leaning

Tower of Pisa. Glory, Lena, and the rest of North Forty-Ninth Street, Wallingford, swam up to the tops of their houses and continued the party until the roofs started caving in.

Surprised to not be dead, most of the survivors were eventually rescued and transported to less damaged parts of the lower forty-eight. Lena ended up back in Butte with her family. Derrick Park, who was in his mostly unscathed Washington, DC, apartment that night, arranged to have Glory sent to him, where she endured what she described as "a *watts* stupid junior year of high school" living with him and her stepmom, Madison. Lena eventually returned to Seattle and her work helping to design and implement the Seattle Floating City Project, an effort to rebuild Seattle in the style of a modern Venice, with canals and plastic-wrapped edifices—a project which was ultimately yanked when the US government declared the entire western half of the country in a state of emergency, stripped the states of their very existence, renamed everything Post-A——Zone——(my favorites would be Potato Zone 1, formerly Idaho, and Seagull Zone 2, the northern half of what once was Utah), and sent in the military to keep people from drowning each other over food and clean water.

Sopping, outlaw Seattle, stripped of its name, government, and most of its personality (probably due to the scarcity of coffee and the fact that half of its populace had either drowned or moved away). Post-asteroid, the post-A world, the post-A movement, or the post-A post-punk music scene generated a band called the Marshmallow, fronted by hip twentysomething siblings Eddie and Vi Kildare, who'd spent four years of their childhoods living at the Johnston manse in Macon, Georgia, before Milo and Jodie managed to get them back to Portland, where Jodie worked as a psychotherapist and Milo taught high school music and social studies. Glory bragged that she was close, personal friends with the Kildare kids, which is apparently something that I set up. "They're spiral-famous," she explained, while we were working out our plan: me skipping forward nineteen years to be with Lena.

Patience is a virtue, but I wasn't willing to wait nineteen years to be with my family. Also, why not be fifty-nine with the body of a forty-year-old? Admittedly, my forty-year-old body was a busted mess of bloated liver, fading tattoos, and graying beard, but still. There was also my loneliness, which led to impatience, which led me to want to do brave, crazy things. I could have just started an online dating profile or taken to bed one of the average-seeming women who came to my bar in the hope of hitting the sheets with an average-seeming guy. But I was in love with this hot, smart physicist with a cool teenage daughter.

As I was settling my affairs, Glory texted me and explained that she had been reassigned at Post-A Teen Corps from drywalling to the Teen Oral History Project. The first person she set about interviewing was none other than Milo Kildare, that old friend of her stepdad's, who had fronted a once popular indie rock band that her mother liked very much.

HE TOLD ME IN AN INTERVIEW TO FILL MY HEART WITH LOVE, THAT YOU COULD LOSE SOMETHING YOU LOVE AND FEEL LIKE YOU DON'T DESERVE THAT, AND THAT I SHOULD GIVE YOU ANOTHER CHANCE BECAUSE YOU'RE A GOOD GUY. THAT PEOPLE LOOK AT LIFE WITH DIFFERENT EYES AS THEY GET OLDER AND I DON'T KNOW THAT YET WHICH IS OKAY BUT TO TRY TO UNDERSTAND HOW MUCH OF THE WAY YOU TREAT LIFE CHANGES AS YOU AGE. EDDIE KILDARE'S DAD, YOUR FRIEND MILO, SAID THAT.

Glory sent the photo of me and Lena that I'd seen on my snooping trips to the post-A apartment, a close-up on our faces, our lips pressed together, lit by the cigarette lighters each of us held in our hands. Our faces were streaked with dirt and sweat and other "nast," as Glory might say. But we looked goofily happy, content amid the chaos, connected, not alone, shiny in that love way you just can't fake.

I'M CRYING, GLORY.

HA HA! YOU TWO GOT MARRIED IN A HOSPITAL WAITING ROOM IN BUTTE A WEEK AFTER THE ASTEROID. THE POWER WAS OUT WHICH IS WHY YOU HAVE THE LIGHTERS. NO NEED TO CHANGE THIS. AS FAR AS STEPDADS GO, YOU'RE GOOD SO COME ON DOWN. THIS WAS A SWEET WEDDING! GRANDPA DAVID AND GRAMMA JUDY WERE THERE, TOO.

THIRTY-SIX YEARS AFTER THE FIRST TIME WE MET, TECHNICALLY. SAME ROOM.

I KNOW. CRAZEE! SORRY ABOUT TRYING TO KIDNAP YOU. I GET EMOTIONAL SOMETIMES. DON'T TELL LENA, K?

For the final time I closed up my bar. Then I set the controls on Wayne's old program and disappeared with a flash into the post-A future.

HOURS BEFORE THE asteroid was scheduled to hit Siberia, Seattle was a mess of traffic. The electric brokenness of impending municipal doom had made the citizens behave horribly. It was the end of the world as they knew it, and so the angry hordes set alight the ancient, blighted record stores that made no money but existed on the backs of community love, destroyed underperforming burrito shops (Glory had told me that there would be no more tomatoes by 2029; salsa and ketchup, rest in condiment peace), and set free every cat, dog, turtle, and parrot housed in the local animal shelters. Violent screams and the echoes of glass being smashed, very much on purpose, filled Seattle's ears. Cars (very round cars seemingly still run on gas engines) slammed into other cars, into trees, into houses, fences, and decimated burrito shops. Shop owners boarded up their windows. There was a lot of unintelligible yelling over loudspeakers by both authorities and independent rabble-rousers. Some denizens of this doomed city were calmly enjoying the last moments of their lives by partying on their overgrown lawns. People wearing very long, brightly colored T-shirts (down to their knees—really, 2029?) collected in groups and embraced. An old man kissed the top of a small child's head, even though the child was trying to run away. An elderly couple handed out free pizza, and along a trash-strewn side street, people had moved their couches into the center of the road to sit and eat pizza and watch a rock band play what, on a more safe and solid day, I would have termed a dreadful cover of "Heart-Shaped Box" by Nirvana.

"Heart-Shaped Box." If this were 2010 instead of asteroidal 2029, I would have made gurgle and gag noises, motioned my index finger in and out of my mouth, cursed these young musicians, still a long time coming when Kurt placed that gun to his head, for thinking they had the right—the right—to play Nirvana.

THEY DON'T TELL you how to behave at an end-of-the-world party. I was taken by the serenity. By the love and need, the burning smells and the human vulnerability. I also wanted to kill the idiot who, a few streets over, was firing a gun into the air.

"You're not all going to die," I said to no one in particular, although my statement did prick up the ears of a gentleman in a too-long T-shirt who was playing one half of a chess game atop a card table in the middle of the street, seated on what looked like a stack of tires. "The asteroid is far enough away that all of your infrastructure will crumble, and the streets will run with filthy water for the next three years, and things will get a little postapocalyptic for a while, but you're not all going to die. Just ask Dr. Lena Geduldig."

"Who are you?" the chess man asked. He wore dreadlocks and was clad in a bright purple knee-length T-shirt with all manner of silvery threadwork around the collar. "Soothsayer motherfucker?"

"I come from the past. I know the future. And I know Lena Geduldig. This is her asteroid. She's been tracking it for years."

"That's what Lena has been saying," the guy said, pointing to Lena, whose older face I knew from snooping but which, on this day, April 27, 2029, looked vibrant and vital, radiant with her grapefruit-colored hair, ready to receive her apocalypse boyfriend, I hoped. Dr. Lena sat on an outdoor couch with her arm around an elderly woman wearing a Pixies T-shirt, dipping into a shared carton of ice cream with a big spoon.

Glory, age fifteen, tall and lanky with her black hair piled atop her head in a bun, saw me and waved. She looked happy and bouncy, even though the world was ending, and she, too, was wearing one of those freakishly long T-shirts, hers bright pink and with more coils of silver reflective thread (solar power for charging your wrist phone?). She ran to her mother and pulled her off the couch, dragging her to where I stood, next to a tipped-over mailbox and a woman with a stroller shouting into her wrist phone.

Glory waved me over. With a pit in my stomach as big as half an asteroid, I walked toward mother and daughter. My feet became heavy.

Glory grabbed my hand and Lena's and stuck the two together. "Okay, you two. Kiss and get married, like, right now."

Lena, rightfully, looked spooked. No one should rely on their teenage daughter to be a cross-time matchmaker, but here Lena and I were, staring at each other like goobers, all dopey grins, me studying the age in her face. New lines, all of them beautiful, and her eyes, big and brown behind her glasses, just how I remembered them.

"My daughter tells me that you're the pin and I'm your cushion," she said, and then pulled me into a warm, strong hug. "I've spent the last two weeks eating ice cream."

I fought tears. Asteroids make a guy mushy on the inside.

"We've all been pigging out," she said. "Food might be weird to nonexistent for the next few years, so there has been some serious dairy consumption around our house."

"You're beautiful," I said.

"So are you," Lena said, smiling like a nervous schoolgirl trying to flirt.

"Glory and I decided that this should be the day we meet. I know you've been working really hard lately on tracking the asteroid. I guess the day has come and you're ready to, uh . . ."

Lena blushed. Gosh, what an awkward remeeting. Even our first meeting, at the Dictator's Club, didn't feel this weird. Or the meeting that happened after/before that, in the hospital in Butte. Lena didn't appear to be mad that I'd abandoned her at that bar in Seattle in 2010. Perhaps her daughter had explained to her why.

"Um, yeah. Glory is all in on you and me being together. She told me not to blow it." Her cheeks turned redder. "This is ridiculous, you know. I've known you forever, it seems like, even though I don't know you at all. And my work on the asteroid is done. We could have evacuated, but there's no good place to evacuate to, except for the middle of the Atlantic, so here we are."

Glory put her arm around her mom. She was a few inches taller than Lena. "Daughter," I said.

Glory made a yuck face. "Uh, maybe not just yet."

"Look," Lena said. The street band's amps were abruptly cut off. A police helicopter flew overhead and someone on a loudspeaker yelled down to break up the party. "I generally don't enter committed relationships on the first date, but Glory has convinced me to be brave and just go for it. And with the asteroid, well . . . I'll toss out the old rules for the asteroid. When her dad left me a few years ago for one of his students, Glory wasn't that upset. I mean, she was, but she told me that it was okay, that Karl would show up and marry me and that we'd be okay."

I said, "It's nice to know that Glory is, you know, on my side. I never would have done anything with the wormhole to make her go away, Lena. That's why I'm here now, and not, well, earlier."

Lena exhaled and pressed her hand to her chest, where once there had been red and black loops. "I'm fine with being single, but Glory seems to think you're a good guy, and that it would be nice to have you around. We can fly in the face of convention and just do this. I know you knew me some other way, some other time, that you were breaking and bending time long before we were. I'm flattered that you would be so into me as to leap forward to when the time was good for me, which is right before everything breaks. That's my house by the way. At least for the next couple of hours." She pointed to a plain-looking one-story house painted dark blue with white trim. The mailbox stood upright, but there appeared to be an orgy in progress on her lawn.

"I don't know who those people are," she said. "I haven't hosted an under-tarp sex party on my lawn in years. At least not since I had Glory. Should I make them move? They won't believe me if I tell them that we're not all going to die. You don't want to join them, do you?"

I laughed at this Lena, slightly different from the one I knew. Maybe it was that her youth had turned out differently. Maybe it was her being in her fifties, being a mom, being successful, or even having her heart broken in a different way. This Lena had a sense of calm. She still liked the same bands, which I was hoping would carry us through some of the difficulties of marriage, of living in a watery disaster zone, of raising our kiddo, and all the other goodies for which I'd skipped over nineteen years of my life.

"I'm just here to be with you. And Glory. . . ."

"But, uh . . . where are you? I mean, if you're fifty-nine . . . the fifty-nine-year-old version of you . . . if you skipped nineteen years . . ."

"I guess he doesn't exist. I think it's just me, getting to look like a busted forty at the age of fifty-nine."

I looked at Lena's collarbone, where I remembered the swirls of her red and black tattoo, which was now plain, slightly papery skin. Her arms were free of tattoos and scars. Her never-purple hair was a plain, graying brown. This Lena, the older, the more self-possessed, the less fragile, and to my eyes, beautiful, excited me just as much as the Little Trouble Girl I had known nineteen summers earlier.

She looked into my eyes and I looked into hers and I didn't see sorrow. Or fire, for that matter. But we would soon have all the fire and water we could handle. Together, we would have different trouble, some of our own making. I took her hand and she took my hand and some friend of hers, a man with ass-length dreadlocks and blind-man sunglasses, yelled, "Hey, Doctor Lena. End of the fucking world, baby."

Lena knew, as I did, that tonight was not the end of the world, but how cool is an end-of-the-world party? Say and do whatever you want. Huff gas, fuck, eat twelve pizzas, punch the shit out of a mailbox. So, in this spirit, Lena turned and walked up to this shirtless, sight-impaired guy sucking on a bottle of Jim Beam and bent over, put her butt in his face, and released a rather glorious, reverb-rich fart five inches from his sunglasses. And there it was: the fire of Lena, slightly different, dirty, silly, naughty, reborn. Everyone who saw this momentous application of butt wind applauded as if she'd just delivered the virtuoso performance of a lifetime. Lena bowed and waved. The shirtless man stood up and gave her a hug.

She bounded back toward me, her face drunk with joy, and whispered in my ear, "I hope that turned you on."

"Weirdo," I said, leaning down to kiss her.

Then, nearly toppling me down to the ground, she grabbed me and pressed her lips against mine so she could kiss me first, to the sound of thunderous applause and shouts.

"Whoo-hoo! Go Lena! Yeah!"

"Who is this guy?"

"All prayers will be answered in the order in which they were received."

I gasped for breath. Lena wasn't done kissing me in front of all of Seattle. "Lena, you have a wormhole, yes?"

Lena giggled and then recalibrated herself to some level of seriousness. She sat up, straddling me across my belly. "Sort of. I guess I should tell you sometime what happened with all the government regulation stuff regarding the wormhole, but maybe not tonight. Tonight we ride this out together, as a community." I wasn't sure what she had in mind in terms of "community." She was sitting on top of my crotch.

"Do you think we should . . . the three of us . . . get out of here?

Jump forward? Or backward? I've got my phone. And my wormhole just kind of travels with me. I can't seem to get rid of it."

Lena, still seated on top of me, shook her head no. A vehement no. She clasped her hand over her wrist and leaned in to whisper into my ear, "No. I'm happy. I've got my daughter and all these people, these neighbors who are like family since we started preparing for the asteroid. Look how together everyone is. I barely knew my neighbors until a year ago, and then word got out that I was the asteroid scientist and we started having meetings and block parties, and Glory found out that there were three other fifteen-year-old girls on the street. We had a variety show last night. I juggled! It was ridiculous. Even my ex-husband says that the asteroid has brought together his community in DC. What, other than regular old physical safety, would we be going toward? The past? The time travel business is so heavily regulated by the government that it's mostly just a function of the military and a tourist plaything of the extremely rich. Besides, I'm not even part of the GloWorm research team anymore. I've been paid off handsomely and I'm pretty sure that the FBI tracks every word that comes out of my mouth. My wristlet is tracked. They'd know if I travel." She uncovered her wrist and smiled at me. "I'm so glad you're here. I get to marry the guy from my favorite band! Give me another kiss."

Lena and Glory and I sat outside with the neighbors for hours, in plastic lawn chairs that would soon melt. We let the sky turn black and held each other and waited and partied and drank with all of these future people, the good citizens of Seattle before the asteroid. I missed my bar. Oh, what a temple I could have built on a night like tonight.

In the hour before the asteroid hit, I pulled out my phone.

WAYNE? I texted. HELLO FROM 2029. THE SKY LOOKS LIKE A WHITE SHEET OF PAPER AND THE TREES ARE

DEAD AND THE STREETS ARE PAVED WITH GARBAGE, BUT I GET IT. YOU AND YOUR 980. LOVE AND COMMUNITY. PEACE, LOVE, AND UNDERSTANDING. BUT NO FISH. NOT EVER AGAIN. THEY'RE ALL DEAD.

I kissed Lena. She kissed back. She was an A-plus kisser.

Glory gobbled some chocolate from 2010. I had to hand it to the kid: the world was about to get scary and she looked calm. Teenage time benders knew the ends of all the stories.

"Two moons," Lena said, and pointed up to the sky, and turned to her daughter, who we were totally making out in front of (sorry, Glor). "Look for them, Glory. Just like in 980."

"One of them's not a moon," Glory said, and put her arm around her mom.

I was prepared to have a full-blown emo episode on my putative stepkid—that release, the sweaty satisfaction of finally, finally getting your heart's desire—but she wouldn't have any of it. Glory wouldn't even let me give her a hug. "No crying, Karl. You're welcome. Gosh, I have to do everything for you, and I'm only a kid."

After the hugs and the kisses and the introductions to Lena's neighbors as her "hot, sexy boyfriend" came the moment we'd all been waiting for. The flash—everything turned white—and when our eyes came back, the sky was pink. I could feel on my skin that the temperature of Earth had risen by at least thirty degrees. The ground beneath us dropped a few feet. Shingles from the neighboring houses flecked off the roofs like dead skin. Screams echoed off the freshly made canyons, and the great groan of the rush of water filled our ears.

"Is everyone okay?" Lena yelled, as the street began to fill with warm, grayish water. "Glory?"

"I'm fine. Are you fine, Karl?"

"I'm better than fine. This is the happiest day of my life."

Lena laughed at me. "This is the worst natural disaster ever, Karl."

"But we're going to live. This is the first time I've loved the future. I love the future because I love you."

"You're very sweet, but look around. Holy shit."

Our pants were soaked with grungy water, and soon we were swimming up to the rooftop. The sky had turned a cotton candy pink, foreboding and delicious all at once. The air smelled of burning electronics, and smoke collected where the treetops used to be. The light from the flash mixed with the smoke and created a gauzy veil across the white night sky.

Wayne's second moon had returned. And that's how I felt at this moment. Just like Wayne's chosen sky, perfect and undamaged and full of sparkle and promise. That was the strange thing about the wormhole. You could, if you wanted, go somewhere where the sky was completely different. You could choose the color, texture, and moon quantity of your sky. You could choose your family, your 980, your home.

My phone buzzed, even though it was soaked with water.

> TOO BAD ABOUT THE FISH, BUDDY. YOU'VE GOT TO HAVE SOMETHING IN YOUR LIFE LIKE THE FISH. THE FISH IS THE VERY BEST PART.

Glory and Lena were my fish, my very best part. I'd found my 980. My 980 was this crumbled city, gauzy sky and gray water, and my family's heads bobbing above the surface, breathing, me holding on to them so they wouldn't float away.

Acknowledgments

My deepest thanks go to Eileen Pollack, Michael Byers, V. V. Ganeshananthan, and Nicholas Delbanco, with all the mushy love, mad respect, and stunning admiration I can muster. And thank you kindly to Helen Zell, Andrea Beauchamp, and the Hopwood Program at the University of Michigan (an earlier draft of *Every Anxious Wave* won a Hopwood Award in 2012), and my brilliant Michigan fiction cohorts: Rachel, Nina, Amielle, Gina, Sheerah, Eric, James, Jide, Henry, and both Dans. You managed to create Writer Heaven on Earth in Ann Arbor and I am so grateful to have been a part of it.

Thank you Jenni Ferrari-Adler for your faith and wisdom, and to Brenda Copeland, and Laura Chasen at St. Martin's for your wit, fine taste in literature, and impeccably worded e-mails.

Thank you to my cadre of early readers: Cortney Philip, Wayne Alan Brenner, Katherine Kiger, Sarah Wilkes, and fellow writers at the Vermont Studio Center and the Squaw Valley Community of Writers.

Thank you to the real-life physicists who helped me make Lena sound like she knows what she's talking about: Dr. Cindy Keeler, and Dr. R. Jeffrey Wilkes.

Thank you Bob Apthorpe for years of support and encouragement, and for figuring out how Karl knows Lena, but Lena doesn't know Karl (on graph paper, like a real scientist!).

Thank you Julie Gillis, Heather Black, Cassi Nesmith, and Abe Louise Young for the gift of your friendship.

Thank you to Austin, Texas, the city that nurtured me for so long. Special shouts to the friendly and fashionable coffee shops that let me sit and write for hours: Bouldin Creek Café, Bennu, Cenote, and Thunderbird on Koenig. Thank you also to these important local institutions: The Hideout Theater, *Bedpost Confessions,* and BookPeople.

Thank you *Sassy* magazine (RIP) for the teenage cultural influence whose longevity continues to astonish me two decades on, and to Lou Barlow for being cool with the title of this book.

Thank you most of all to my mother, Christine, for the childhood typewriters, book-buying trips to B. Dalton in Fresno, patience, love, and understanding. It took me thirty years to do it, but here's my book, just like I promised.